**SOMERSET SECRETS:
A SERIES OF SHORT STORIES:
THE ADAIR CLASSROOM MYSTERIES
Vol. III
BY T.W. MORSE**

**SOMERSET SECRETS**
*by T.W. Morse*

Copyright © 2020 by T.W. MORSE

All rights reserved. This book or any portion thereof may not be reproduced or used in any manner whatsoever without the express written permission of the publisher except for the use of brief quotations in a book review.

Printed in the United States of America

First Printing, 2020

E-book
ISBN: 9781513664408

Paperback
ISBN: 9781513664392

Adair Classroom Mysteries
Naples, Florida

https://adairclassroommysteries.sitey.me/

*SOMERSET SECRETS*
*by T.W. Morse*

**This book is dedicated to my wonderful editor, Megan Ryan**

**THANKS TO MY TERRIFIC WIFE AND KIDS!**

**SOMERSET SECRETS**
*by T.W. Morse*

INTRODUCTION

ULYSSES

THE DOUBLE DATE MURDER

ULYSSES

I.

II.

III.

V

BOB'S GRANMAMA'S GOT A BIG...BIG PROBLEM

LOGAN

I.

II.

III.

IV.

V.

VI.

HANNAH FLIES SOLO

HANNAH

I.

II.

III.

## IV.

## THE CASE OF THE MISSING BEAT

### ULYSSES

#### I.

#### II.

#### III.

#### IV.

#### V.

#### VI.

#### VII.

## SCHOOL NEWSPAPERS: REPORTING TRUTHS—NOT FAKE NEWS

### ULYSSES

#### I.

#### II.

#### III.

#### IV.

#### V.

#### VI.

#### VII.

## FIELD TRIPS ARE MURDER

*SOMERSET SECRETS*
*by T.W. Morse*

## LOGAN

I.

II.

III.

IV.

V.

VI.

## THE CASE OF BOB'S UFO SIGHTING

## ULYSSES

I.

II.

III.

IV.

V.

## BOB AND I ARE IN A TEACHER WORKSHOP FROM HELL

## LOGAN

I.

II.

III.

IV.

*SOMERSET SECRETS*
*by T.W. Morse*

V.

**OUR CHEATING CLASS PRESIDENT?!**

**ULYSSES**

I.

II.

III

IV.

V.

VI.

**HORRIFIC ADVENTURES IN BABYSITTING**

**ULYSSES**

I.

II.

III.

IV.

V.

VI.

**THE CASE OF THE EMPTY CHURCH**

**ULYSSES**

I.

II.

## SOMERSET SECRETS
### by T.W. Morse

III.

IV.

V.

**WAKE UP! IT'S MURDER!**

**LOGAN**

I.

II.

III.

IV.

V.

VI.

VII.

**WEDDED TO MURDER:**
**THE ADAIR CLASSROOM MYSTERIES VOL. IV**

-SNEAK PEAK-

PROLOGUE

**ABBEY AND THE WASP**

*SOMERSET SECRETS*
*by T.W. Morse*

# Introduction

## ULYSSES

My name is Ulysses Adair. My widowed dad, Logan Adair, and I have had a long school year. Dad teaches U.S. history at my high school, Mangrove High, where I'm a freshman.

Dad and I lost Mom almost six years ago in a car accident on our move down to Somerset, Florida, which we now call home. Dad and I miss Mom every day. Dad recently began to date again, though—so there's that. He's been dating Hope Henderson, a doctor of physical therapy, for most of the school year. I think she might be the one, other than Mom. Maybe there are wedding bells in the future—who knows?

Dad and I live in a cramped condo since Somerset is a very expensive, very touristy city on the Gulf of Mexico. It's home to a lot of the 1 percenters—you know, the super-rich and famous people of the world. It's like Beverly Hills on steroids.

This year, Dad and I discovered a knack for finding our way into problems. Oh—I didn't tell you?! We are amateur sleuths. We've already solved a few murders, and my freshman year isn't even over yet. But those are other stories. Along the way, we've made a frenemy of our local sheriff, Detective Brute. The police often frown on meddling, and Dad and I love to meddle. Word to the wise: if you solve murders or like to meddle in other people's problems, your principal may not like you either. Principal O'Leary has it out for both Dad and me. I sometimes can hear his annoying screech of a voice in my dreams.

**SOMERSET SECRETS**
*by T.W. Morse*

Of course, we don't work alone. My hot-tempered, half Cuban girlfriend, Hannah Reyes, is always by our side. Don't let her delicate frame fool you. Believe it or not, she's a second-degree black belt. We always hang out at her parents' coffee shop, Penny University Café. The Reyes family named it after the first coffee shops in London. It's in a big warehouse on the Somerset docks. My dad and I often play guitar and sing at their open mic nights.

Unfortunately, we are also aided by Bob Nelson, Dad's bumbling, track-suit-wearing best friend who is Hannah's and my physical education teacher. Dad always describes Bob to other people like this: "Imagine if Barry White and JJ Evans from *Good Times* had a love child—it would be Bobby Nelson." Whatever that means? Dad is such a boomer. Bob means well and has a good heart, but often face palm emojis are required when talking about him. His antics can often get us into trouble, but they've gotten us out of problems too.

Somerset, Florida, is a great place to live; white sand beaches, huge homes, perfect weather year-round. But whenever you have this much beauty and wealth, you're bound to have deceit, deception, and mayhem. We've come across all kinds of weird cases in our meddling. Some spooky, some thrilling, some even out of this world. What dark mysteries lie around the corner? It's your lucky day! Dad and I have never told anybody some of our greatest adventures this year, and I'm about to share them with you now. I hope you enjoy some of Dad's and my more extraordinary cases in *Somerset Secrets*.

# THE DOUBLE DATE MURDER

## ULYSSES
### I.

I have never been on a double date. I always thought it would be lame. Despite this, Dad, Hope, Hannah, and I walk from the burrito restaurant to the cinema to see the new superhero action movie, *Scarlet Ninja II*. Dad and Hope share their favorite scenes from the first *Scarlet Ninja* movie, which they both have a strange obsession with. They're going back and forth like comic book nerds.

"Can't wait to see *Scarlet Ninja II*. The first one was so lit!" Dad comments, baiting us with his use of our slang.

"Dad!"

"Oh—Mr. Adair!" Hannah admonishes.

"What?" Dad teases, feigning a confused expression at Hope.

"Dad—we've gone over this. You can't say lit."

"Yeah, Mr. Adair, it's weird."

"Oh—okay," Dad says, defeated. He suddenly lifts his head and, with a sly smile, says, "Why? Is it—cringy?"

"No, no!" Hannah and I say in unison, covering our ears.

Hope and Dad walk in locked arms, and he notices her carrying the thick jacket that she purchased for our Christmas in Maine. "Hope, you know it's like 85 degrees out. Aren't you going to be hot with that jacket?"

"What? Oh, no, I get cold really easy, especially in movie theaters."

She has something there. Movie theaters in Florida are notorious for being frigid. I think they do it for the elderly.

# SOMERSET SECRETS
## by T.W. Morse

"Who's ready for *Scarlet Ninja II*?" Dad asks, making karate chops in mid-air after buying the four tickets to the 3D showing.

The ticket lady looks weirded out as she speaks through the intercom of her booth. "Don't forget your 3D glasses," she reminds us as she passes them through to Dad, who turns a little red.

Hannah and I need to escape this super nerd fest.

"Oh, I wish I was seeing that new romantic comedy called *Lost Love*. It's about a new neighbor that moves into a small quaint Carolina town. She loses her dog, and the guy next door helps her find him, and they fall in love," Hannah says, sighing.

"The way these nerds keep geeking out, I might agree, but we promised them a double date," I remind her as we move out of earshot of Dad and Hope.

"Ulysses Adair, they are really cute together. You're just jealous," Hannah teases, taking my hand and swinging joyfully while we walk to our assigned theater seats.

"Of what?" I snicker.

"You're jealous that we aren't the only cute couple anymore," Hannah says with a warming smile.

I smile back at her and realize she may be right as we sink into our reclining leather theater seats.

"Where's Bob tonight?" I ask, feeling like we're short a member of our group.

"Haven't seen him much these last few days. He's been spending a lot of time with Sarah. I actually think he said he was going on a date too. I'm surprised he's not with us; he loves action movies," Dad replies. Sarah and Bob have been dating since Christmas, and we've been seeing less and less of him—which isn't a bad thing.

Before getting too comfortable, I stand up and offer, "I'll spring for popcorn." Leaving Hannah with Dad and Hope, I speed back into the lobby.

"Argh!" I exclaim under my breath as I notice an ever-growing line at the concession stand. I decide to make one last pit stop at the bathroom before getting into the long line. Hopefully, it will die down by the time I am done. I swing open the door to find—another line.

"What?!" I comment. Only the women's room usually has lines like this. To add to my frustration, some guy cuts in front of me just as it is about to be my turn.

"Hey!" is all I can muster.

When the guy steps up to the urinal, he says in a low, sarcastic voice over his shoulder, "Deal with it, kid."

What the hell! All I can do is stand there pissed off. He is a tall, muscular guy, so I don't say anything more. He looks a little shady too with an old khaki rain jacket like they wore in the old classic movies and a red ball cap lowered down over his face, preventing me from seeing his facial features. His only definitive feature is his lame circa 1985 mullet that sticks out the back of his cap. Mr. Mullet is going to be my nickname for this villain. He's probably one of those jerks who secretly records the movie and pirates it out to people.

After finally doing my business in the bathroom, I get back into the concession line. The line has dwindled, but to my surprise, I am right behind the cutter—Mr. Mullet. He orders his popcorn, keeping his head down as he orders in a whisper. That is weird. When he is done, he walks by me with a jumbo size popcorn bag, quickly checking the time on his watch and looking down once again so that his hat shades most of his face from me. I only get a glimpse of a dated Freddie Mercury mustache that distracts me from his other features. His watch is nice, nicer than his clothes. It's one of those old Omega divers' watches.

"What can I get you, son? Son?! What can I get you?" an old lady behind the concession stand repeats, breaking me from my obsession with Mr. Mullet.

"Um—ah—yeah. I'll order two large popcorns and, um—ah—four waters to please," I order before paying and heading back into the theater.

Dad, Hope, and Hannah are all wondering what took me so long, so I relay the events in the bathroom and lobby. Dad then points at the front row and asks, "Is that your Mr. Mullet?"

I look up quickly, almost dropping the popcorn, and nod in disgust.

"Ulysses, you need to stop letting your anger get the best of you. Maybe you should have an outlet like me," Hannah suggests.

"What? Karate? Can you really see me doing karate?"

"Why not?"

"Well, if I did, I wouldn't need you to protect me all the time. And what fun would that be?" I ask before kissing her on the cheek. She blushes as the lights dim and the movie starts.

The movie is awful. I look at Hannah with raised eyebrows. I know we're both thinking that other movie, *Lost Love*, may have been a better selection. I look over to Dad and Hope, who are on the edge of their seats squirming during the fight scenes and even cheering when the Scarlet Ninja overpowers his opponent. Wow, they are so lame.

About a third of the way through the movie, a tall man slips into the theater unnoticed by everyone but me. He is so thin his red t-shirt hangs on him like a clothes rack. His gaunt face scans the audience as he slowly makes his way to the

**SOMERSET SECRETS**
*by T.W. Morse*

front of the theater, slinking into a seat right next to Mr. Mullet in the front row. They sit and whisper into each other's ears like they are old friends. Why would this guy be so late to a movie? I look at my Apple Watch, 9:00.

Hannah squeezes my arm and whispers, "What's wrong?"

"Nothing—nothing," I whisper back and refocus on the painful task of watching the movie, which has a typical action movie plot. The hero has to save his family before the big bad villain kills them. In this case, Japanese gangsters kidnap the Scarlet Ninja's long-lost daughter he didn't know about until this sequel. Everyone gasps when the gangster almost kills the daughter, but instead he goes into a long monologue, which gives the Scarlet Ninja time to come up with an escape plan. Wow, haven't seen this before—yawn. Just then I hear a click. And it wasn't from the movie. I look over and find Mr. Mullet leaving the gaunt, thin man behind and walking out the theater's emergency exit door. After he steps outside, Mr. Mullet continues to hold the door with one hand, leaving it open just enough so the door won't close and lock behind him. I nudge Hannah.

"What's he doing?" she asks.

"I don't know; maybe letting in someone for free? But why isn't the alarm going off?"

Hannah shrugs in confusion as I lower my 3D glasses to get a better look. My watch now reads 9:30. It's hard to see what he is doing. His hand is all that is visible as he props the exit door open. It seems like he is speaking to someone outside in the parking lot, but I can't quite make it out from my vantage point.

"Should we get security?" Hannah asks, taking my attention away from the door for a moment. In that brief moment, I look back and find Mr. Mullet already heading back to his seat next to the gaunt man. They say nothing to

**SOMERSET SECRETS**
*by T.W. Morse*

each other. Mr. Mullet just starts eating the popcorn, and his attention returns to the movie. Hannah looks at me and shrugs. We too turn our attention back to the movie.

The rest of the movie continues as expected. The Scarlet Ninja saves the day, gets his daughter back, and kills the gangster. Dad and Hope, along with other Scarlet Ninja nerds in the audience, clap as the credits roll. "Cringy." I have never understood why people clap at the end of movies. The movie stars can't hear your admiration.

As the lights go up, Dad asks, "So what did you kids think?"

But before Hannah and I can respond, we hear a woman a few rows in front scream. "Ahh!! He's got a knife!"

We frantically look up to where she is pointing. In the front row stands Mr. Mullet, with his Freddie Mercury mustache and trench coat, holding a large bag of popcorn in one hand and a knife covered in blood in his other hand.

Mr. Mullet is shaking his head yelling, "Help!—Help! This man is dead!" As he drops the knife, two burly looking middle-aged guys tackle Mr. Mullet to the ground while Hope, Dad, Hannah, and I run up to the front row. The man, now tackled to the ground, doesn't look quite the same as the guy who cut in front of me in line. As we watch him unsuccessfully squirm from his captors, I realize he has the same mustache and mullet as that man, but something's not quite right. I quickly relay this to Dad as he looks back at me puzzled.

When we arrive at the front of the theater, we all turn and find the tall, gaunt man slouched in his seat with blood seeping through his red t-shirt.

Dad says, "I'm calling 911. Hope, does he have a pulse?"

Hope gingerly leans over the body and feels his neck for a pulse. She shakes her head, discouraged. "He's—he's dead," Hope says before recoiling into Dad's arms.

Hannah crosses herself and grabs my hand tight to hers. I look at Dad, and we both have the same expression of dread.

## II.

Detective Brute's lanky frame moves into the theater like a marionette, his elbows flailing beneath his gray seersucker suit. All the audience members huddle in the back rows of the theater, guarded by a pacing deputy with a name tag that reads Miller.

After looking over the dead body, Detective Brute turns his bony elbows to the row where we sit and in his long, drawn out deep Southern twang exclaims, "Gr—eat, the A—dairs!" He then rolls his eyes in indignation. I guess he still hasn't gotten over our involvement in his last case.

"Good evening, Detective," Dad greets him with a twinkle in his eye.

Detective Brute shakes his head in response. "Deputy Miller!" The pacing deputy in an evergreen uniform snaps to attention and immediately marches over to Brute. "I want—state—ments from every—one pre—sent during—the mov—ie, you—hear? Do those—characters—last," he says, pointing at us. "I don't want them goin' no—where, ya—hear?" His deep Southern draw lingers on every word.

The deputy sheepishly nods.

The detective blows by us and approaches the handcuffed Mr. Mullet sobbing in the corner.

## SOMERSET SECRETS
### by T.W. Morse

"Detective, I can help!" I yell after him, leaping out of my seat.

"Quiet!" the deputy snorts, gesturing for me to sit myself back down.

After talking with the supposed Mr. Mullet for a few moments, Detective Brute looks over at me and comes striding our way with his pointing elbows flailing about.

"What?"

I quickly relay the night's events as they unfolded, from Mr. Mullet cutting in line in the bathroom to his chummy relationship with the victim, and then his opening of the exit door.

"What has this Mr. Mullet said so far?" Dad inquires, looking at him with a cocked, confused face as Mr. Mullet rises from his seat.

Detective Brute smirks. "You A—dairs,—al—ways putt—ing your nose where it should—n't be goin'."

"Hey, we solved a bunch of cases for you!" I exclaim.

Brute's smirk darkens at this. He looks over his shoulder and says, "Perp's name is Green. Chris Green. He said he does—n't know any—thing."

Brute doesn't finish his thought because Dad interrupts, "He said he was paid to sit in the front, next to the victim. He found the knife in the popcorn bag."

"What? How did you?" the deputy sputters before Brute can respond.

"That is corr—ect, Mr. A—dair. How did—y'all know—that?"

"When the exit door was opened. The first Mr. Mullet snuck out. Replaced by this guy dressed up like him," I conclude, a little confused, looking at Dad for confirmation.

Dad nods in agreement. "Ayuh. You can see his mouth where his Freddie Mercury mustache is coming off."

"Who is this Freddie Mercury? Is he a suspect?" Deputy Miller mutters to Dad.

Dad shakes his head and rolls his eyes in my direction, "Lead singer of the band Queen—rock god …" Still Miller and even Brute look a little confused. "Never mind," Dad says, giving up in disgust.

We all slowly walk over to Chris Green, sobbing, cuffed, and sitting in the second row only a few feet from the victim.

He looks up at us, but it's hard to return his gaze without giggling. His mullet wig has done a 180-degree turn under his red hat and his mustache is now hanging like a hinge above his lip. The victim's blood still stains his hands.

The detective slowly drawls out, "So Mr. A—dair, is this—the ma—n you saw?"

I look to Dad because I heard "Mr. Adair," but then realize Brute was speaking to me.

"Ah, sorta."

"Ah, sor—ta. Son, that ain't re—assuring," Brute says, putting his hands on his hips in disgust while his bony elbows spread out like bird wings.

"Well, I think Mr. Mullet and this Chris Green were both wearing disguises. This guy doesn't sound like the guy who cut in front of me in the bathroom line. Oh …" The memory pops back in my mind like a lightning crack. "This guy—Green isn't wearing that Omega divers' watch."

"You don't say," Deputy Miller says, smiling at Detective Brute, who looks amused by my revelation too.

"Yeah—what he said is true," Chris Green sputters, wiping away tears and the remainder of his disguise. "Some guy dressed in this same getup approached me a few hours ago down by the canal bridge. That's my spot, great fishing down there."

Hannah, who has been quiet through most of this ordeal, says emphatically, "Wait, are you homeless? I know that spot. It's near Penny University Café. My parents often bring everyone food there on Sunday mornings. I recognize you; you're always down there."

Chris aggressively nods, "Yes—see. I only wanted a buck. This guy with a mustache and mullet gave me an identical disguise with strict instructions to be at that exit door"—Chris points at the door with his cuffed hands—"Be at the exit door by 9:30 sharp, he said. He gave me $300 to switch seats with him and said I'd get another $200 after I left the theater. He told me I'd need to sit down next to the man in the front row and eat the bag of popcorn." Chris relays this with such a naïve voice, not fully realizing the trouble he has stumbled into.

"After the lights went up, I was directed to leave the same way I came—through the emergency exit door, but before I did, I found the knife. It had blood on it." At this recollection, he looks down at his sticky red hands and tries his best to unsuccessfully wipe away the blood from his shackled hands. "I looked down and the guy I was sitting next to was dead. I could see the stab wounds. I swear!" Chris pleads, "I didn't do it."

"Eat the bag of popcorn," Dad whispers to himself. "And you said you found the knife in the bottom of the popcorn bag?" Dad asks.

"The murderer must have hidden the knife at the bottom and planned for you to eat it through the remainder of the movie and find the knife at the bottom. Then the lights come on and you see the dead body, but you're holding the bloody knife with your prints all over it, so you're implicated. I bet the real Mr. Mullet used a glove," I add.

"This is absurd. The exit door being opened would've set off the alarm," Deputy Miller spouts.

Detective Brute just replies, "Ri—ght." Like it was a word longer than five letters. "Sooo, where—is the popcorn bag? And why did the alarm not go off?"

"I don't know. Maybe the killer dismantled the alarm. Wait—you mean you didn't see any popcorn bag?" I ask.

"Ah—no." Brute confirms.

"What? I mean, it was here. I know it was," I add.

Brute turns back to Chris, "And you did—n't notice he was—dead un—til the lights went—on?!" Brute laughs with a louder than necessary snicker. "That boy's—all hat and no cat—tle."

I look at Hannah and mouth in confusion, "All hat and no cattle?" She shrugs.

"Yes, I swear. Look, I didn't kill him. Please help me. You believe me? Right?" Chris asks, desperately looking up at me and Dad.

"So, the real Mr. Mullet met this man at the theater, killed him, and then switched places with this guy, Chris Green, and dressed as him? Why?" Hope exclaims, sounding confused.

"Alibi," Dad infers. "Detective, who is the victim?"

"Y'all will find out soon—er than la—ter. It's Roger Swan—son." Brute's sunken eyes look at us like we should know the guy by name. We all look blankly at each other. Dad is the first to respond.

"I'm sorry, sir, is he someone we should know?"

"You A—dairs. Think you know so—much but don't know anything. He's a Somer—set city council—man."

This takes us aback. What the hell is a Somerset city councilman doing meeting with a shady character like the real Mr. Mullet during a showing of *Scarlet Ninja II*?

## SOMERSET SECRETS
### by T.W. Morse

"Je—sus! We're wide o—pen as a case—knife. Mil—ler, I don't have ti—me ta deal with these folks," Detective Brute says before ordering Deputy Miller to take us back to the rear of the theater with the other witnesses.

We sit, hunched over in our seats, as Deputy Miller starts the interviews, leaving us for last.

"So, what do we know so far?" Dad offers, rallying the team for another mystery.

I start by saying, "We know the murderer was in disguise. He doesn't have a mustache or a mullet. We also know he paid Chris Green to impersonate the persona he created."

"We also know the murderer let him in at 9:30 through the exit door, leaving the murder weapon at the bottom of the popcorn bag," Dad adds.

"Yeah, for Chris to find, poor guy," Hannah interjects.

Hope shakes her head and adds, "Why? There have to be easier ways to kill someone."

"To give the murderer an alibi, so he could pin it on Chris. He probably used a rubber glove on the knife, and then left the knife so Chris would hold it with his prints. I bet he wore gloves the whole time so he wouldn't leave any evidence that could reveal his true identity," I reason.

"Yeah, and his plan worked. It appears that Detective Brute doesn't believe Chris's story. He probably thinks that, because Chris is homeless, he killed the councilman for money to feed an addiction. It certainly doesn't look good for Chris. He was found with the murder weapon, and he was seen sitting next to the councilman. Ulysses and Hannah may be the only ones who saw him go to the exit door, and we can't guarantee that the switch actually took place. It won't hold up in court," Dad works out with his analytical mind.

"So, we have to clear Chris, then?" Hannah clarifies.

"Yeah. We have to," I repeat before starting to rapidly type on my iPhone.

"What are you looking up?" Hannah asks.

"I'm looking up this Councilman Swanson. He has to have made enemies as a politician."

"Good. We don't have much time," Dad adds.

"Why?" Hope asks.

"Because I just figured out something. If the bag of popcorn was here when Chris found the knife, and we saw him hold both in the air before he was tackled, then where is that bag now? Why haven't the police found it? It would be covered in blood and prints."

Dad has a point. We all look puzzled as he lays this new issue out for us.

"What are you getting at, Dad?"

"I think the murderer is still here or an accomplice. Someone picked up that bag and disposed of it prior to the detective and the officers controlling the scene."

"What?!" Hope exclaims, a little too loud. She quickly covers her mouth before starting to whisper again, "The murderer is still here?"

Dad nods as we all quickly look around us in fear.

## III.

"We need to look for a used popcorn bag?" Hannah asks in disbelief, "In a movie theater? That's worse than a needle in a haystack."

"I know—right? Also remember to keep an eye out for that Omega watch. Those aren't worn much anymore. People either go without watches or wear smartwatches," I add.

"Hope and I will look for the popcorn bag and subtly question the other audience members. While we're at it, we'll also try to spot if they have the Omega watch you described. Hannah and Ulysses, you guys keep researching the councilman. Did Swanson have enemies? Take bribes? Was he investigated for anything that could warrant someone murdering him? Then you can join us in looking for the popcorn bag. No one has left the theater except a few police officers who have been in and out."

"The police won't hold everyone here forever. After they are done questioning people, they'll send us all home," Hope adds.

"Right. Look." I point to Detective Brute reading Chris his rights, which is excruciatingly slow with his drawl. He then orders two deputies to escort Chris from the movie theater to a squad car waiting outside. "We better hurry."

"Where should we start?" Hannah asks as I quickly type into my phone.

"I'm looking right now at the Somerset Daily News. I put in a search for our victim, Roger Swanson." Hannah leans into me, and her hair brushes against my cheek as she anxiously awaits the slow speed of the theater Wi-Fi. This momentarily distracts me from the situation we, once again, find ourselves in.

"This looks interesting. The headline reads *'Somerset Hardware Closes After Thirty Years.'* I read further and relay the article's highlights to Hannah. David and Marylyn Parkinson started Somerset Hardware back in the eighties. They were one of the few businesses still active from before the city grew in population—and wealth. A new, young city councilman, Roger Swanson, was spearheading a new condo complex on their exact spot.

"He wanted to bulldoze their shop?"

"According to this, last year he convinced the City Council to agree with him. But wait." I google David and Marylyn Parkinson. A picture pops up. "Do they look familiar?"

"No, but Ulysses—I do remember the store, though. It was right next to the ice cream stand we used to go to."

"Oh yeah. You're right; now Sunshine Manors sits there. The ice cream place was bulldozed at the same time."

Hannah gasps, "Yeah, and read the article under the picture of the Parkinsons."

"'David and Marylyn Parkinson took their lives in an apparent murder/suicide late Tuesday evening.' The date is exactly year ago today," I gasp, horrified.

"Do you think someone murdered the city councilman as retribution for their deaths? The date certainly fits with that scenario, given that their deaths happened exactly a year ago. This can't be a coincidence," I reason.

"No, and look at this! The only surviving relative was their foster son, Sebastian. Huh," Hannah says, pointing to her phone.

"What is it?" I ask. After Hannah makes her exclamation, a look of confusion comes over her.

"Well, this Sebastian, they don't put his age or his last name. Did he take their last name or did he keep his birth name?" Hannah says.

"Good questions, but this guy certainly sounds like a person of interest."

"Ulysses, this kid could be five years old."

"Or 25, we don't know," I say, pressing my point.

"Any other search results for the victim or this family he destroyed?"

## SOMERSET SECRETS
### by T.W. Morse

"Negative," I add with a sigh. "Nothing relevant anyway."

"Should we start looking for the popcorn bag?" Hannah asks.

"I was thinking that a bag like that could easily be folded up and put in a pants pocket," I add.

"Yeah—same as the watch, if the murderer overheard your description to the detective," Hannah adds.

I look around to see the deputies interviewing the last of the other witnesses. Dad and Hope are talking to the two guys who tackled Chris after he found the knife. Detective Brute is examining the exit door. Good, maybe this means Brute believed my story after all. Hannah and I stand up and walk over to sift through some of the disposed popcorn bags on the floor. Deputy Miller rushes up to us and says through gritted teeth, "Kid, sit down!"

"Sorry, Officer, we were just stretching our legs. Sitting for the movie and now for all of this."

"Deal with it, kid; this is a crime scene."

I am taken aback by his anger. What a jerk. Dad and Hope make their way back to us.

"What did you guys learn?" Dad asks.

Hannah and I take turns telling Dad and Hope about Somerset Hardware and Councilman Swanson bulldozing the Parkinsons' shop to erect the Somerset Manors condo complex. We also relay the murder/suicide of the Parkinsons a year ago on this very day. Dad softly whistles under his breath at this revelation.

"That's motive for murder," he says.

"Yeah, and they had a foster kid named Sebastian," I add.

"What was Sebastian's last name?" Hope asks.

"We don't know. We don't even know his age," Hannah confesses.

**SOMERSET SECRETS**
*by T.W. Morse*

"It's little to go on, but it's something," Dad says with a frown.

"Dad, what did you find?"

"Two things. First, the guys who tackled Chris after the lights went up swear that Chris was, in fact, holding a popcorn bag. Second, they agree that no one who was in the theater at the time of the murder left the theater. Deputy Miller arrived on the scene first, ushered people to stay in their seats, and waited for backup to arrive."

"One of the guys who tackled Chris could've taken the bag," Hope exclaims. "They were a little shady."

Something strikes me. Something that's lingering in the back of my mind, something that Dad just said. What was it?

"Ulysses, you okay?" Hannah asks.

"I got something. I just can't put my finger on it."

"Do you know who killed the councilman?" Dad asks, perplexed by my behavior.

I proceed to use Dad's technique and begin to review all the facts and moving parts in my head. I sit in the theater and watch the police move around us, dusting for prints and questioning witnesses. Then it hits me like a boulder.

"Dad, Sherlock Holmes always says when you eliminate the impossible, whatever remains, no matter how improbable, must be the truth."

"Yeah. Why? What you got?"

In a whisper I reveal, "It's Miller."

## IV.

"The deputy?" Hannah whispers back, with her mouth dropped in utter shock.

"Ulysses, we can't accuse the deputy of a crime. If we do, we need proof," Dad chimes in.

"Why do you think it's Deputy Miller?" Hope hisses while looking up at the deputy, who is pacing once again with a fake smile and appreciative nod.

"The way he said, 'Deal with it, kid.' It was the same voice and phrase that the real Mr. Mullet used back in the bathroom before the movie started: 'Deal with it, kid.'"

"That's not much to go on," Dad adds.

"He was the first to the crime scene," Hope adds. "He could've taken that popcorn bag and folded it up, putting it in one of his pants pockets. Maybe that's what he had planned all along."

I nod in agreement. "I bet the disguise is in his squad car too. He wouldn't have had too much time to get rid of the evidence," I relay.

"Yeah, but what's the motive? You think he's the Parkinsons' foster son, seeking revenge on the one-year anniversary of their deaths?" Hannah hisses out as our voices become lower and lower, afraid to be caught.

"Like I say to my students, we've got the world wide web at our fingertips. Let's investigate Deputy Miller," Dad adds.

Hannah is already on it. "The sheriff's department has bios on their website." She is clicking and typing twice as fast as any of us can. "There is not much here. Ian Miller, age 25. Loves to hunt and fish and has lived in Somerset his entire life. Nothing else. He has no children, and I believe he is single."

Dad is starting to go deep into his mind trance. He often pulls everything together in his head, working out the details of the evening and putting together this bloody puzzle.

"We need more evidence," he states, breaking from his trance. "If we're going to take this to Detective Brute, we need more to go on."

"I think the police are finishing up in here too and will start dismissing us soon," Hope adds.

"So, we don't have much time," I emphasize. I leap from my seat and march down the aisle to a pacing Deputy Miller. I imagine him with a mustache and mullet and can definitely say for sure that he is our guy, but I need proof.

"Kid—get back to your seat," the deputy calls out.

"I just want to know the time. My smartwatch just died, and we need to get back to our dog. Could you tell me the time?"

Instinctively, the deputy looks down at his left wrist, but it is bare, except for a distinct tan line—just the right size for an Omega divers' watch. He looks up at me, startled, and grunts, "Must have forgotten my watch at home." The deputy takes out his phone and says, "11:00." I thank him as his eyes drill into mine. I rapidly head back to my seat, feeling his eyes penetrate the back of my head as I exit.

Now I know for sure—Mr. Mullet is really Deputy Miller, and he suspects that I'm onto him. He must have taken off his watch after I described it to Brute.

I relay my test to Dad, Hannah, and Hope. Dad shakes his head. "It's still not much to go on," he adds as I catch a glimpse of the deputy now nervously looking at us.

"Oh my god! I got it," Hannah exclaims in a loud whisper, while keeping her head down below the seats so no one can hear her. "My cousin Sebastian," she hisses in a loud whisper.

"I don't think your cousin Sebastian killed the councilman," I joke, smiling.

"No—don't be *estupido*," Hannah says in Spanish. "My cousin, Sebastian, his nickname, it's … !" Before she can finish, Dad finishes for her.

"Ian."

She nods silently in affirmation, as we all swallow hard.

### V

"Miller must be his birth name. He must have been raised by the Parkinsons and is now seeking revenge on the man he blames for the death of his foster parents."

"What the …" Hope exclaims under her breath before Dad dashes for Detective Brute, who has just snapped off two rubber gloves in the front of the theater.

"That's enough for Brute; everyone stay here," is all Dad can say before clearing the aisle and making his way over to Detective Brute.

We watch Dad whisper rapidly in the detective's ear. First, we notice Brute sigh and emit negative body language as his wing-like arms snap back as if he is about to take flight, placing his hands on his hips. But then I see Brute's hard gaze focus on Deputy Miller. Maybe Brute knows about his foster parents, or maybe he suspected Miller all along. Suddenly Deputy Miller stops and turns, locking eyes with Detective Brute. His face turns pale white as he panics and sprints past us, exiting the back of the theater and into the lobby.

"Stop Deputy Mil—ler!" Detective Brute shouts to his other deputies. They all look stunned and barely move.

"Let's go!" I say, grabbing Hannah's arm.

"Wait, kids—no!" we hear Hope shout just as Detective Brute gets on his walky-talky, "Apre—hend Deputy Mil—ler!"

We run to the lobby to find Deputy Miller with his gun pointed at several other deputies, who, in turn, are pointing their guns at him. Hannah and I run right into the scene. Before we know it, Deputy Miller shifts his gun to aim it at Hannah and me.

"Put your guns down—or these damn kids will get what's coming to them," Miller shouts at the deputies. Dad and Detective Brute burst through the door we had just come out of. Brute, who had his gun drawn, now lowers it when he realizes this is a hostage situation, caused by our stupidity.

Damn! What an idiot I am for leading Hannah and me into this mess is all I can think about.

"Brute! You're going to let me leave this theater," Miller demands. "I don't know how this kid figured it out!"

"What? That—you mur—dered a city council—man to a—venge the death of your foster pa—rents? You won't get a—way with this; you're sur—rounded," Brute says as he and Dad creep slowly toward both of us. With each step they take, Deputy Miller backs his way toward the next theater over. The marquis says *Lost Love*, that romantic comedy Hannah wanted to go to. I now really wish we went to that instead of *Scarlet Ninja II*.

Deputy Miller's back is now just a few inches from the swinging door of the theater. "We figured it all out. Well, Ulysses and Hannah did at least. The only part I don't get is how you lured Roger Swanson to the movies in the first place. And how did you disable the exit door alarm?" Dad asks, continuing to creep forward with Brute.

"Paid off some little usher to disable the alarm system. As for Swanson, we were on a date," Deputy Miller hisses. "I lured that fool from a dating website. I knew he was gay, and he thought we had hit it off. Oh, that bastard didn't know what was coming. He arrived late because of traffic. I almost thought he wouldn't show." Every word of this diatribe is accompanied by a spray of saliva that hits Hannah and me smack in the face.

"Yuck," Hannah protests.

"He killed my parents!" His primordial rage is now bursting through. "He took everything! For what? A god damn condo complex! That business was their life!" Tears are now falling as he waves the gun in the air above our heads.

Hannah looks pissed, like she is about to make a karate move, but just then our luck pivots. For in that moment, the 9:30 *Lost Love* movie ends, and we can hear people getting up to leave the theater. The swinging doors behind him burst open like a gale force wind, knocking the back of Deputy Miller's head, crunching against his skull and forcing him to drop the gun as he crumples to the ground. I kick it out of the way as Detective Brute rapidly moves in to cuff him.

The first person to exit the theater, knocking out Deputy Miller, is talking in a deep Barry White-like voice, "Let me tell you somethin', baby—that was one funny movie." To our shock, Bob Nelson exits the theater with an arm around his girlfriend, Sarah Evans. After seeing all the deputies with their guns drawn, he quickly puts his hands up in the air. "Whatever happened, I didn't do it."

"Bob!" We all exclaim in unison. "You saved us." Hannah gives him a quick hug.

"What? Ah—okay. Yeah, that's what Bobby Nelson does—you dig," Bob says, first confused, but then using the situation to his advantage. "You know that's right. Mmm—mmm."

While frisking Deputy Miller, Detective Brute pulls an Omega watch and a folded up, bloody popcorn bag from Miller's pant pockets.

"Nice job, Ulysses!" Dad says, placing a hand on my shoulder.

"I bet his Mr. Mullet outfit is stashed in his police cruiser too," I add.

"You A—dairs are some—thing, I reckon," Detective Brute mutters before hauling Deputy Miller away.

"What is going on?" Sarah questions. "Bob, your friends are always getting into trouble."

Dad puts his arm around Bob, hugging him from the side with his other arm braced around my shoulder. "And Bob is always getting us out of it. We'll explain the whole adventure over some drinks back at Penny University Café."

"Yeah, drinks are on me," Hannah adds.

"Sounds good to me. I could use a coffee. And Dad—Hannah and I are picking the next date night movie," I insist as we all laugh.

*SOMERSET SECRETS*
*by T.W. Morse*

# BOB'S GRANMAMA'S GOT A BIG...BIG PROBLEM

## LOGAN

### I.

"Where are we going, Bob?" I ask, stirring in the driver's seat of my old silver Prius as it putters up highway 75.

I am growing impatient with Bob's cryptic request, which is leading Ulysses, Hannah, and me on a possible wild goose chase.

The three of us were all on our way to get lunch on this fine sunny Saturday when Bob showed up, panicked. "Dude, I need your help. It's a family thing in Cape Coral. I'll explain on the way."

I'm done waiting for him to explain. "So what is it? What is your 'family thing'?" I ask, frustrated that my lunch was interrupted.

Bob starts to wring his hands. His black Adidas tracksuit makes him look like he is about to attend some warped funeral. Bob tends to be a nervous guy, even anxious at times, but this level of anxiety is worrisome. "Mmm—mmm, let me tell you somethin', Logan. I sure hope y'all can help."

"No worries, Mr. Nelson—I mean, Bob. We can help," Hannah gently reassures him.

"Yeah, Bob. But we can't help if we don't know the problem," Ulysses adds.

"Y'all so good to me. Helping Bobby out all the time. You guys are like family to me."

I put an arm around his shoulder. "I know, buddy. So, what can we do?"

"Well, it's like this: my Granmama Nelson is in a little bit of trouble. I mean, nothing too bad. Let me tell ya somethin'—she's a tough old lady. For a while, according to Latesha—"

"Who's Latesha?" Hannah asks before Bob finishes his thought.

"My niece, my sis's kid. Now she is quite the troublemaker—you know that's right," Bob snickers to himself.

"Bob, back to the story," I interrupt to get him back on task.

"Well, according to Latesha and her momma—my sis Shellyann—Granmama has been ah—into a little, um—um, how do I put this?"

"Anyway—just get on with it!" Ulysses yells from the back seat.

"Well, Granmama Nelson, according to Latesha—you know, Shellyann's daughter—my sis." We all roll our eyes in frustration as Bob takes excruciating amounts of our lives away telling his story.

"Bob!"

"Okay—okay. Well, Granmama has a bit of a gambling problem," he says as he puts his face into his hands. "Logan, I don't know what to do! She's in for ten large."

"Ten thousand dollars!" I blurt without even thinking while I hear Ulysses whistle in the back.

"Who does she owe ten thousand to?!" I inquire, a little concerned myself.

# SOMERSET SECRETS
## by T.W. Morse

"Ah—according to Latesha, some bookie in Cape Coral. His name is Eddie Money. I tried looking up this dude on the computer but couldn't find him anywhere."

"Bob—Money is probably not his real name. He's a bookie. It's probably an alias, you know, a fake name. Your granmama is in some real trouble. This Eddie could wreck her life or worse."

"I know, Logan. I need my crew to figure this one out." As Bob releases this tale, his black freckled face grows pale.

"We got this," Ulysses confidently encourages him.

"Yeah, you can count on us," Hannah adds.

I feel a little out of my element: what the hell do I know about gambling and dealing with bookies? But I nod reassuringly anyway.

"I'm worried about Latesha. She has been living with Granmama awhile, on her gap year before college. Mmm—mmm," Bob explains, sounding more concerned and frightened than I have ever heard him before.

The rest of the trip to Bob's granmama's house passes in silence as we traverse the expansive bridge over the Caloosahatchee River to Cape Coral.

I rack my brain on how to help a grandmother, in debt ten grand, negotiate with a bookie. How do you do that? One thing I know is Bob has helped me and Ulysses more times than I can count. So, if we can help—we will.

## II.

Granmama's house is bigger than I expected. It's an expansive ranch, nestled in a quiet cul-de-sac, and, like most homes in Cape Coral, it sits directly on a canal. The house looks new and pristine, except for a broken mailbox post. "What did Granmama do before she retired?" I ask as we approach a bright red lacquered door with a camera doorbell.

Bob just shrugs. "Ah—banking, I think." I raise my eyebrows at this as we are greeted by a young African American woman, most likely Bob's niece, Latesha.

"Uncle Bobby!" she screams, jumping into Bob's arms.

"Hey La-La." I notice Ulysses mouths La-La to Hannah from the corner of my eye as we all step into the house. "This my best friend, Logan Adair; his kid, Ulysses; and Ulysses's girlfriend, Hannah Reyes."

"Nice to meet you. I've heard so much about you—La-La," I greet her, causing Latesha to blush at my use of the pet nickname Bob most likely gave to her.

"Uncle Bobby has called me La-La since I was able to speak. I had difficulties pronouncing my name and would often say La-La instead of Latesha. Of course, Bobby thought that was so cute, so it stuck," she says with a shrug.

"That Bobby can be so cute," I laugh, chuckling and elbowing Bob.

"Mmm—mmm. La-La, where is Granmama? I brought my friends to help her out with her—ah—problems," Bob grunts in explanation of our visit as Ulysses and Hannah shake hands with Latesha.

"Bobby—Granmama is not goin' to like these white folk gett'n all up in her business!" Latesha now drops the pleasantries, showing her true thoughts to Bob. "I told you about the money she owes in confidence!" She tries to communicate in a whisper to Bob; however, we all hear her loud and clear.

Bob pleads, "La-La. They good. This is my crew. Together we've solved murders and mysteries from Somerset to Maine. You read about us in the newspapers, remember?

**SOMERSET SECRETS**
**by T.W. Morse**

They helped me solve the murder of that rich guy and the Mangrove High Principal who were murdered. We solved that together. I know we can be of use with Granmama too."

I turn to roll my eyes at Ulysses and Hannah at Bob's insertion of himself in our crime-solving escapades: a bit of a stretch there, Bobby.

"But this Eddie Money is a bad dude. Him and his guys are always dealing in the back of their store," Latesha explains.

"I know we can help," I add as I give a confident glance to a worried Bob.

"Okay, I guess you guys couldn't make it worse." Latesha says, gesturing for us to follow her.

Granmama's house is decorated with dozens of glass figurines, entire shelves of them. With chrome and glass shelving, the whole place looks like something out of *The Golden Girls*. Added to this look is the wicker furniture with its floral cushions. I almost expect Betty White to pop out of the kitchen.

Latesha brings us out to the lanai. It too is dotted with dated, floral-covered furniture. The canal is just a few steps away, beyond the end of the pool cage, looking muddy in comparison to the sparkling pool. In the middle of the pool is a large blow up chair holding up a round and fairly old black woman wearing a bathing suit that matches her furniture. She is sipping a giant margarita while wearing rhinestone encrusted sunglasses. She is so engrossed in her drink, she doesn't notice her new guests. She holds the straw of her glass with long, bedazzled pink fingernails that appear to be twice as long as Hope's manicured nails.

"Granmama! You have visitors," Latesha says before ducking out of the lanai, not wanting anything to do with what is about to transpire.

"Granmama!" Bob bellows.

"Boo-Bear!" she exclaims in a high-pitched voice, oddly reminiscent of Bob's when he is frightened, as she ungracefully exits the pool. It is my turn to mouth Boo-Bear to Ulysses and Hannah as they try their best to hide smirks.

"Boo-Bear. It has been too long!" she says with a huge grin as she tightly consumes Bob into a wet hug, leaving his black tracksuit soaked. "How's my Boo-Bear?" she asks, rubbing her nose to his.

It takes everything in my power for me to not laugh out loud with this new bit of information. Ulysses and Hannah look like they are about to burst from holding in laughter.

Bob introduces us to his gran as we all take seats around a large patio table.

"To what do I owe my sweet Boo-Bear's visit on this fine Saturday? Bringing his friends too! Are you guys here for a pool party? Lunch? I can whip up some egg salad for y'all."

"Mmm—mmm, that does sound good," Bob says looking at us. I nudge him and nod to get on with it.

"Granmama. Um—Latesha told me about your gambling problem."

"She what!" All the smiles and affection suddenly drop as a stern, old, serious woman is now staring at Bob like she could murder him with her eyes. "Latesha! Latesha! You get out here girl—now!"

"Granmama! Enough! It is not La-La's fault. You are in some serious trouble. I brought my friends to help you."

"Boo-Bear. I can handle it. What your white friends goin' do anyway? This Eddie Money character is big time."

"Mrs. Nelson. How much do you owe Mr. Money?" I ask. She looks at me like I hadn't been there before and waits for Bob to introduce me.

# SOMERSET SECRETS
## by T.W. Morse

"Granmama, this is my best friend, Logan Adair; his son, Ulysses; and Ulysses' girlfriend, Hannah." Bob uses the same spiel he gave Latesha about our adventures and how we solved murders. "We know what we're doing, and we're here to help. They've even saved my life a time or two."

With this, her gram demeanor returns and a sparkle comes back to her eye. She then gives me her full attention. "Logan, my dear. I have heard of you. What a sweet boy." She takes my hand, pushing past Bob, and gives me the adoration he had just moments ago. "You can call me Granmama."

"Okay," I cautiously reply, now flustered.

Ulysses seizes the opportunity for some questioning. "Where can we find this Eddie Money?"

"Oh dear—yes. He runs a small racket out of a pawn broker store on 15 South West Street, in an old run-down strip mall."

"Did this Eddie break your mailbox?" I add.

"Yes! He sure as hell did!" Now Granmama is holding back tears. "He sent one of his thugs. He's got two of them. The Bowmans. Twin brothers who each got only half a brain between the both of them. They are his muscle, and they don't take no for an answer. They said if I don't pay by next Friday, they will take everything I own."

"How did it all start? What happened? Ten grand is a lot to be betting," Ulysses adds.

With this, Granmama's tears start falling. Her mannerisms mirror Bob's. He tries to console her, but she turns to me instead.

"Start from the beginning," I say as I pat her back, at which time I receive a surprisingly jealous stare from Bob.

"Well, I had some items that I wanted to sell at the pawn broker awhile back. One day I was in there selling Granddaddy's old watch."

"You sold Granddaddy's watch?!"

"Hush, child, let Grandmama speak." I nod, agreeing with her. "This nice man, Eddie, had a TV on watching horse racing. I love horses, so I asked him about the race. He said he loved horses too. So we hit it off. He told me how I could make some money by picking the right horses and leaving the bets with him."

"Oh Granmama!" Bob cries out.

"Hush, Boo," Granmama admonishes.

"Yeah, hush, Boo," Ulysses and Hannah say in unison, holding back their laughter.

"After weeks of betting, using my savings, I won! I won a lot. I loved the thrill of betting and watching my horses win. Eddie helped me with my bets, guided me to the right winners, week after week."

"I bet he did," I inject. "Then—just like that—you started to lose," I surmise.

She nods. "I kept losing too. I lost big. I wanted to get out, but I didn't want to lose what I put in! And now I owe Eddie ten thousand dollars! He knows that Latesha is living with me, and he even hinted at hurting her! Oh—what am I gonna do?!" she wails with tears now pouring down her plump cheeks.

Hannah places a hand on Granmama's shoulder. "We can help. Are those glass figurines worth a lot? Is there anything we could sell to get the ten grand you owe?"

"My glass figurines. No, child! Good heavens, no—I've collected those since I was your age, dearie."

"Gran—we might have to. They could hurt you or Latesha," Bob adds.

**SOMERSET SECRETS**
*by T.W. Morse*

"Not with my Boo-Bear and the Adair men on the case. And you too, dear," she says, including Hannah as an afterthought as she stands and gives us all wet hugs, leaving us as soaked as Bob.

### III.

The strip mall housing Eddie Money's pawn shop is only a few miles from Granmama's house, but the canals force us to travel in a roundabout way, causing much longer drive times, typical for Cape Coral. It ends up taking about twenty minutes for Bob and I to drive there.

The mall itself has seen better days and is as sleazy as you can get. The atmosphere is a clear indication of the type of business Eddie Money conducts. I park my Prius in the middle of the busy parking lot, far enough away so that we're hidden from the people in the store, but close enough that we can get a good look at the comings and goings from the store. I take out my binoculars that I had stashed in the glove compartment. Bob takes them out of my hands and puts them up to his face.

"Mmm—mmm. What's the play, Logan? We bust in there and threaten them? Maybe they back off?" Bob suggests, anxious to get into the store.

"Ah—no," I reply, ripping the binoculars back in frustration. "We aren't going to do this by intimidation. What criminals would be intimidated by us? We get the lay of the land, and we divide and conquer. I had Latesha drive Ulysses and Hannah back to my place for supplies, remember?"

"What kind of supplies?"

"Bob, it's best you don't know the plan."

"Wait, so you got a plan?"

"Ah—well, I have the start of one at least. It really depends on Eddie and his goons. We'll wait here for Latesha to arrive with the kids, and then we'll make our move."

The waiting seems to take several hours of sitting in the Prius with a whining Bob, but in reality, it only takes Latesha about an hour to return with the kids. Latesha's beat up Ford Escort drives up slowly. Ulysses runs out of the car and hands me a paper bag, saying, "Good luck, Dad," before dashing back into Latesha's car.

"Good, my first phase is ready to go."

"What first phase, Logan? Why you bein' so cryptic? Let me tell you somethin', Granmama is in some big trouble, and you said you could help! What you got planned?"

"Bob—I have a plan, trust me. I think we got this." As I say this, Latesha's car rolls around to the back of the strip mall. I count to 100 then take a deep breath before saying, "Okay—let's go."

"What? Inside?" Bob squeaks. I bolt out of the car, and he tries his best to catch up.

"Where did Latesha go?"

"Hopefully, by the time we're done, we will rendezvous with them at the back of the store."

Before we can be viewed by the shop keeper, I pull Bob aside and explain to him that I'll go in first and he is to follow after thirty seconds. Under no circumstances is he to look in my direction or give any hint that we know each other.

"You do all the talking, but pretend like you don't know me. I got a plan," I whisper into Bob's ear before stepping into the store.

"What? Really?"

"Yeah—you got this, buddy."

**SOMERSET SECRETS**
*by T.W. Morse*

"You know that's right," Bob says confidently in his Barry White voice.

I casually make my way in. "Just window shopping for a guitar," I announce. The pawn shop looks like a garage sale threw up in a ratty old store. Everything from guitars and brass instruments to many ornate vases are spread throughout. Glass floor cabinets are chock full of silver and gold jewelry.

An unshaven man with a terrible Hawaiian shirt and thick gold chain hanging from a leathered tan body looks up. His fish lips swim around a toothpick that needs replacing. I deduce that this is the Eddie Money character we're looking for. He stands behind the register, leaning on a tall stool. He licks his right hand and wipes back his greasy hair before turning the page of the newspaper he's perusing.

Two men, almost identical in appearance, come to the front of the store through an old saloon-style swinging door. Both men have to turn sideways to make it through the doorway because they weigh about six hundred pounds together. Their vacant expressions cause me to conclude that they weren't read to as children. The Bowman twins, I presume.

Bob strolls in like a bull in a pawn shop—literally. It is hard for Bob to hide his emotions, but that's what I was counting on.

Eddie awkwardly folds his newspaper and asks, "Can I help you, son?" Even his voice sounds greasy. The Bowman twins just sit down on two flimsy metal chairs behind the counter. I actually feel sorry for the chairs, as they look like they have been holding up these two loads for a while.

As Bob approaches the counter, I drift away to stand behind him. Luckily, there are no other customers in the store. Bob walks up to the cash register, staring into Eddie's slanted eyes for a long minute before saying anything. "Do you know Roxanne Nelson?"

"Roxanne, Roxanne—'fraid—not—boy."

I cringe with that comment. I hope Bob doesn't get too angry. I step further behind him, pretending to be unassuming as I fiddle with one of the guitars hanging high on the wall facing the cash register.

"What the hell did you say? I am nobody's boy! I will knock you down off that stool," Bob spouts.

With this, both twins rise from their crippled chairs and move behind Eddie.

"I may know of a Roxanne Nelson." He looks back at the twins with an even greasier smile. "Yeah—doesn't that old broad owe us ten large?" Both Bowman twins nod, or I think they do; their necks are so fat I can't be sure. I am watching most of this exchange through reflections off of the hanging brass instruments as I feign interest in one of the electric guitars.

"Why you takin' advantage of a little old lady?" Bob exclaims with increased tension in his voice.

"She likes to bet. I merely provide the service to meet her needs. I am just a facilitator of her unfortunate addiction. What do you care?" Eddie inquires with a greasy, condescending tone.

"I'm her grandson, Bob, and I want to pay back the money for her."

"Grandson? She never mentioned you. Well, debts can't be transferable—yet. I'm sure her great-granddaughter she has living with her could pay the debt. What's her name? Oh—yeah, Latesha. What a fine—girl. I'm sure we can find a way for her to work off the money owed," Eddie threatens while his lips twitch around the old toothpick.

## SOMERSET SECRETS
### by T.W. Morse

"What you say?" Bob shouts in a rage as he lunges over the counter and grabs Eddie by the collar, lifting him off the stool. This action would've been super heroic, but he is stopped, almost as quickly as he starts, by the Bowman twins. They take Bob's big head and smash it hard against the counter, pinning both shoulders so he is unable to move.

Eddie leans up against Bob's ear and hisses, "You listen here, grandson. I catch you around here again, I will have my associates kill you, your grandmother, and your niece— you understand? Tell your grandma that I want my money by Friday! Or else I'll pay that Latesha a visit! You understand me?"

At this, I make my way out of the store unseen and wait at the Prius for Bob.

A few minutes later, Bob emerges, looking like the life has been sucked out of him. He's holding the left side of his face, which looks red but not bruised. I crack the window and instruct him to get in quickly. Bob jumps in as I peel out of the parking lot.

"Where were you in there? You didn't have my back! We could've taken them. I thought you always had my back!" Bob complains in a voice varying between yelling and cracking.

"Bob! That was all part of the plan."

"Oh—yeah! The plan was for my best friend to abandon me like that? That was your plan?"

"Ah—no. The plan was for you to distract those jerks so I could unassumingly place my camera on an empty outlet. It's motion activated and set to record everything. Ulysses handed it to me before we went in. We had bought one for a surveillance job our neighbors hired us for but never used it. I'm glad we now have a chance. I thought I wasted my money, but I guess not."

"Say what?! A camera?"

"Yeah, they look like typical white USB outlets that you plug a charging cord into, but they have a motion-activated, built-in camera lens. They don't have audio, but I got a terabyte SD card, so it should capture a lot. I'll go back in a few days and retrieve it, and no one will be the wiser. I planted it on the floor outlet, right below the guitars, while you were in your scuffle. Those wise guys are now under our surveillance. You were great, by the way! You showed real chivalry protecting your granmama and niece like that," I praise, causing Bob to grin widely in response.

"Logan, you're a genius!"

## IV.

"It was a success!" Ulysses exclaims exuberantly as we sit in the back of Latesha's car with Ulysses struggling for breathing space between me and Bob in the cramped back seat. We met Latesha at the opposite street facing the back of the store.

"Ah—what was a success?" Bob asks with his face tilted in confusion.

"Ulysses, Hannah, and Latesha had a separate mission," I inform Bob.

"Oh—yeah, it was lit. We planted our old wireless security camera on a tripod out back of the strip mall. Latesha said they do drug deals there daily. And we'll catch them in the act," Ulysses adds.

"Yeah, the cops don't know anything about it. I know a few of my friends are involved in that crap. They say Eddie keeps his client list short, so they stay under the radar of the police," Latesha injects.

"We got a perfect angle, a real tight shot on the back door of Eddie's shop. Here, let me show you," Hannah says while opening our old laptop on Latesha's car dash. She brings up a live video feed of the back door of the strip mall. "We just have to be under 150 feet away; that's why we parked so close."

"Come on, son. I don't see nothin'," Bob whines.

"It's motion activated," Ulysses explains with a sneer. "As soon as we have some movement back there, it will turn on, just like the one Dad planted inside."

"If nothing happens tonight, we'll check back tomorrow. If we haven't seen any action in three days, we'll remove all the cameras inside and outside the store. Then we'll double check the footage and find out if we have enough to take to the police. Eddie and the twins can't collect from Granmama from behind bars," I reassure Bob.

"So this is like a stakeout? Mmm—mmm," Bob says eagerly.

"This is a stakeout," Ulysses affirms, shuffling around. "And I wish we had a bigger car, like a van. How did I get the back seat? The girls and I should be back here."

"I got something!" Hannah exclaims, looking over her shoulder with excitement.

"That was quick," I add. We watch the video to see the Bowman brothers head out of the back to greet a hooded figure, and they are soon joined by Eddie.

"It looks like a drug deal," Latesha adds.

"Good, we'll catch them red handed," Ulysses says, now very anxious to get out of the backseat.

The hooded figure gives Eddie a packet of money. Eddie then gives the hooded figure a large brown bag, and the hooded figure walks away from the strip mall.

"We got him," Ulysses exclaims.

"Maybe. I'm calling the police on this hooded figure," I say, proceeding to dial 911 and report a possible drug deal, giving the description and whereabouts of the subject. "Okay, Hannah and Latesha, take the laptop with the video and follow the hooded guy. Hopefully, an officer will be responding soon, and when they do, you can show them the video. He's on foot and shouldn't go too far, but be careful. Bob, Ulysses, and I will go back to the store to retrieve the camera so we can check for any relevant footage. There's enough of us that we can go back and replant the camera if we need to."

Bob, Ulysses, and I pile out of Latesha's tight backseat. I quickly scribble a message on a piece of paper for Hannah, handing it to her and reminding her, "Be careful."

## V.

We get to the Prius and return to our former parking spot in the strip mall. Close enough to run back to, but far enough away not to be seen. "Okay, Ulysses and I will go in; we'll distract Eddie and the twins while we retrieve the camera."

"Ah—Whatcha—want'n me to do, Logan?" Bob asks nervously.

"You're the getaway driver. Hop into the driver's seat once we leave and keep the Prius purring so we're ready to split at the first sign of trouble. Here, let me call you on my phone and I'll just keep it in my pocket. That way we can keep a line open between our phones. You'll be able to hear everything."

"Right. Okay. I got it," Bob affirms.

I share the whereabouts of the camera with Ulysses, explaining that it's near the guitars on the wall facing the counter. "I'll let Eddie know that I'm in search of a new acoustic guitar for you when we arrive."

"Wish that were true," Ulysses says under his breath. I only can shake my head at this. I call Bob on my phone before entering. "You there—good buddy?"

"Loud and clear, Logan." I turn the volume all the way down on my phone so Bob won't be heard on our end, set my phone to record, and place it in my back pocket before entering the pawn shop for the second time.

Eddie and both twins eat behind the counter, looking more thuggish than usual. I guess drug deals induce hunger.

"How can I help you, sir? Ah—you were the one earlier today looking for a guitar—right?"

"Yes. That was me. Actually, it was for my son here. He is in need of a new acoustic guitar." I turn to Ulysses and say, "Why don't you check out those ones over there?" I point to the wall where I planted the camera. Ulysses nods and walks over while I join Eddie at the front counter. The Bowman brothers stand on either side, and they look hungry—even though they're already eating.

"Do you recommend a certain model? Or should I go with one of those Spanish ones?" I point to the antique guitar directly behind the counter, and all three men turn their heads, hopefully giving enough time for Ulysses to complete his task. "How much for that one?" As the pleasantries volley back and forth about the price of Eddie's guitars, I feel a tug on the back of my shirt from Ulysses. I turn to him and he gives me a startled look and mouths, "it's gone."

I turn back to the counter, and Eddie's greasy smile is looking through me. "I think we better get going. The prices are too high here. Thanks anyway."

"What's the rush—Mr. Adair?" Eddie asks as I hear a clinking sound of metal to glass. I look down to the counter and find Eddie is now pointing a very large gun in our direction.

"How dumb do you think I am?" Eddie sneers.

"Pretty dumb, if you ask me," Ulysses spouts. I gesture for him to be quiet.

"You brought your pesky son too. Ulysses and Logan Adair. When I saw that bumbling idiot Bob Nelson in here earlier, I did a bit of research, and sure enough, he's associated with a father and son set of amateur sleuths that like to investigate crimes. So I had my boys here do a search of any cameras or recording devices that you may have planted." He pointed to the Bowman twins, who have, quickly for their size, come from behind the counter and are now standing on either side of me and Ulysses.

"Wish we had Hannah," Ulysses mutters in my ear.

I can only smile at this statement. But then my smile quickly fades as I fully realize the extent of our trouble. Once again, we are in danger for our lives. Definitely not going to get Dad of the Year. I've got to keep Eddie talking so my plan has time to work.

"So, Eddie, you're not as dumb as you look," I say as he pours our camera from a box onto the glass counter—what was left of the camera anyway. Several camera fragments clatter against the glass counter.

"As soon as you left, I found this. The twins found the camera out back too. We left that one for you guys. We left it for you to waste your time with—ha—ha. Like dangling a carrot." Eddie's greasy laugh gives me a chill.

"Wait, that drug transaction was a fake? You and these two douchebags thought that up. All on your own? Not bad for a few drop-out thugs," Ulysses injects.

"Watch your mouth, mini Adair. We pulled a fast one on you two, and you fell for it. You think you're so smart? I'm going to kill both of you, and then I'm going to collect the ten grand from the old lady and work off the interest with that little great-granddaughter," Eddie threatens as he waves his gun in satisfaction.

"So a step up from drug dealing and gambling. Murder or even attempted murder will put you away for a very long time, Eddie," I say, trying to make him talk a little longer.

"The police have got to prove it, Mr. Adair. Some lousy classroom teacher snoop and his mouthy son can't stop me. I want to increase my drug operation. This store is just a front. We don't even sell most of the merchandise here. The vases are all stuffed with several pounds of cocaine—police don't know Jack." Eddie sneers again as the Bowman twins chuckle. "Get rid of them. Shoot them out back, but take down that camera first."

Just then, like a superhero, Bob comes thundering through the door holding a tire iron. "Let my friends go!" He suddenly spots Eddie's gun and drops the tire iron.

"And kill this joker too," Eddie adds, cocking his gun and motioning it at Bob, as both of the Bowman twins put us in bear holds.

"Logan, Ulysses, I'm so sorry for bringing you in on this. It's all my fault. I heard what you guys were saying in the car and had to come in and help you."

"Wait, they're recording this?! Frisk them," Eddie demands.

"Bob!" Ulysses shouts.

"I don't know why your plan failed. Your plans never fail," Bob whines.

Ulysses looks up at me through the bear hold with a confused expression, just as blue lights appear outside and a half dozen police officers parade through the front and back of the store yelling, "FREEZE!! FREEZE! POLICE! You are under arrest!" Eddie places his gun on the counter, and all three thugs raise their hands in the air.

Hannah and Latesha race in behind the officers. Hannah gives Ulysses a hug before giving me one too. "We came as fast as we could after I read your note," Hannah informs us.

"What note?" Bob asks, stunned.

"Ah—well, this was all part of my plan," I sheepishly confess.

## VI.

"This was your plan the whole time?!" Ulysses exclaims while Hannah and Latesha stand back and smile. Bob is still dumbfounded. "I kinda knew, but wasn't 100 percent sure, until Bob said your plans never go wrong. They don't, so I figured this must have been the plan all along."

"Afraid so. I knew the only way to get Eddie caught and in prison, away from Granmama, was to show the police who he really was: a drug dealer with the potential to become a murderer. Being a bookie was just a side gig. I knew he would be suspicious of a man entering the store a few seconds before Bob and thought it likely that he would research Bob. In doing that, he'd find the news articles and pictures of me and him together solving one or more of our mysteries, and he'd put two and two together. So, I deduced that the camera was going to be compromised, and Eddie would be onto us."

"You knew he would be onto you?" Latesha finally speaks, a little confused.

"My plan involved keeping everyone in the dark. I needed everyone to do their parts and not give away the master plan. This was key considering that Bob doesn't have the best poker face. I also know Eddie would want to put on a show for us so we would think he was performing a drug deal in the back of the store to lure us in. So my plan all along was to confront him and record him confessing. Idiots like that always monologue their misdeeds."

"Yeah, the bag was empty. I showed the cops the video and led them back to the store. When we arrived, we could see through the window of the store that Eddie was holding a gun on you guys," Hannah says, out of breath.

"What was in the note Dad gave you?" Ulysses asks. I am about to answer, but Hannah shows it to him smiling. 'The bag will be empty. Eddie knows we are onto him and will try and kill us. Get the police back to the store ASAP. This is the real plan.'"

"And what if she couldn't get them back in time?" Bob asks incredulously.

"I suspected that the police had their suspicions of Eddie for a while, so they were just looking for a reason to arrest him. Seeing a gun trained on us helps too. In seeing that, they wouldn't need a warrant and would be free to search the store for contraband."

"A little too dangerous, if you ask me," Bob says.

I smile and nod in agreement, "Maybe—maybe. It seems to be our way lately. How about we don't tell Hope about this adventure?"

"We got a recording of Eddie's confession. Blackmail, attempted murder, kidnapping, and drugs. Eddie and the Bowman twins are going away for awhile," Ulysses says as the police pour small, plastic wrapped bricks of cocaine from the vases in the store.

"You and Latesha go back to Granmama and tell her the good news. Bob, you and Latesha take all the credit. She's got quite the superheroes in her grandson and great-granddaughter," I add.

Bob grins from ear to ear and in his best Barry White voice says, "Mmm—mmm, let me tell ya somethin'—you know that's right."

*SOMERSET SECRETS*
*by T.W. Morse*

# HANNAH FLIES SOLO

## HANNAH
## I.

"**O**h my gosh, Ulysses is going to freak!" My exuberance resonates through my marketing class. I smatter blue paint over the screen, scraping it evenly across the template as I create the new Penny University Café t-shirt. I lift the frame off the burnt orange t-shirt to reveal our new logo. A steaming cup of coffee sits in the middle of a college crest with the words Penny University Café written in cursive font wrapped around it.

"Hannah, that is lit!" Amanda says, snapping a picture with her obnoxious oversized phone before posting it to Snapchat. Then I see her tilt her head and take a picture of herself holding up a peace sign and puckering her lips like a fish.

We were partnered with each other in marketing, assigned to design t-shirts for businesses we would rebrand. My t-shirt was a two-for-one deal, as my parents' business was my marketing redesign project.

Amanda Cho works with me as a waitress at Penny U.

"That's better than those polos your parents make us wear," she chides, laughing at her own joke. I pretend to laugh along, but I actually like those polos.

Amanda is a sophomore, and we take marketing and P.E. together. She is now taking another pic of herself, this time resting her round face on one of her palms while blinking her eyes in distress.

"Ms. Cho, put the phone away," Mrs. Barnes, our marketing teacher, bellows from the front of the class. Amanda sticks the phone down her tank top, using her bra as a phone holder. I can only imagine how uncomfortable that must be, especially since Amanda's bra is already failing to do a good job of holding in her chest. Papa would never let me out of the house looking like that.

Amanda is going on and on about something, spilling tea about her boyfriend, Roberto Gomez, Mangrove High's very own star soccer player. Roberto is a senior, and they have been dating for a few months now, almost as long as Ulysses and me. I am only half listening to her, which is another thing that would drive Papa and Mama crazy. As I place the orange shirt on the drying rack, I turn to pack up my bag, still half listening to her go on about how Roberto keeps posting photos on Instagram with a strange woman.

"All of his Instagram posts have some woman. I mean, she's not our age—she's, like, ancient." Ancient in Amanda's eyes is probably mid-thirties.

I act like I care, but I really don't. I'm only friends with her because we work together and share a couple of classes.

"What?" I say, looking and acting shocked. "How could he? So, you've never met this woman?" I say, feigning interest.

"Never! I've met Roberto's family too, and she is definitely not one of them. She better not be some cougar moving in on my man," she snaps with ferocity.

"What does Roberto have to say?"

"Well—um, I haven't exactly asked him about her yet."

"Oh—Amanda, she could be anyone. A friend of his parents, a relative. You are so overreacting."

She lets out a small scream of frustration as the bell rings and we head for P.E. "Ah!!"

**SOMERSET SECRETS**
*by T.W. Morse*

"You got the pics?"

"Yeah, right here," she replies, discouraged.

I look at her obnoxious phone that is almost the size of our home TV. In the photo, Roberto is dressed in a Manchester United jersey and his muscular arms are wrapped around a beautiful, petite Latina. She is very vivacious for her size, probably in her mid-thirties—so I was right about Amanda's age classifications. They were both gleaming with joy, looking like they were very happy at whatever they were doing. The backdrop looks like Somerset's pier. The post says four days ago. I see another post with Roberto and his parents in which Amanda points out the same woman again. Everyone is still smiling, and once again, the little Latina is in a hugging embrace with Roberto. According to Amanda, this was taken at his house.

"Huh" is all I can muster.

"Huh. That's all you got?! What do you think? I'm freaking out, Hannah. What do I do?"

I gulp. I am starting to feel sorry for her and think about giving her a little advice when we find ourselves in front of my locker where I meet Ulysses every day between classes. Amanda takes back her phone and lingers impatiently behind me as I wait for U.

Ulysses rounds the corner and greets me with a kiss as I try my best to fix his unruly hair. He smiles down at me. How can I resist those sparkling blue eyes that urge me to kiss him back? So I do. Amanda rudely coughs and nudges at me.

"I'll see you after school," Ulysses adds, giving a side glare and slinking away covertly.

"See you after school," I smile back. Ulysses doesn't care too much for Amanda and her "me, me, me all the time" attitude.

"That's it!" Amanda says loudly, giggling to herself. "Why didn't I think of that before?" She takes me by the arm and pulls me to the lockers. "Damn, Hannah, your arm is like solid rock." I blush at this. I always try my best to not make a big deal about my strength, but striving for excellence in my karate dojo sometimes interferes with that.

"I just thought of this when I saw Ulysses. You guys have solved crimes and stuff—right?" She says this while waving her hands frantically in front of me and nodding for reassurance.

"Ah—yeah. Why?"

"Because you can investigate, ask around without it looking like I'm a jealous, crazy girlfriend."

"But you are." Oops. I shouldn't have said that out loud—my stupid mouth.

"Hannah, I thought you were on my side?!" Amanda pouts. "If I ask Roberto who the woman in his pics is, he'll think I'm a crazy stalker girlfriend, but if you investigate and find out what's going on—well, everyone wins."

Yeah, everyone but me. "Fine," I say with hesitation, "I'll do it."

As we change for P.E., Amanda gives me the lowdown on Roberto's movements and schedule. "Twice a week he claims he does something with his family at their home. Then on those nights, a new picture of him and this woman appears on Instagram."

"Ladies, hustle it up! Let me tell you somethin', you all gonna be late!" Mr. Nelson blares through the locker room door with his blow horn.

"We're coming, Mr. Nelson!" I yell back through the door, eager to leave Amanda to play some volleyball. "So he is going home after practice tonight for a family event. That's all he says. What time does he do this?"

**SOMERSET SECRETS**
*by T.W. Morse*

"He is done with practice around 6. He's got a big house on the beach, just a few blocks from Penny University Café."

When she says big house, I picture a castle because of the exuding wealth of Somerset, Florida.

"He walks home, so he should be home by 6:15. You don't mind doing this alone? If he catches me, he'll dump me for sure."

"Argh! ¡Que demonios! Fine." My Cuban temper wants to do a roundhouse kick at her head.

"And don't spill the tea to Ulysses. Please … ! Keep this mission a secret, okay?" she pleads, taking my hand in hers.

"Ulysses and I don't keep secrets, Amanda."

"Okay, but just say you're doing a favor for me."

"And what am I supposed to do when I get to his house?"

"I don't know. What you always do—snoop."

This deal is getting worse by the minute. I pick up a volleyball and distractedly serve the ball out of bounds.

## II.

My old Trek bike is getting harder to ride. Either I am growing out of this bike or it is growing out of me. I better ask Papa if a new bike could be in my foreseeable future.

I approach Roberto's house on Somerset Beach. Ah, house is an understatement. It is the size of a small castle. You could fit a few Penny University Cafés in this so-called house. My parents' apartment above the café is about the size of one of their five-car garages.

"¡Está volao!" I say. "That's amazing!" I follow it with a low whistle. I often use my Cuban Spanish and English interchangeably since I grew up with a Cuban papa and American mama.

"Never forget your heritage," Papa always says in what Ulysses calls his raspy hit-man voice.

I hide my bike in a towering, perfectly manicured, landscaped bush and round the house to the beach side.

The house has a grand veranda in the back facing the pristine white sand beach of the Gulf of Mexico. I'm sure the veranda is so big that nobody would catch me out here. My nerves are getting the better of me, though, as my hands start to shake.

"I wish Ulysses was here." I fed him some excuse of how I was hanging with Amanda and couldn't meet up. I hate lying to him. Hopefully, I can easily find out if this woman Amanda is obsessed with is moving in on Roberto or if it's just something silly.

The veranda is made of very nice polished stone and littered with lawn chairs, couches, and a wet bar that I plan to hide covertly behind.

I look at my phone. It reads 6:30. Everyone should be inside. I creep closer as the sinking sun is rapidly descending. I notice a large set of doors open as I am making my way across. I can hear people's voices ringing out over the surf of the waves, which crash only a few feet away. I watch as figures cross the threshold onto the veranda. I freeze.

"Just look at this—what a beautiful evening," a woman's voice says as I drop to my stomach, unnoticed as I crawl slowly under a beach chair. The woman speaking is my thirty-year-old target who appeared in Roberto's Instagram pictures.

She is talking to his parents. All three of them make their way onto the veranda and sit down on the sectional couch, not even two feet away from my hiding position, trapping me on the veranda as they watch the sunset. Estoy en problemas, how am I going to get out of this one? I could be arrested for trespassing. And to make matters worse, I hear Mrs. Gomez yell, "Roberto, we're out on the veranda, dear!"

"Sorry, Ma and Pa. My practice ran late." He hugged and kissed them both. "Hola, Daniela," he greets the target and gives her a long hug. A little too long if you ask me. And then a prolonged kiss on each cheek. So the woman's name is Daniela, and Amanda was right. ¡Maldito!

### III.

My right leg is falling asleep and I am getting cold in my hiding position under the beach chair against the polished tile—just a few feet from Roberto, Daniela, and his parents while they all watch the sunset.

I have seen hundreds of sunsets with Ulysses from our canal view at Penny U. They often happen very quickly. This sunset is not. It seems like I have been under this beach chair for an eternity. But it's worth it. Roberto sits on the same cushion as Daniela, his arm loosely wrapped around her. I still can't believe that nut job Amanda was right.

"So how was your day, Roberto?" Daniela asks in heavily accented Spanish while fixing his hair. What! I pull out my phone and take some pictures. I really am feeling like a genuine private investigator. Ulysses would be so proud, but Papa and Mama would probably lock me away in my room for the rest of my life. I feel a little dirty too, hiding under this chair and snooping around.

## SOMERSET SECRETS
### by T.W. Morse

"Soccer is going well, and how about you? I never hear about your life."

I shake my head at this as I hear Daniela talk about going back to school. Wow, Roberto. I mean Amanda is annoying, but you're going to cheat on her with a thirty-something college student? And your parents, who are obviously very wealthy, are okay with this? This is cray-cray!

Finally, the sun has fully set. I decide that after the veranda becomes dark enough, I will make my escape. Papa will be starting to get worried soon. I try shaking my leg awake. It is hard to do from where I am lying. If I am going to make a run for it, I will need both legs operational. I have my pictures as proof that Roberto is a two-timing scum. Jamonero is what Papa would call this guy. A creep.

I look around and realize it is dark enough. I have to make my move, so I roll from under the beach chair and burst into a run, retracing my steps back the way I came. Easy enough, right? Except for a stray side table in my running path. I hit it hard and fall even harder. "¡Maldito!" Damn, my Spanish comes out more and more when I'm angry. I recover quickly, just as Mr. Gomez says, "Who the hell is that?"

I start running again, hurdling over chairs as I descend the veranda steps. I hear rapid footsteps behind me. "¡Maldito!" Damn, it's Roberto, and he is stinking fast! I increase my speed, but my ankle was bruised from the fall and it's slowing me down.

"Hey, you! Stop!" comes from behind me as Roberto continues to gain on me. I am finally off their property. I have to make a split-second decision: run on the beach and lose Roberto in the crowd watching the sunset or make for my bike and lose him on my wheels. I stupidly dash toward my bike. I regret that choice as soon as I make it. Sweat is

## SOMERSET SECRETS
### by T.W. Morse

making my hair stick to my face, and it's blocking my vision. I can see my bike in its hiding place, but I can also feel Roberto's breath behind me. I finally conclude that this needs to stop. I put the brakes on and turn to Roberto. It is dark and he can barely see me, so I have a good chance that he won't recognize me.

I stop, turn, and perform an open-palm hand strike to Roberto's chest. It works and he buckles in pain. I then grab his arm and twist him around, twisting his wrist as he wrenches in pain to his knees. "Stop! Please!"

"You stop cheating on Amanda!" is all I can say as he submits, writhing in pain.

"What?!" he gasps in a pained tone.

"Don't play dumb with me, Roberto," I sneer in a condescending voice. "Daniela? Don't deny that. I saw you guys together. I got the pictures to prove it."

"You're wrong," he mutters, still in pain.

"Right ... I saw how she looked at you, and fixed your hair, and hugged you." Man, I sure was lucky to have a good guy like Ulysses, not like this jerk.

"She. Ah!" Roberto is just about to say something when I get a better hold on his wrist and twist it harder.

"Watch it, buddy. One wrong move and your wrist is broken," I remind him with a smile. I don't know why I'm taking so much joy in Roberto's pain. Maybe because I hate cheaters so much. I feel his weakened body writhe in pain as my karate hold keeps him in place.

"She's my mother!"

## IV.

Roberto manages to explain in a quick exhale—"She's my mother." He sputters in pain as I loosen my hold on him, spin him back around, and release my grip. He drops to one knee and nurses his twisted wrist.

"Right! Ha! Your mother. That's a good lie. I'm sure Amanda will believe that."

"Hannah Reyes?!" Roberto blurts out, just now noticing his attacker's identity for the first time. Oh crap! I forgot I was trying to remain incognito. He could bust me now for trespassing and assault. ¡Maldito!

"Did Amanda put you up to this? Are Ulysses and Mr. Adair here too?" Roberto asks, looking around for my usual backup.

"Yes, Amanda put me up to this. And no—I don't need a man to do this job," I exclaim as I put my hands on my hips, trying to look intimidating. "Talk, Roberto, or I'll hurt the other wrist."

He stands up, now fully recovered. "Daniela is my mother."

"Explain!" I order.

Before he can, Roberto's phone rings. "It's my parents. They're probably wondering if I'm okay." I nod my head, indicating that he's free to answer it. "Yeah, Dad. Just a friend from school," he reassures them, reluctantly looking at me in the shadows of the night. My eyebrows raise as I whip back my hair in disgust. "I'm going to walk her home. Yeah, yeah. Everything's good. I'll see you in a few minutes. Love you."

**SOMERSET SECRETS**
**by T.W. Morse**

I grab my bike and we walk to Penny University. It is about a ten-minute walk, but tonight it feels ten times longer. As we walk, Roberto explains the whole story about his mother.

"A few weeks ago, my parents told me I was adopted at the age of one. I don't remember Daniela, but she was my parents', my adoptive parents', maid. She and I lived in one of the wings of my home. Then one day, immigration came knocking at our door ..." With this recollection, Roberto's voice cracks. I don't need light to understand that this part in his story is really upsetting to him. "They got a tip that Daniela was in the United States—illegally. That was true, but she just overstayed her green card. She didn't want to be here illegally, but life got in the way and she couldn't afford citizenship. She was happy here before she was forced to leave. My adoptive parents—"

"Mr. and Mrs. Gomez?"

"Yeah, Mom and Dad. They volunteered to adopt and raise me. I was born in the U.S., so I was a legal citizen. I wasn't part of the deportation order to return to Guatemala, where Daniela is from." He chuckles a little. "Where my family's from. Daniela wanted a better life for me because Guatemala was—is—a difficult place to live and receive an education."

"So how did she get back to the U.S.?"

"My dad owns a large agricultural company and works with different Central American governments. Her deportation order barred her from returning to the U.S. for fifteen years, but once that time passed, Dad was able to find Daniela and get her back here legally, with a proper green card this time. They waited to tell me until they were sure they could find her. She is enrolled at Lee Community College in Bonita, and my parents are paying for her tuition.

Hopefully, she'll be a full citizen someday. She visits a couple times a week and things are—good. She would visit more, but we're trying to take it slow. It's so much to process right now, especially balancing school, soccer, and Amanda. I wanted to have more time to come to terms with it before I told everyone, especially Amanda. You know how she can be!" Roberto says with a laugh.

"Wow" is all I can say. I feel like such a fool. I invade this guy's life, almost break his wrist, and for what? A busybody girlfriend. I hate what I did. I feel so ashamed as we walk back home in darkness. "I am so sorry, Roberto. I was wrong and made some dumb choices and assumptions tonight."

"It's all good. I know how jealous Amanda gets. If I had a friend who was an investigator, I would've hired them too."

"You're pretty understanding. I don't know if I would feel the same way in your position. But now you do have friends who are investigators. Let me or the Adairs know if you ever need our help," I say with a smile as we approach Penny University Café with its large Edison-bulb-lit sign.

"Thanks."

"Are you going to tell Amanda?" I ask sheepishly. "If you like her, she should know."

He smiles. "You're right. I will. You tell Ulysses he's got one tough girlfriend."

I smile at this. "Oh—he knows."

*SOMERSET SECRETS*
*by T.W. Morse*

# THE CASE OF THE MISSING BEAT

## ULYSSES
### I.

"What the hell, Nick!" I yell over the electric hum of our instruments and microphones. Our version of "Running Down A Dream" by Tom Petty sounds more like "Running Down A Nightmare."
"Argh!"

"Take it easy, Ulysses," Dad calmly states, while putting a hand on my shoulder. Our playing has screeched to a halt.

Maybe it is the heat of Bob's garage, which is a tiny building detached from his condo. It's our temporary practice space and is hotter than hell, even with fans going and an open door. Could be the heat, but maybe it's just—Nick.

Bob sits on an old crate labeled trophies, sipping a beer and acting the part as our biggest groupie. "Let me tell ya somethin'—you guys aren't sounding too good," Bob injects before taking a long gulp of beer followed up by a roaring belch.

"I know—right? Nick, you're not in rhythm," I explain.

Nick sits slumped behind his glittering drum set; his skateboarding Flock of Seagulls hair cut covers his right eye while his left eye stares out into space.

Dad exhales in a long sigh and gives Bob and me a long leer. "We should take a break. That's enough for the day." Dad walks over to Nick and puts a hand on his shoulder, saying, "You okay?" He sounds very concerned, not only as a bandmate but also as a history teacher showing concern for one of his students.

**SOMERSET SECRETS**
*by T.W. Morse*

Nick Lyons has been our drummer lately when we play at Penny University's open mic nights. He's usually lit, but his playing today has been cringeworthy at best. Actually, cringy doesn't do it justice. He has been awful.

"I don't know," Nick says as his eyes come into focus. After a long pause, he finally explains, "It's my dad." He continues his explanation as he slumps over his drum set. Dad, Bob, and I listen intently. "He has been missing lately."

"Missing?" I ask. As Nick tells his story, his body rattles with adrenalin. (Is it any wonder why he is such a great drummer? His ADHD gives him a lot of pent up energy.) His leg shakes with an unknown beat.

"Well, I mean, nobody, like, kidnapped him, but at night he's—he's, like, missing. He's missed two of my band concerts. Like, Mom is really concerned too. She won't dare say anything. He always says he has to work late, but when she called his work, they said he hasn't been in for awhile. Weird, right?"

We all nod.

"I think my mom, like—thinks he's having an affair or something. I don't know what to think. My dad's great—he loves my drumming and wouldn't miss a concert in like a bazillion years. I know you guys look into stuff like this. Could you help?" he asks, straightening his shaking frame.

"I've known Johnny—your dad—for a while, and he's a stand-up guy. Your mom hasn't confronted him about where he goes?" Dad asks.

"No. My mom is pretty quiet. Doesn't like confrontations." As Nick describes his mom, I remember her from the couple of times I met her. She did indeed seem to be a frail, meek woman who could be afraid of her own shadow.

"Let me tell ya somethin', your dad is gett'n somethin'—somethin', you know what I mean? Mmm-mmm," Bob grunts,

***SOMERSET SECRETS***
*by T.W. Morse*

talking out the side of his mouth and grunting in his deep Barry White voice.

"Bob!" Dad and I sternly admonish in unison.

"I'm sure your dad isn't having an affair," I say to comfort Nick after Bob's inconsiderate remark. I feel pretty lousy for criticizing him a few minutes ago. Just then, Hannah shows up, dropped off by a waving Mrs. Reyes. We all wave in return.

"Hola," Hannah says, kissing me on the cheek and greeting everyone. "Wow, who died?"

We fill her in on what is going on with Nick, and she walks right over and gives him a huge hug.

"We'll definitely look into this for you, Nick. You can count on us," Hannah reassures him while looking back at Dad and me for confirmation while we nod in agreement. We know better than to question Hannah's decisions.

"What does your dad do for a living?" Dad asks.

"He's a bartender at Rascal's Sports Pub."

"Love that place! Logan—Logan, remember those chicks…" Bob doesn't finish his sentence because Dad gives him the sign to stop talking. He coughs loudly while Hannah, Nick, and I all look at him with raised eyebrows.

"Ah—all before we started dating Sarah and Hope," Dad reassures us.

"Where should we start?" Hannah asks.

"Me and Hannah can follow him from Nick's house tonight. When he claims to go to work, we can follow him on our bikes," I offer, with Hannah nodding in agreement.

"Bob and I will check out Rascal's," Dad says while Bob nods a little too enthusiastically. "Just to ask questions, Bob," Dad warns.

"Meet back at our home. It's near Rascal's," I add.

"Go team Adair!" Dad says in a very cringeworthy way.

## II.

Hannah and I sit on our bikes across from Nick's house, a small yellow ranch with too many blue and red fat gnomes. We chat about what I know about Mr. Lyons. He was at our first gig at Penny University Café. Since then, he has always eagerly cheered us on and seemed like such a stand-up guy.

"That's how I remember him too," Hannah says. Just then, a short blonde man, with traces of punk that have faded through years from the responsibility that comes with fatherhood, darts out the front door.

"There's Mr. Lyons," I exclaim. He is dressed like he is thirty years younger with a Nirvana t-shirt and ripped jeans. "Someone's in denial of his age."

I nod to Hannah as he pulls out of the driveway. He drives a silver Jeep Wrangler. Easy enough to follow, I think as we set off. We're able keep up easily with his Jeep because most of the streets in Somerset are twenty-five mile an hour zones and have wide enough sidewalks for bicycles. We stay a couple cars back just in case Mr. Lyons recognizes us.

Hannah and I glide down side streets, racing at breakneck speed reminiscent of Mikey and the gang in the classic movie *Goonies*. Mr. Lyons heads straight, then left, right, another right and then makes a U-turn. I yell over to Hannah, "Do you think he knows we're following him?"

"I don't think so!"

"We should hold back a little—just in case!" As soon as I state this idea, the Jeep goes through a yellow light at the intersection. "No! We're going to lose him!" I yell as both of us have to screech to a stop at the red light as the do not cross sign for bikes and pedestrians goes up. After an excruciating amount of time, and Hannah hitting the crosswalk button about twenty times in frustration, we get the countdown clock to ride on. We continue on for about a mile more, but we instinctively know that we have lost Mr. Lyons.

"Maldito!" Hannah exclaims.

"Yeah—Damn!" I say as an afterthought, smiling over to Hannah. "He couldn't have gone too far. The only thing down here are a few warehouses."

"Yeah, Papa mentioned that one of the warehouses was converted into shops, restaurants, and a community school. Another into brewery and the third—" She stops in mid-sentence.

"What? What did your dad say was done with the other warehouse?"

"Nothing. It's condemned. A lot of bad things go down there. The city wants to tear it down because it's such an eyesore, especially since the other two warehouses are being used and updated. But it was too costly to tear it down, and now it has a lot of homeless people living in it," she says with a nervous look.

"So, what's the big deal? He probably went to the other warehouses."

"No entiendes."

"Hannah, you know my Spanish is weak."

"I said you don't understand. They are homeless and living down in the warehouse because they have opioid addictions. The drugs prescribed by their doctors have become severely addicting to them. Ruining their lives, forcing them to live on the street if they don't get the help they need—in most cases, they overdose. Everyone turns a blind eye, unwilling or unable to help them." I knew of this happening in the United States, but I never thought opioids were a problem here in Somerset.

"I hope that's not the case for Mr. Lyons. Hopefully, Dad and Bob come up with more at the bar where he works." As I say this, we swing our bikes through the warehouses, scoping them out. On one side of the road stand two warehouses, nicely redone with a new marquee showing off a list of trendy shops and restaurants. There's even a large engraved marquee that reads Somerset Community College in cursive writing.

On the other side of the street stands a run-down warehouse. Its steel frame is rusted from age and neglect. We get a glimpse of a few people inside, as parts are open to the elements. They leer at us with tired eyes. They live in makeshift tents, keeping all their belongings in grocery carts. My heart saddens to think that one of the richest cities in the richest country can't do more for these poor souls.

We find Mr. Lyons' Jeep parked in the lot between the two warehouses. "Great! Which one did he go into?" I ask to a stunned Hannah.

"I don't know. He could've just gotten a new job at one of these restaurants." I cringe and really hope Hannah's optimism pans out.

"Yeah, but why the charade, lying to Nick and his mom?"

### III.

I search through Mr. Lyons' Jeep while Hannah anxiously acts as my lookout. "Ulysses, hurry," she impatiently exclaims. "What do you hope to find?"

***SOMERSET SECRETS***
*by T.W. Morse*

"I don't know, but we sure are lucky he took off his Jeep's coverings." The Jeep currently has no roof or sides, exposing the entire front and back seat and making it extremely easy for me to search without having to shimmy a lock. As I rummage, I find an old picture of him and Nick. Must have been a couple years old, Nick's hair looks way less punk. He looks quite prim and proper, as Dad would say. Looks like a different kid. I find some loose change and then I check the glove compartment. I find a stack of envelopes and show this to Hannah.

"What do you make of this?" I ask, showing Hannah.

"It looks like old bills," she responds.

I nod in agreement. "All unpaid bills. Why have this in his car?" Hannah shrugs in response as I feel my phone vibrate.

"It's my dad," I say before answering.

"Hey, Dad. What did you and Bob find?"

He has me on speaker phone and I can hear Bob in the background, "Mmm—mmm, I remember this place have'n a lot better-looking women. Let me tell you somethin', these women look—" Bob doesn't finish that lovely observation because Dad hushes him in frustration.

"Yes, unfortunately, found out that Johnny Lyons—is no longer employed here."

"What!" Hannah and I say in unison as I have switched my phone to speaker so Hannah can hear Dad's information.

"For how long?" I ask.

"According to the Rascal's manager we interviewed, Johnny had been fired about six months ago," Dad replies.

"Six months!" Hannah repeats with a gasp. "What has he been doing this whole time?"

I shrug.

"The manager also states Johnny was a model worker."

"Why fire him then?" I ask.

"My thoughts exactly. Johnny is most likely collecting unemployment pay through the government because he was fired, but it wouldn't be much," Dad adds.

"This explains the unpaid bills we found in his Jeep," Hannah reasons.

"What did you guys find out?" Dad asks.

I explain the situation and how we followed him to the warehouses and searched Mr. Lyons' Jeep. "That's where we found the unpaid bills," Hannah adds.

We also inform Dad and Bob about the warehouse with all the homeless.

"Don't go in there," Dad insists. "We'll come and join you guys; we'll be there in about ten minutes. Don't move."

We agree and hang up, now having more questions than we had started with.

"Ulysses, why wouldn't Mr. Lyons tell his wife or Nick that he has been unemployed?"

"I know—right? Why would he keep the bills in his car too?" I say this as I look at the old, rusty warehouse and hope he's not in there.

"Poor Nick," Hannah sheepishly exclaims under her breath. "If Mr. Lyons got a new job in one of the restaurants or stores down here, why not tell his family?" she pleads.

"All of these are great questions that we have to find the answers to," I acknowledge, feeling a little bit of a knot forming in my stomach. "I think we should check out the rusty warehouse first."

"Ulysses Robert Adair, your father told you not to; he thinks it's not safe."

"I know—but when have we ever done the safe thing?"

## IV.

We cross the threshold of the old warehouse. The front door, located near large garage doors, is old and rusted like the rest of place. Opening it releases a loud whiny creak, making me hope I'm up to date on my tetanus shot. When I close it behind me, it leaves us in partial darkness. Dust and soot fill the air as nesting birds scatter with our arrival, startling us and making me realize—this was a bad idea.

Darkness mixes with rays of sunlight streaming through the Swiss cheese roof. Most of the warehouse is open to the elements; a drip—drip—drip can be heard all around us, giving off an unnerving feeling throughout. Hannah grabs my hand as we wander further into the structure.

We come across a young woman sitting in the corner near some pitched tents speaking with an older woman. Both of them look like they've lived difficult lives, and they're dressed in ragged clothes with haggard faces. The younger woman jumps up from her sitting position. "What the hell are you kids doing here?!"

Her voice echoes throughout, vibrating off the metal walls of the warehouse. Her lip piercing flutters as she speaks. The woman only appears a few years older than us. It makes me wonder about the family and friends who worry about her, or maybe they have given up on her. She's wearing shorts and I notice ACL surgery scars on both her knees and cringe. That may be the reason she has an addiction to opioids in the first place. I bet there is a story behind her addiction, but I put it from my mind to focus on other pressing concerns.

"Get out!" she screams as she comes stumbling over to us with immense rage.

Hannah instantly gets into her karate ready position, prepared to defend us 'til the end. But I put my shaking hand on her shoulder to calm her down.

"We're looking for a friend," I say with polite confidence as my insides are becoming scrambled eggs.

"He's a tall blonde man with a black Nirvana t-shirt," Hannah explains, relaxing her ready stance.

The woman fumbles about in a drug-induced state. "I haven't seen anyone looking like that," she mutters. Hannah and I take a deep breath. "You kids better freaking go. This is a dangerous place," she insists, retreating back to the older lady who laughs as she rocks back and forth, exposing missing teeth. Her heckle rings around us in a repeating eerie echo, "He!—he!—he!—he!"

"Ulysses, I don't think Mr. Lyons came here and this place is giving me the creeps. Let's get out of here," Hannah says, taking my arm. I feel her nerves resonate over to me.

"Yeah. I guess you're right," I agree, dejected. I was hoping we would find him and prove to Nick what he's been up to. But I'm glad whatever he's up to does not involve this place.

We head back the way we came, but the path back is now darker than when we came in. The sun coming through the cheese-holed roof has shifted and now it is getting harder to see our way out. We turn on our cellphone flashlights. This helps a little but also adds to our already stressed nerves as the occasional addict or homeless person passes us, some looking like zoned out zombies. Hannah gasps as another drug-induced man stumbles by us, nearly knocking into her.

"All these poor people—they just need help," she says as she grips me tighter.

Then all of a sudden, a hand grabs my shoulder from behind. "Ah!" is all I can say before dropping my phone. I scramble to the ground, in search of it so I can reveal our attacker. Hannah immediately reacts to the potential danger by instinctively swinging around and executing a fist punch, swinging blindly in the dark. I can see she is just about to do a roundhouse kick toward our attacker when we hear a scared, whiny, "No!"

## V.

I frantically feel the ground for my fallen phone. As I find it, I rapidly shine it front of us to reveal a hurt and squealing—Bob, rubbing his shoulder after being hit by Hannah. Dad rushes up, having been a few yards behind him, holding his phone's flashlight.

"Mmm—mmm, girl—you nearly killed Bobby."

"Hey Mr. Adair. Sorry about the arm, Bob," Hannah says as we swiftly exit the warehouse. Outside the sun shines down on us with Florida intensity. After being inside the dark, creepy warehouse, it is a welcome relief. Dad has to block out the sun with his hand while chastising Hannah and me.

"I said not to go in there! Ulysses, that was a dangerous move by you and Hannah!" His anger is overflowing now.

"We're always doing stuff like that" is my lame defense.

"Let me tell ya somethin'. The boy's got a point there. You Adairs are always doin' stuff like this," Bob decries.

"You're not helping, Bob. The people in there can be very desperate and could have hurt you two."

"But they didn't and we're okay. Also, Hannah was there to protect me," I reiterate, smiling.

"Yeah, thanks for that," Bob adds, rubbing his shoulder.

"Don't creep up on us then," Hannah says, giving Bob a playful shove into Dad.

"I don't think Mr. Lyons is in there," I add.

"I know. That's another reason why I told you to not go in there," Dad says.

"Wait, you knew he wasn't in there?" I ask.

"Yeah. Nick never said his dad was acting different. He just said he went missing. Johnny Lyons doesn't have a drug problem. Some of the tell-tale signs of cravings, sweating, discontent, and slurred speech would have been noticeable to Nick or Laura—Mrs. Lyons—or even us. Johnny has none of these. Nick said he's been missing. According to Nick and Laura, he has been telling them he's been going to work, but when Laura called his workplace, Rascal's bar, he hadn't been to work in awhile. We also just found out he was fired six months ago. So he must be coming down here to that warehouse," Dad says, pointing to the better renovated one with restaurants and shops.

"Yeah, but why not tell his family?" Hannah asks while I nod in agreement.

"Maybe he's not making the same bank as before," Bob adds. This sounds reasonable, but it still doesn't sit well.

Dad walks with us in silence, and I can tell he is in his typical deep thoughts again, rolling the case around in his head, trying to put all the pieces together.

The entrance and front door to the other warehouse across the street are night and day different from where we just came from. The front door is newly painted, and the metal is complemented by a nice stone façade. They managed to take an old, dilapidated warehouse and transform it into a modern chic business. We enter into the lobby and are greeted by a rushing waterfall and stylish artwork, the stylings catering to the ultra-rich 1% of Somerset, Florida.

"Where do we start?" Hannah asks as she looks at a sign of all the businesses that's in the lobby on a large, ornate wooden sign above a spiral staircase leading to the second floor. "We have five restaurants and three shops and a school."

"We'll look pretty silly going all together, and we can cover more ground if we separate. Let's meet back here when we're finished," Dad says as we divvy up which places Hannah and I and Bob with Dad will investigate.

"We'll take the upstairs," I decide.

"We'll take the downstairs." Dad goes off with Bob, who is still rubbing his shoulder and muttering to himself. This causes me and Hannah to giggle as we race up the stairs.

While upstairs, we separate to search each of the restaurants and stores. The second floor has two stores and two restaurants. Our plan is to ask to use their bathroom and accidentally go into kitchens and back rooms that are labeled "staff only."

"Nothing!" I say as I come back, holding up my hands in disgust.

"Me too," Hannah says with an irritated, impatient deep breath. Then my phone comes to life in my pocket. The song "Summer Wind" performed by Frank Sinatra blares out of my phone. I picked it as Dad's ringtone since it's his favorite song.

Before I answer, I put my phone on speaker so Hannah can listen in too. "What's up?"

"I found him. You'll want to get down here, U."

"Where are you, Mr. Adair?" Hannah asks, grabbing my arm in silent relief.

A long pause comes over the speaker. "He's at the school."

I hang up and give Hannah a look of shock before we bolt downstairs to join Dad and Bob at Somerset Community College.

## VI.

The school isn't much more than a hallway with five or six glass doors leading to small, but nicely decorated, classrooms. The carpet in the hallway puts off a school smell. I could be blindfolded and know I am stepping foot in a school.

Hannah and I find Dad and Bob stealthily trying to stay concealed, but they only look awkward, like two teens ducking out of class.

"What are you two doing?" Hannah asks like she is too cool for Dad and Bob's sneaking around. They are now in squatting positions right outside a classroom.

"Girl! We try'n to not get caught," Bob hisses.

We squat down close on carpet to stay out of sight of the classroom to the right of us.

"We started to check the restaurants and shops down here, but then it hit me. I remember Johnny mentioned way back when we first met that he only had a high school degree. I had told him it was never too late to go back to school when he said he was interested in higher education." My eyebrows raise with Dad's recollection, knowing my Dad is probably the biggest spokesperson for higher education.

"Good job, Mr. Adair," Hannah adds.

"Do we know what class? Or what degree he's going for?" I say, peeking up and looking into the window.

**SOMERSET SECRETS**
*by T.W. Morse*

"I think it's some math class," Bob says. He is closest to the door and can hear a lot of the conversation inside. All I hear is a muffled Peanuts cartoon teacher voice: "Wa—wa—wa."

Then, all of a sudden, like a bull in a china shop, Bob attempts to stand from his stealth squat position. "They're coming. The class is being dismissed."

But before we can all get up from our squat position, Bob adds, "My legs are asleep," and falls to the side like a sack of potatoes, knocking into Dad, who in turns knocks into me. Hannah, quick and agile, is able to escape our domino of bodies. We sound like a herd of elephants stuck in mud. It must be a sight as a dozen adult students file from the classroom looking down on us in either disgust or pity. Hannah crosses her arms, her face looking cherry red in embarrassment.

The last student who exits the classroom is Johnny Lyons. He looks down, puzzled. "Logan? Ulysses? Mr. Nelson? What are you guys—doing?"

"Um—um" is all that comes out of our mouths as we lay tangled like we were playing a mean game of Twister.

"Nick! He was worried!" Hannah blurts out, now looking more red.

Mr. Lyons tilts his head in utter confusion. "Hannah Reyes?" This gives me, Dad, and Bob enough time to untangle and stand up from our Three Stooges mess.

"Nick had you follow me?" Mr. Lyons asks with hurtful astonishment.

"Ah—yeah. I'm afraid so, Johnny," Dad adds bashfully, looking ashamed.

"He said you have missed his band concerts and his performances at Penny U. He didn't know where you had been going. He knew you hadn't been going to work. He was worried," I interject.

We face a silence that is extremely awkward—until it is broken by the loud grumbling of Bob's stomach. "Dude! Did you hear that? Mmm—mmm, I've gots to eat. Logan, Johnny, let's conclude this little meet and greet down at that wing joint," Bob says.

"I think that's a great idea. Are you okay with this, Johnny?" Dad adds.

At this point, Mr. Lyons looks like someone kicked him in the gut, but he manages a slow nod in agreement.

We enter the overly loud wing restaurant, with blaring big screen televisions covering the walls. This place could make even the chillest person feel like they have ADD, as voices and games from around the world drown out the conversations from the other tables. The hostess shows us to a booth where Bob and Dad flank Mr. Lyons on one side, appearing stuffed together like my school locker. Hannah and I sit across from them, leaning across the table with intrigue.

I am just about to ask Mr. Lyons what his deal is when the waitress slinks up to our table. She is fair skinned with deep purple hair and a shiny nose ring. "Can I get you guys something?" she asks with a nasal tone that really said, "I don't want to be here, and I'd rather be skateboarding with my boyfriend."

"Mmm—mmm, you sure can, girl. I'll have a tall pitcher of—" Bob quickly asks before getting cut off by Dad.

"Bob, no beer."

"Ah—come on, son. Alright—alright, I will order a basket of twenty wings. Extra hot sauce. You guys want anything?" Bob asks as we all shrug no and our purple haired waitress collects the menu and fetches Bob's wing order.

Hannah just stares at Bob with wide-eyed amazement, shaking her head with what I presume is disgust.

"Okay—you good, Bob? Are we okay to proceed?" Dad asks with a sprinkle of sarcasm.

"Logan, I'm good. Bobby Nelson just needing some nourishment."

"So," I say, breaking the awkwardness once again. "Mr. Lyons, why didn't you tell your family you went back to school?"

With this question, he puts his face into his hands and starts to sob. "I know—I know. Poor Nick. Why didn't he say anything?"

"He probably knew you had your reasons," Dad adds.

"Reasons? Yeah, I got reasons. They aren't good. They aren't worth missing my son play the drums. You know I taught him? We used to play together all the time. But you know how teens get. They want less and less to do with their old man. They are off with friends and girls." He says this with a grin as Hannah passes him some napkins to wipe away his tears.

"Were you fired from Rascal's?" Hannah asks as the waitress arrives with Bob's wings.

"Yes. That's where my problems started. I bartended at Rascal's for many years. The money was pretty good. But we had changed managers recently, and he did not like me. He wanted Rascal's to go in a new direction, have all female bartenders. Thought more guys would like that. Not some ex punk rocker." Mr. Lyons slinks down in the booth while Bob mows on chicken wing bones.

"All women bartenders? Mmm—mmm," Bob manages to say between bites of chicken.

"Bob!" Dad admonishes sternly.

"So you went back to school?" I prod.

"Yeah. I've been collecting unemployment. It's not as good as bartending, but it pays enough. I have a buddy that just opened his own electrician business. He said if I get certified, I can apprentice with him. He's looking for help, so I enrolled at Somerset Community College. And I'm almost done. When I graduate, I'll be able to make twice as much at being an electrician as I was as a bartender." With this, Mr. Lyons' posture straightens, proud of what he has accomplished.

"Then why not tell Mrs. Lyons or Nick?" Hannah asks.

"I was first ashamed of being fired, and I was also wary of going back to school. I've never been a great student, hence the bartending, and I was scared of failing again. I wanted to get back on my feet again before I let them know. But I guess I made it worse. Ah! What do I do?"

"You tell them the truth," Dad reassures him, patting Mr. Lyons on the back.

"Yeah, Nick and Mrs. Lyons will understand. Hell, Nick is a wiz in math. He could probably help you study," I say, grinning while Hannah puts her arm through mine.

"That sounds nice. It's been hard doing classwork in secret. I've had to spend most of my days at the school library," Mr. Lyons adds.

Just then, Bob unzips his buffalo stained tracksuit and pats his stomach. "Mmm—mmm. Let me tell ya somethin', those are some bone-smacking good wings."

With this, we all laugh and shake our heads with amazement at the same time.

"Oh, Bob," we all say in unison.

## VII.

The following weekend we are able to spend some time with the Lyons family. Nick has a gig with Dad and me at Penny University Café. His family looks so happy. Nick thanks us profusely before we go into our set. He even mentions how he had helped his dad with his math homework.

It was a pretty special night at Penny U. The converted industrial warehouse is hopping; the crowd is swelling. Half of Mangrove High is here. The smell of oversized cappuccinos and greasy Cuban sandwiches fills the air. Edison bulb lights are strung throughout to light the stage that Nick, Dad, and I just took. We start our set with a great rendition of Neil Young's "Old Man," a nice classic about older people and younger people being similar in the needs and wants of life.

Dad chose the song as a way to commemorate our experience with Mr. Lyons. Nick has found his beat once again, sounding sick on the drums. He also found his dad. I look out over the crowd and see a glowing Mr. Lyons, grooving proudly to his son's playing. We sound lit! It's amazing how fortunate we all truly are.

## SCHOOL NEWSPAPERS: REPORTING TRUTHS—NOT FAKE NEWS

### ULYSSES
### I.

The Mangrove High bell rings—loudly. It startles me awake as I jerk my head up from its resting position on my arm. The imprint from my arm on my face feels hot and red from the pressure of skin being pressed together for so long. Is that drool? Yup. I hope nobody saw that. Damn, if Dad knew I had fallen asleep in Spanish class, he would lecture me until my ears bled. Hell, if Hannah knew I fell asleep, I would probably have some sort of ancient karate medieval torture hold put on me until I lost consciousness.

I need to get to bed earlier. Damn, these late nights are killing me! I continue to lecture myself as I rub my eyes while stumbling from my Spanish class to my locker, trying my best to not bump into anyone or anything.

"Ulysses! Ulysses!" I hear through the clamor of the hallway. Hannah is excited about something as the crowded hallway parts like the Red Sea, exposing her delicate features and brown hair whipping while she almost skips up to me. I greet her with a light kiss.

"Luces enfermo," Hannah says, holding my face with her hands.

"What? Please, I've had enough Spanish for one day," I say in an arrogant tone.

# SOMERSET SECRETS
## by T.W. Morse

"I said you look sick. Ulysses Robert Adair, first, you can never have enough Spanish in your life. I'm proof of this. Second, you need to get to bed earlier."

"I know—I know. Sorry. I've been up late these last few nights."

"Why? And why didn't you say so, silly?"

"Mrs. Carol in guidance said a couple days ago that I'm not doing enough extracurricular activities. What-eve!" I respond, slamming my locker in frustration.

"She's loca. You run cross country, you get pretty good grades, and you work at Penny U. What more does she want!?"

I shrug at this, already feeling tired again after listening to Hannah list all of what I already do. "She said if I want to attend a good college, I need to be 'well rounded.'" I say this with sarcastic air quotes.

"Well, mister," Hannah teases, poking me in the chest playfully. Hannah is a strong female, and her pokes to the chest hurt like hell. "It's perfect!"

"What's perfect?" I ask, rubbing my chest.

"What I was coming to tell you, silly: some good news, and it so happens to coincide with what Mrs. Carol wants you to do. There is an opening for two photojournalists at the school newspaper, *The Manatee Times*. It's perfect."

"Photo—journalists? What? We don't know anything about photojournalism."

"Yes, we do, silly. We like to write. We go where most people don't go, and you have that great camera your mom left you."

I nod at all of Hannah's counterpoints and slowly wrap my brain around her idea.

"Mr. Scott, the teacher assigned to oversee the newspaper, had two seniors drop out of the program and told me we would be perfect. I don't know if he has read some of our mystery exploits and thinks name recognition sells papers or what. But it's a win-win for us. We both have an open period, you get the extracurricular hours, we'll have some fun doing it, and the paper sells more copies because the two best sleuths are now on the case." Hannah finishes by pulling me in and kissing me just as we hear the shrill screech of Principal O'Leary from down the hallway.

"PDA! Mzz. Reyes! And Mr. A—dair!"

We quickly slink away, not wanting another confrontation with our principal from hell.

## II.

"Hannah, hold up!" I plead as Hannah drags me along the corridor as we exit the cafeteria, making our way to *The Manatee Times* classroom.

"Hey guys," we hear from behind us. "What's the rush?"

Dad is sprawled out on the stairs chilling with one hand behind his head and the other holding a half-eaten apple. Next to him is Mr. Nelson, who's sitting upright bent over his phone in his bright kelly green velvet tracksuit. Today he looks a bit like a fat leprechaun. I blink rapidly, unsure why they are both on the stairwell. "Hey Dad ... hey Mr. Nelson. What are you guys doing?"

"Yeah." Hannah stops for a moment between breaths as she stares in confusion too.

"Let me tell ya somethin'—mmm mmm—our fearless leader, Principal O'Leary, heard they'd be some shady business going down over here—in this particular hallway—and wanted us check'n things out on our planning period—

our planning—period!" Bob huffs with his head down while he rapidly texts on his phone.

"Bob, what are you complaining about? You're doing exactly what you'd be doing on your planning period," Dad says while taking a bite of his apple.

"Mmm—mmm."

"Yeah, I guess we're playing security for O'Leary. Where you guys off to? Isn't this your open period?" Dad adds between chomps of apple.

"Yeah, we're on our way to *The Manatee Times* classroom," I explain, relaying my extracurricular conundrum and Hannah's idea to become photojournalists.

"That's great! I think it will be a wonderful addition to your future college applications," Dad says, smiling.

"Mmm—mmm, watch out, Logan; they may want to investigate this business," Bob warns without looking up from his phone.

"What do you mean, Bob? I mean, Mr. Nelson," Hannah corrects herself, remembering we were in school, where we had to adhere to protocol. "Ulysses, this sounds like our first case as photojournalists."

Bob coughs uncomfortably while Dad quickly steps in, "This is a school matter. If O'Leary knew we spoke to you kids about this, he'd have both our jobs. Bob shouldn't be opening his big mouth." Bob waves a hand to this to symbolize "big whoop," still remaining engrossed in his phone.

"So, that's a no comment?" Hannah presses further. I smile at her for already showing the persistence of a reporter.

Dad raises his eyebrows and says, "No—comment. Watch out for the slippery floor." Dad points to the yellow caution signs stationed on the floor.

# SOMERSET SECRETS
### by T.W. Morse

"Walk slow, please," an old man requests as he rolls a cart to the custodial closet behind the staircase. It is Mr. Maxwell, our ancient custodian. His liver spots have liver spots. "Hey Ulysses and sweet little Hannah."

"Hey Mr. Maxwell," Hannah and I say in unison. I reflect on the fact that if Hannah had been called little by anyone else, they probably would've been drop kicked.

"Remember when the caution signs are up you have to walk slow," Mr. Maxwell chimes a reminder.

"Here is our faithful relief," Dad says, looking behind us as Ms. Thatcher and Mr. Cortez come through the cafeteria door.

"Hola Ulysses," Mr. Cortez says from behind, startling me.

"Oh, hey Mr. Cortez." Mr. Cortez is my Spanish teacher, and I am now a little worried he may tell Dad I slept through most of his class this morning. Ms. Thatcher sits down next to Bob on the stairwell.

"Hey Bobby—nice tracksuit," the petite, round, Japanese American science teacher says, warming up next to Bob. I think Dad mentioned awhile back that Bob had a fling with her, but he never called her back. Oh—Bob.

"Hey Helen—long time," Bob replies nervously before giving the nod to Dad to make a rapid retreat. Both Bob and Dad stand and say their goodbyes to me and their security relief before retreating into the cafeteria for lunch.

After Dad and Bob escape, Hannah and I walk up the stairway. As we distance ourselves from the adults, we begin to move at a slower pace. Hannah then whispers to me, "What do you think that was all about?"

"What, the teacher security patrol? I don't know but must be pretty big if Mr. O'Leary pulled Dad and Bob off of their planning to watch a hallway."

"Ulysses, I think this should be our first case."

"I don't know," I say with extreme reluctance. "*The Manatee Times* usually has fluff pieces like who did our football team lose to, or where's the debate team going next. I mean, this may lead to next-level stuff."

"I know!" Hannah eagerly clamors, rapidly clapping her hands in quiet delight as we march into *The Manatee Times* classroom.

## III.

*The Manatee Times* is literally in a makeshift classroom. About a dozen students I recognize, from freshmen to seniors, bang away on laptops and smartphones, so intently working that they don't lift their heads from their cherished devices. No windows and dim lighting give the classroom the appearance of a cave.

"There they are!" A pudgy, bearded, middle-aged man, looking like a white Bob, joyfully approaches us, smacking us on the backs as he heartily shakes our hands, which leaves my hand sore.

"Mr. Scott, I told you I could convince him," Hannah says, beaming up at me.

"My two new photojournalists!" Mr. Scott announces to the rest of the newsroom. We only hear a pathetic "Yeah" and a sarcastic "Whoopi!"

Mr. Scott definitely wants us for our fifteen minutes of fame. I do remember Dad saying to me over dinner one night that Scott could lose his job if more *Manatee Times* papers weren't sold. He even mentioned that, at one time, people from the community would buy copies of *The Manatee Times* to get the goings on at Mangrove High. That sounds pretty cringy to me, but what-eve.

"Mr. Scott, we got the perfect story." Hannah recalls the meeting we just had with Dad and Bob. Mr. Scott first looks intrigued but quickly changes to a leering cringe.

"Oh, I don't know, Hannah. A story that involves Mr. O'Leary and a problem with security may not be the best direction the newspaper should go," Mr. Scott warns, now looking pale. "Here, this can be your desk. And Ulysses, Hannah says you have a camera?"

"Yeah. An old Olympus digital SLR. My—my mom left it to me before—she died."

Mr. Scott winces when I say this. "Sorry to hear that."

"Well, it was a long time ago," I add, trying to make him feel better.

"Okay—then. I'll let you kids get to it. Andy! Do you have that article about the away soccer game last night?" Mr. Scott barks before leaving us to our new extracurricular activity.

Our desk holds two older laptops with a small partition that blocks the view of other desks. We both sit in the hard chairs and log on to the laptops.

"Ulysses," Hannah whispers. "This is so lit. I think this is what I want to do when I grow up."

I smile. "What, work for a school newspaper?"

Her smile gives me a flutter in my gut. "No, silly, I want to be a journalist."

"That would be exciting," I say in agreement.

"I also disagree with Mr. Scott. I say we investigate what and why your Dad and Bob were guarding in that hallway. We need to find out what they know and take it from there."

"You heard Mr. Scott. He doesn't want that. It may hurt the paper," I plead.

"Ulysses Robert Adair!" she hisses in my ear. It is never good when she uses my full name. "How many times have I risked my neck to help you and your father? How many times have we put our noses where they didn't belong?"

"Okay—okay. You've convinced me."

"Good. I better have." She says this while furrowing her eyebrows at me with a rage I had never seen before. "Any thoughts of where we should start?"

"Oh, I got one," I say with a wide smirk.

"Your dad?"

"No, the weakest link."

"Bob!" we say in unison. Just then, the bell rings.

"Damn! Last period. How do you want to do this? We can't let my dad know we're investigating this."

"Agreed. Let's try and meet Bob up at his office after school."

## IV.

Bob's office is above the gymnasium overlooking the basketball courts. I had been there a few times, but this was Hannah's first time up there. We knock when we approach the door and hear a "What's happenin'?" As we enter, we see Bob sitting in his bright green tracksuit, with his feet up on his desk. He is excessively typing on his computer, but I know he is probably playing a video game. Hannah tries her best to not plug her nose in response to the stank odor of locker room mixed with very potent cologne.

"Ulysses, my man, and Hannah. To what do I owe this wonderful company?"

It is Hannah's turn to speak; for some reason, Bob always does what Hannah asks. I think it is because he is secretly scared of her. Seeing her black belt moves firsthand, on actual bad guys, gives you a better appreciation of what this unassuming Latina can do.

Hannah fills Bob in on our new jobs and extracurricular activity.

"Mmm—mmm, nice. Let me tell ya somethin', I always love reading *The Manatee Times*. It's the only newspaper I read." I hold back a smirk as I know this to be true. Bob isn't much of a reader.

"Well, Mr. Nelson, I mean Bob, that's why we are here. We want to hear from *Manatee Times'* most dedicated reader. We are trying to ascertain why you and Mr. Adair were patrolling the hallway and providing, as you state, added security."

"Ascertain what?"

"Why did Mr. O'Leary place you and Dad in the hallway during your planning?" I explain, frustrated with Bob. Hannah glares up at me as we each sit in chairs in front of Mr. Nelson. I think we may be here awhile.

"Bob, we thought we could get the scoop from an avid *Manatee Times* fan," Hannah says, trying to butter him up.

"Oh my! Let me tell you somethin'. This is serious business," Bob quips in the Barry White voice he usually reserves for his girlfriend, Sarah. "Bobby Nelson could get in trouble sharing that with you kids. If that got in the school newspaper, they would know it came from Bobby."

Even more frustrated with Bob's attitude, I spout off, "We could keep you as an anonymous source."

"Yeah," Hannah agrees. "Principal O'Leary, or Mr. Adair, wouldn't know you are our source."

"Oh, I don't know," Bob says, playing with his tracksuit zipper and exposing a classic RUN-D.M.C t-shirt beneath.

"Don't you think the readers of *The Manatee Times* would want to know?" I ask.

# SOMERSET SECRETS
## by T.W. Morse

"Don't you think they have the right to know? Mean old Mr. O'Leary shouldn't keep something like this a secret," Hannah adds as we both do our best to coax the information out of him.

"Mmm—mmm," Bob grunts. "Okay—okay. Let me tell ya somethin'. What I have to say will be anonymous—you dig?" Bob's Barry White voice is coming through again.

We both nod in agreement while Hannah gets out a black composition notebook and a pen while I hit record on my iPhone. We sit back and listen to Bob's story.

"It all started out a few days ago. Mr. O'Leary—you know, the principal."

We sigh in unison. "We know that Mr. O'Leary is the principal," I say with impatience.

"I know; I was just making sure your readers know," Bob adds.

"Bob!" I try to hold back my frustration. "Our readers are the students!" Hannah places a hand on my shoulder to quiet me.

"Continue on," Hannah says in her sweetest demeanor, while I know full well she wants to drop kick Bob.

"Well, Principal O'Leary kept busting kids in that hallway on drug possession this last week."

"Drug possession?" I clarify.

"Yup. He's caught several of the buyers right after the sale with Deputy Diaz's drug sniffing dog—you know that cute German shepherd Maximus? But O'Leary can never locate the seller. He can't afford to cover that particular stairwell with cameras, as there are so many blind spots, so he has positioned teachers to patrol it until the selling stops."

"That's it?" Hannah asks, not impressed. "How do they know the transactions are happening there?"

Bob shakes his head in disagreement. "Because they have a gazillion cameras in Mangrove. They can track kids even to the bathrooms where we even have cameras on each bathroom's exit door. And Maximus has been sniffing every kid coming up those stairs. The stairway also only goes one way," Bob pauses and takes a frustrated breath. "The students and staff come through the cafeteria on the opposite side. That's how O'Leary knows it's that corridor, and that's why he had me and your dad guarding it during our planning. Other teachers he trusts are doing the same thing during their planning when O'Leary can't use Maximus's sniffing ability."

"Why wouldn't the seller just move the drop-off point?" I ask.

"Good question. It is one of the only places where students and faculty aren't on camera coming and going. It's a busy stairwell and corridor. It might be the only blind spot of the school. O'Leary has had that Maximus sniffing all around this school to exhaustion." Bob says this with a shrug, clearly frustrated at the inconvenience.

"That corridor leads to the cafeteria. Maybe the seller needs to sell there and only there," I add. "O'Leary doesn't think they've been buying and selling in the cafeteria?"

Bob again shakes his head in disagreement. "Mmm—mmm, Ulysses, my boy, you don't understand. There's cameras in the cafeteria. If Maximus smells the drugs on kids coming up the stairway, then O'Leary can now follow those kids on the cameras and rewind to where they have been throughout the school. All that comes up empty. According to O'Leary, the only place those kids could get those drugs is in that area coming from the hallway outside the cafeteria and on the stairwell." Bob leans in closer and whispers, "O'Leary thinks it's a faculty member."

"What! Impossible!" I gasp.

Bob puts a finger to his lips to hush me. "Your dad disagrees with him. He doesn't believe it's a faculty member either, but O'Leary keeps putting teachers on patrol and the drugs keep getting handed off. He has caught five kids in the last four days and they ain't talk'n. All they say is, 'Snitches get stiches.' I really hate that saying. Man, Deputy Diaz and Principal O'Leary are worried they may have to stop the surveillance before a culprit is apprehended."

"What kind of drugs are being sold?" Hannah asks as she furiously writes.

"I think prescription drugs. You know, those painkillers that doctors prescribe. Gets people really hooked. Bad stuff," Bob says, looking dejected.

"My dad hasn't looked into this?" I add.

"He was talk'n about that today but was worried about O'Leary. You know how him and your dad butt heads."

I am the first to break the silence as we leave Bob's office for work at Penny University. We're both feeling stunned and fearful for Mangrove. We hate seeing drugs get into our school.

"This isn't enough to go on, Hannah. We can't bring this to Mr. Scott; he wouldn't publish it in a million years. And we could get Bob in trouble. Anonymous or not, Mr. O'Leary will know his loose lips were our source."

"True, but what should our next move be?"

"I say we regroup. I'll grab my camera at home tonight, and tomorrow we'll stake out that hallway."

"Ulysses, how are we going to do that? We have classes all day."

Then it hits me, and I grin down at her and whisper, "Dad's hidden video camera. He just bought one, just in case we had to do any future surveillances. We can hide it outside the cafeteria doors. It should be able to film enough of the corridor and stairwell to give us an idea of what's happening. The camera has a time lapse feature. We can review the footage at the end of the day."

"That's brilliant!" Hannah says before she hugs and kisses me. "Should we tell your dad?"

"Ah—I don't know. He definitely wouldn't approve. I don't like keeping stuff from him—ah, maybe after we find some evidence."

## V.

The air is thick with humidity, and it smells like rain as Dad and I drive to school together. I figure that if I go in early with Dad, I can get to that corridor before anyone else, plant the camera, and then wait until after school to retrieve it. Hopefully, we'll get some hard evidence.

"What're your plans after school?" Dad asks after turning down the volume during an AC/DC song. I take this as a warning sign that something is up. Dad loves AC/DC and would never turn down the volume during one of their songs.

"Not much," I say, trying to hide my guilt. "Just hanging with Hannah probably, at her place."

"You're always at Penny U. If you're not working there, we're playing there. When we aren't playing, you're still there because of Hannah."

"Ah—so?"

"Well, I've barely seen you. You've been hanging out a lot with Hannah, and I just thought we could have some father and son time—alone."

"Dad, we see each other at school, during our band practice, and when we jam at Penny U. We are always together." I suddenly feel guilty. Maybe he's feeling lonely. "You have Hope and Bob," I quickly say.

"Gee—wiz." Oh man, Dad using his dorky sayings isn't a good sign either. "I was just wondering if we could do something, you know, just the two of us. I don't know, go fish or something."

"Fish! Dad, you don't fish."

"I know, but I was just wanting to spend more ..." But before Dad can finish his sentence, we pull into the parking lot at Mangrove High, and I exit the car quickly.

"Sorry, Dad. I got to meet with, ah—Mr. Cortez—yeah. I got to turn in paperwork," I shout from behind me as I jog away. Why is Dad being so cringy? We spend all kinds of time together. I put it from my mind and concentrate on my mission. I sneak down the corridor that leads to the cafeteria. The cafeteria is full of early risers hunched over their books at the daily before-school study hall. I wave to a few friends before moving on through the overly fluorescent grub hub, and I open the door on the far side. After the heavy door closes behind me, I release a sigh of relief because no one is present. "Nice!"

I dig deep into my backpack and pull out Dad's time lapse video camera. "Where should I put you?" I say to myself as I twirl in a circle. "There." Right above the heavy door into the cafeteria is an exit box. I stand on my backpack. The geometry, U.S. history, Spanish, and biology books inside give me an additional six inches.

"Damn! Not tall enough," I exclaim as I reach and stretch my body as far as it can go. "Almost there." But no, I can't reach to the height needed. I can just touch the lettering, but it isn't enough to place the camera safely above it.

"Looks like you need a boost." A voice comes from behind me, startling me and making me lose my balance. I fall off my backpack and crash to the floor.

"Ah!" is all I can muster as the pain of the cement floor vibrates through my body. When the pain subsides, I open my eyes to see Dad standing alongside Bob. Both of them smile and look down at my pathetic situation.

"I didn't believe you for a moment about Spanish class, and after seeing Bob's guilt-ridden face this morning, I knew you were onto this case," Dad says with a cocky grin.

"You got me. I can never get anything by you," I say, rubbing my sore arm. I take Dad's outstretched hand, allowing him to help me up.

"We're here to help too. I'm hurt you wouldn't come to me about this."

"Well, Hannah wanted me to, but I told her to wait until we had evidence."

"Mmm—mmm," Bob mutters.

"Well, that's water under the bridge. Let's get that camera in place."

Dad and Bob both boost me up. I almost hit the ceiling. I position the camera perfectly and push record. Just as my feet hit the ground, Mr. O'Leary bursts through the cafeteria door, giving us a suspicious eye.

"Mr. A—dair and Mr. Nel—son! What are you doing here?!" His high-pitched screech rings through our ears. Some people's voices sure can get to you, and Principal O'Leary could definitely do that to us. "Mr. A—dair, why is your son down here?"

"We were just passing by on our way to Mr. Nelson's office," Dad replies for all of us because Bob and I are frozen in our tracks.

"Reeeeaaal—lllyyyy?" Mr. O'Leary is about to say more, but just then, Mr. Maxwell the custodian comes out from under the stairs.

"Good morning, boys," he says in his ancient grandpa voice. "Principal O'Leary, I got to mop this floor before the kids start arriving." With this interruption, Dad quickly leads Bob and me back through the cafeteria door and safely away from O'Leary.

## VI.

After school, Dad and I retrieve the camera from its perch above the exit sign. It was a little easier for me this time. We tell Bob and Hannah to rendezvous at Dad's classroom, near the front office.

"Let's see what we got," Dad says hopefully as he hooks the camera to his laptop. We all position chairs in a semi-circle around him. Dad keeps the lights off, and our faces are lit with the intense monitor screen. The footage runs quickly in front of our eyes because it is time lapsed. Dad brings the speed down a little, but it is still very, very fast.

"Logan, man, this is like watching paint dry," Bob says in disgust, putting his hands behind his head and tipping his chair back.

"You got to have patience, Bob. It is a virtue you know," Dad quips.

"Maybe we should speed it up a little, Mr. Adair," Hannah asks.

"Righty-O, full speed ahead," Dad adds as Hannah and I shake our heads in embarrassment.

SOMERSET SECRETS
by T.W. Morse

The video now is moving at about double speed. The timer clicks through the morning and then into the afternoon in a matter of minutes.

We see Maximus sniffing students going up the stairs as Deputy Diaz, our school resource officer, stands on the bottom step. Then the corridor explodes with students. "Lunch must have just gotten out," I say, interrupting the silence.

"Yeah, keep your eyes peeled for anything shady," Dad adds as he slows it again.

"Nothing," Hannah says after the herd of students leave.

"Maximus was there the entire time. He didn't get a whiff," Bob chimes. "I'm just surprised that dog hasn't gotten nose blind having to smell teenagers all day," Bob jokes as he continues to tip in the chair with his eyes closed.

"There you are Dad, with Bob." Dad and Bob arrive on the stairway after a lunch session. Only a few passersby come through. Bob comes to attention and stops tipping, presumably to check himself out on the screen.

The video proceeds to show Ms. Thatcher and Mr. Cortez again taking over for Dad and Bob.

"There is Helen and Edgar," Dad says under his breath. We even see Mr. Maxwell coming out of the cafeteria with three students. One of the students goes over to Mr. Cortez and starts chatting with him. Another student, a girl, starts speaking with Ms. Thatcher, while the other stands near the bottom step and starts to tie his shoe.

"Do you know any of them?" I ask Dad and Hannah.

They shake their heads to indicate that they do not.

"I know those three," Bob quips. Bob, being the P.E. teacher, seems to know every student. "Yeah—yeah, the girl, that's Katie Hillard. The boy speaking with Edgar Cortez is Jason Simmons, and the kid tying his shoe is Mike Johnson."

Just then, Mr. Maxwell comes back out from his custodian closet with his mop bucket. He slowly creeps around. It is like watching *Night of the Living Dead*, even at the faster speeds. He places down one of his warning signs to indicate that the floors are slippery.

"There! Did you see that?" I yell, startling everyone.

"No. I didn't see anything," Hannah says.

"Yeah, I saw it too," Dad adds. "Let's rewind." Dad clicks the rewind button on the media player guide.

"Right there," I say with confidence as we all lean into the monitor for a closer look.

"Come on, son. What? What are we looking for?" Bob says, now fully paying attention.

"Keep your eye on the yellow floor sign," Dad says as he pushes play and reduces the speed. Everyone is reduced to extreme slow motion, which makes Mr. Maxwell look like he was standing still because he's naturally in extreme slow motion. Just as he puts down the yellow warning sign, he simultaneously drops what appears to be a clear bag of white pills.

"Damn!" Bob yells. "You mean to tell me the old custodian is Mangrove's drug dealer!"

"He must have used Katie and Jason as his distractors. Having them speak with Mr. Cortez and Ms. Thatcher while Mike retrieved the drugs from the drop-off point," I reason.

"This is going to be *The Manatee Times*' biggest story," Hannah says, just as the lights in Dad's classroom burst on, temporarily blinding us. We all look up, shaken to see Mr. Maxwell in the flesh, liver spots and all.

## SOMERSET SECRETS
### by T.W. Morse

"Oh—I thought this room was empty. I didn't know you were all in here. My apologizes, Mr. Adair," Mr. Maxwell says in his slow grandpa voice.

Dad stands tall and circles around us. As he approaches Mr. Maxwell's cart, he covertly pushes the black intercom button. That button opens up a direct line to the office. If they answered the intercom in the office, it would work like a two-way radio.

"It's no problem, Mr. Maxwell. Um—my trash bins need to be emptied, though. Thanks."

"No problem, Mr. Adair. Hello kiddos and Mr. Nelson. What are all of you doing here so late?"

"Just working on a piece for *The Manatee Times*, Mr. Maxwell," Hannah quickly answers.

I sure hope someone in the office responds to Dad's call. Just then, a loud shriek comes over the classroom intercom.

"What!"

It is Principal O'Leary. I'd know that voice anywhere. Dad quickly whips into action. He first closes the door to the classroom and nods to Bob to indicate that he should block the door for him. Then Dad walks over to his desk where Mr. Maxwell is unassumingly emptying his trash bin. In a loud voice, either to ensure O'Leary hears it through the intercom or just for Mr. Maxwell's old ears, Dad starts to question him.

"Why do you do it?"

"What? Do what?" Mr. Maxwell asks in his confused, joyful demeanor.

"Mr. Maxwell—why are you selling drugs to our students?"

With this, Mr. Maxwell drops the garbage on the floor and stumbles a little, catching himself on a nearby desk. Hannah and I jump up and walk over to assist him.

"I'm fine!" he responds sharply, his grandpa demeanor fading rapidly.

"Where do the drugs come from?" Hannah asks gently.

Mr. Maxwell starts to suck on his lower lip, and he strokes his stubbled chin.

"We know about the yellow warning signs. We know you use students to distract teachers while you do the hand off with your buyers," I say, now standing next to Dad.

"You seem to know everything," Mr. Maxwell says with his lip quivering.

"Why did you do it?" Dad says with a stern voice that I haven't heard him use in a while.

Mr. Maxwell looks up at us and then looks at Hannah with a bashful, guilty look. "My wife, Rosie. She died a few weeks ago. She had been close to death for a while now. Our insurance was so terrible. All of her bills left me broke. I owe thousands!" He shakes his head at this and wipes away a tear with a sleeve. "I didn't let her physician know of her death so—so I could get unlimited refills of her prescription drugs at the pharmacy."

"What drugs could you get?" Hannah asks, still sounding sweet and caring.

"I got OxyContin. I thought I could sell them at Mangrove to make the money I owe the insurance companies and the hospitals. They were going to take my home!" With this last statement, Mr. Maxwell begins to weep.

A few seconds later, Mr. O'Leary and Deputy Diaz are at Dad's classroom door. "We heard everything, Mr. Maxwell. You are going away for a long time!" Principal O'Leary sneers as we look on, a little shaken and disturbed.

"What a shame," Hannah says before burying her face into my chest.

## VII.

A couple days later, Mr. Maxwell was charged with selling and distributing an illegal substance. Hannah and I didn't write the piece about Mr. Maxwell selling oxi to the students of Mangrove High.

We instead co-authored a two-piece article about the opioid epidemic and the healthcare situation in America. It was a little out of place among the 1% population of Somerset, Florida, but with the student body knowing this is what caused their beloved custodian to break the law and be put in jail, hopefully we shed some light on these enormous problems through the article. We think we did because *The Manatee Times* sold out at a record pace.

I also think Hannah and I finally found our niche at school—photojournalism.

**SOMERSET SECRETS**
*by T.W. Morse*

# FIELD TRIPS ARE MURDER
## LOGAN

### I.

I hate field trips. This thought pulsates through my brain as the school bus roars to life. I am stuck in its hard bucket seat while a half dozen teenage girls giggle and boys yell across the aisle at their friends. Teenage boys have no concept of inside voices. Being solely responsible for dozens of know-it-all, narcissistic teenagers out in the community is always a frustrating and daunting task. Our bus rolls out of Mangrove High's parking lot, puttering out of Somerset and onto the highway, leaving our rich 1% city behind us.

I am in charge of taking my freshmen U.S. history students to the Tampa Museum of Natural History. One of my ex-students, Harry Tillerman, is going to school up in Tampa and is interning as one of the museum's docents. For those who don't understand what a museum docent is, in a nutshell, they are the official guides and educators in museums.

He had sent me a couple of emails wanting me to take a school group up so he could practice for his final docent evaluation after he graduates from college this spring. Harry wants to make this a career, and I am all too willing to help out one of my former students. I am glad to see that Harry got into the field of history too. I always admired his love for history and am honored to have had some hand in this choice of profession.

Hannah, sitting with Ulysses in front of me, also is giddy with excitement. "Mr. Adair, do you think they still have the

Colusa arrowhead exhibit? I visited it several years ago, but after reading and researching the Colusa tribe for your essay last month, I have a new love for the indigenous tribes of Florida."

"I don't know, but we'll soon find out," I reply, smiling back at her inquisitive nature. Ulysses just stares blankly like Hannah has two heads. I wish I could've just taken the two of them instead of this whole gaggle of goons. I glance over my shoulder to see two of my freshmen, Margo and Laynie, loudly singing along to a song on the bus radio that I do not recognize. Ulysses has mentioned to me too often my ear for music doesn't extend into what kids these days are listening to.

"Mmm—mmm, Logan! Logan! Tell them to be quiet back there. Bobby Nelson is trying to catch some z's before we get to that boring old museum," Bob chimes in as he nuzzles an oversized pillow against the bus window. I smirk in Bob's general direction, wishing I hadn't asked him to chaperone, but I had more than ten students, and Principal O'Leary stated yesterday in his high pitched squeal, "Mr. A—dair, one chaperone per ten students. That is the law around here."

"Margo! Laynie!" I yell to the back of the bus.

"Yeah, Mr. Adair!" they both yell back in unison.

"Could we keep it down?! Mr. Nelson is trying to get his beauty rest, and he needs a lot of it!" I finish to a grunt and groan coming from the seat behind me where Bob is still squirming into position.

I hear a couple of giggles and "Yes, Mr. Adair!" It was followed by then louder giggles from the back of the bus.

"So what kind of student was Harry Tillerman?" Ulysses says, turning to me.

"He was one of my best. Well, until I got Hannah here."

**SOMERSET SECRETS**
*by T.W. Morse*

Hannah blushes at this, and Ulysses does a little too. "I remember he would always turn papers in early and be the first to raise his hand. He loved showing off his magic tricks too, which were honestly pretty lame. He was a little dorky; maybe that's why I liked him so much."

I sit back in the hard seat of our bus and think back to Harry and what I might expect from his invitation. It definitely will be weird seeing one of my students in the real world, trying to make a life for himself.

## II.

It seems like the two-and-a-half-hour trip from Somerset to Tampa is more like five hours in the hard bus bench seats, but we finally arrive. The museum was a massive red brick rectangular structure, topped with a white dome. It reminds me of President Thomas Jefferson's home, Monticello, up in Virginia. Ulysses and I had visited on our drive back from Maine last Christmas. "Doesn't it look like Monticello?" I say to Ulysses.

"Ah, sure, Dad. I guess."

"Monte—what? Come on, son, let's get going," Bob grumpily says. It looks like his nap was cut too short. I josh him by saying, "Does someone need a Snickers bar?"

"Funny. For your information, I was up with Sarah late last night. Mmm—mmm," Bob grunts in his Barry White voice.

"Mr. Nelson, we don't need the details—TMI," Ulysses chimes.

"I was putting together furniture, you know, that IKEA stuff. Damn, it took four hours to put together a little makeup vanity. Four hours! Mmm—mmm."

Bob's retelling of his eventful night is cut short by my name being called out in the distance. A large, bald man with a bright red jacket pushes through a crowd of elderly tourists.

"Mr. Adair! Mr. Adair!"

Before me stands quite an imposing figure. The name tag on his bright red sports jackets reads Mr. Ellis in big, bold letters.

"I am the head docent and will assist Mr. Tillerman on your tour today," Mr. Ellis says, sounding more like a cowboy from a cheap dude ranch than the head docent.

Mr. Ellis towers over me at about six foot six. His bald head is egg shaped and appears to be highly glossed, reflecting the museum lights and making his head look like a dance floor. His face is stretched beneath a wild, red Yosemite Sam mustache that conceals most of his lower face. His eyebrows look like owl feathers as they twitch and come to life as he speaks. Under his red docent jacket, he is wearing what appears to be rocks but, in fact, are just highly toned muscles. I shake his giant catcher's mitt of a hand, trying hard to find something to say, "Aw, Harry—I mean, Mr. Tillerman was a student of mine back in the day."

Mr. Ellis doesn't look amused but turns quickly and enthusiastically waves at a tall, attractive woman with jet black hair who is walking toward a side door of the museum. She gives him a very provocative smile and wave in return; looks like Mr. Ellis has a workplace flirtation going on. Beneath her white silk blouse there appears to be some sort of device, probably a microphone receiver for museum tours. Mr. Ellis continues to beam at her as she exits the lobby. This, however, quickly fades when he looks back at our group patiently waiting for Harry to join us. "Where is that boy?" he angrily mutters before leaving us for several minutes, slipping behind a side door to look for Harry.

## SOMERSET SECRETS
### by T.W. Morse

Reappearing and rejoining us again, shaking his head in disgust empty-handed still with no Harry.

A few minutes later from a door on the other side of the lobby, I spy my old student Harry Tillerman running over to meet us, out of breath, wearing a jacket like Mr. Ellis but with the addition of wrinkles.

"So glad you and your students could make it. And—Mr. Nelson? You too," Harry says with a drawn-out and uninterested response to seeing his old P.E. teacher in his museum lobby wearing a bright purple velvet tracksuit in Bob's ode to the late singer Prince.

"Harry, this is my son, Ulysses, and his girlfriend, Hannah Reyes." I introduce the rest of my freshmen too, as everyone shakes hands and greets our guide and my former student.

"So glad to meet everyone; you have a great teacher in Mr. Adair. I hope today I can spark a passion for history in you, as Mr. Adair did for me when I was at Mangrove High."

From behind me comes a loud cough. The lobby has forty-foot ceilings, so the cough bounces around and can probably be heard in the parking lot.

In Mr. Ellis's grumpy cowboy voice, he said, "Mr. Tillerman! We should get this group moving!" What are we, cattle?

"Ah, right. Yes, sir," Harry says nervously, tripping into Mr. Ellis. The encounter almost knocks him to the floor with Ellis's mountain-like structure.

Mr. Ellis practically picks him up like a mannequin before putting him back on his nervous feet, and he proceeds to reprimand Harry like a drill sergeant with a cadet.

"Son, let's hope you give a better tour than your appearance suggests. Wrinkled jacket and pants, unpolished shoes," he says while looking him up and down, pulling a string from his shoulder in disgust while puffing his mustache up with equal disdain. I am glad my students are distracted and don't see this teardown. Poor Harry!

"Okay, everyone, gather round," Harry says now in a broken voice.

I feel bad for the guy having to put up with this Mr. Ellis. I guess I can relate since I have to put up with Principal O'Leary.

All my students surround Harry and Mr. Ellis as Harry starts his tour by giving out directions and exhibit information, guiding us through the main exhibit hall.

Bob looks like he's sleeping. He has his eyes shut and he's swaying next to me. "Wake up, Bob!" I whisper in his ear.

"Say what now! Bobby's here! Bobby's here!" Bob loudly echoes through the museum, startled, briefly causing interruption to Harry's tour.

"Bob!" I whisper again. "How can you sleep standing up?"

"I don't know—man!" He now leans heavily on me and, with his raised, wrinkled forehead, looks distraught as he says with a hushed, cracked gasp, "Mmm-mmm. Dude, never buy from IKEA!"

### III.

The museum is really neat. I shouldn't say neat, but it's better than groovy. Ulysses always says I'm trying to bring back old corny words. The museum has a Colusa tribe village reenactment with mannequins. It also has some great exhibits from a sunken pirate ship. Hannah is bouncing from exhibit to exhibit like a kid in a candy store, oohing and ahhing the entire time.

"Isn't this so cool, Mr. Adair? Thanks for bringing us!"
"No problem."

# SOMERSET SECRETS
## by T.W. Morse

"Yeah, Dad, it's always better to be away on a field trip than to be stuck back at Mangrove High," Ulysses says with a cracked, dimpled smile.

Harry is standing several feet in front of us, doing a great job of showing my students different coins recovered from a pirate ship, all under the attentive eye of Mr. Ellis.

Mr. Ellis watches him like a hawk, jotting down notes on a little pad of paper. Probably assessing his tour guide prowess. I give Harry a wink and a thumbs up.

"Oh my god!" I hear from behind me. I turn to see Bob, now awake, leaning over a glass case of coins. He's getting his hands all over the glass, which holds a sign that says "Do Not Touch." "Hey Harry! When we gonna see something cool?" Bob yells with a bored, obnoxious grin. All I can think is that I liked it better when he was half asleep.

"Ah—ah, Mr. Nelson—um, I guess we could go down to the lab in the basement. That's where Margie, my director, should be filing away some of the Aztec artifacts. They are on loan from Mexico, and they are rumored to be cursed. That should be really cool to see, right?" Harry says to an excited group of my students. He receives a bored-looking nod from Bob. Harry looks to Mr. Ellis for reassurance.

Mr. Ellis nods his waxy head with approval, and our large group makes its way down to the museum basement. All the students are smiling and jumping around like we are going to a haunted house or something.

"Mmm—mmm—ah, Logan. I wanted something exciting not something cursed," Bob says, grabbing my arm.

I give Bob my most menacing glare. "Be careful what you wish for, buddy. Maybe you should've just enjoyed the tour and kept quiet."

"This is so cool, Ulysses. I can't wait! We get to see cursed artifacts. Did you know Howard Carter, the archaeologist who uncovered the ancient Egyptian Pharaoh Tutankhamen, was cursed? He and his entire team all died of mysterious causes shortly after uncovering the tomb." As Hannah rambles all this out, Ulysses looks back at me with a plea for help. I don't know if the plea is that he doesn't want to check out cursed artifacts or his girlfriend is a little too eager to do so.

We come to a thick, locked metal door. Mr. Ellis uses his ID badge to unlock it with a wave of his wrist. The locking mechanism cranks open, and we all file into a large room with a half dozen lab tables and old wooden crates piled high on the floor. Bits of straw hang off all sides of the crates. Large magnifying glasses attached to bright observation lamps are strategically pointed at different pottery shards and other ancient artifacts that appear to be from different Aztec dynasties.

Harry gestures at different objects on the table and smoothly leads my students into a tale of how an Aztec priest had cursed the jars and artifacts buried with his high priestess wife. "The curse states, 'Whoever touches the items from her burial chamber will slowly suffocate and die an excruciating death.'"

With this, Hannah gasps and pulls Ulysses tighter. Other students either giggle or look horrified. Mr. Ellis smirks at this; his mustache flops up like a blown feather in the wind with a puff of a non-believer. Bob literally takes an immediate step for the door, but it's locked. He violently shakes the handle in an effort to escape.

"You good?" I ask.

"Mmm—mmm," Bob says sheepishly. "Bobby Nelson is good, sooo—good. That's funny, looks like someone else is catching some z's." I follow Bob's thick finger over my shoulder to a corner of the lab, where it appears the same woman giving eyes to Mr. Ellis earlier is fast asleep at a work desk. Mr. Ellis hears Bob's remark and quickly walks over to her.

"It's just Dr. Kim, our head archaeologist. She probably was up late last night and now is making up for it," he says as he approaches her and tries to nudge her awake. He then lifts her arm and checks for a pulse. By now, the students are starting to look over to that part of the lab. Harry continues on with the tour for a few moments, speaking about the artifacts, but then even he stops speaking to see the cause of the commotion.

"She's dead," Mr. Ellis mumbles, stumbling back in disbelief. My students start to whisper loudly; some of them gasp while others whip out their phones and start taking pictures. Ulysses looks interested for the first time all day. Hannah buries her head into Ulysses's shoulder, shuddering at the realization of the dead scientist.

"Oh—man, we be in it again," Bob sputters, putting his hands on his hips and looking disgusted.

I walk over to the corner, where she is now sprawled on the desk in an unnatural position. "Any signs of foul play?" I ask a bewildered Mr. Ellis. "We need to preserve the scene for the police."

As I say this, I observe broken glass in the corner near her desk. Could it be related? Maybe a poison bottle. Did someone try to get rid of evidence in their hasty exit?

Mr. Ellis finally breaks from his trance and responds to my presence. "Ah—yes, yes, of course. I will call 911," he whispers as we retreat from the body.

I, of course, look back and try to visually examine anything I can. I don't see any exterior wounds, but that was no microphone system on her back. Her blouse has lifted above her pant line, and I can tell right away she is wearing an insulin pump. So, she was a diabetic. Next to her blouse, on her exposed waist, I see a needle mark. That's interesting. Why would she need to inject herself with insulin if she had a pump? And where is the needle? I don't see one anywhere. I look up at Mr. Ellis's face; it is hard to read because of his obnoxious mustache. Is he sad? I can't tell. I walk back to Ulysses and Hannah.

"She's dead?" Hannah asks with concern.

"Yes."

"You see anything?" Ulysses whispers, just as Bob comes over.

I explain the needle mark and the insulin pump and the broken glass. As I relay my findings, I lean in to the three of them and whisper while looking around me to make sure no one else is listening. "I think this was—murder."

## IV.

The police arrive quickly. The Tampa Police Department is led by a shabby looking detective with an equally shabby straw hat chewing on a Juul, clearly wishing it was a cigarette.

"Listen up! I'm Detective Walker, and I am in charge of this investigation. We'll want to speak with everyone, so be patient and sit tight," the detective says, scribbling on a notepad and giving everyone an intense stare-down.

Bob is shaking his head and looking nervous, sweating and unzipping his tracksuit jacket, which reveals his old Prince t-shirt underneath.

"You watch, Logan. That dude gonna blame it on the black man, you watch, Logan."

"Bob! Calm down. Nobody thinks you killed Dr. Kim," I say as we wait with all of my students, Harry, Mr. Ellis, and three other museum staff members who join us in the employee break room. Here Detective Walker assembles us all for interviews, following his inspection of the crime scene.

"Dad, why do you think it's murder?" Ulysses whispers as he, Harry, Bob, Hannah, and I all huddle like a football team in the corner.

"I saw her insulin pump, but I also saw a needle mark on her hip. Why have an insulin pump if you also need to inject your insulin? If Dr. Kim was a diabetic, an added dosage of insulin could kill her."

"I think it's Mr. Ellis. That man has been out to get me since I started to work here," Harry says, looking confident.

"I don't know. Wasn't he with us the whole time?" Hannah asks.

"Yes, and we saw Dr. Kim right before you arrived in the museum lobby," I say pointedly at Harry.

"Well, that counts Harry and Mr. Ellis out—right?" Bob suggests.

"So, it must be one of these three other employees. They are the only employees with security access to the lab. The security system rules out any visitors getting in," I add as we covertly look around the break room. "Harry, what can you tell us about them?"

"Ah, well, Amber Meade, she's widowed, a retired archaeologist. She's harmless, I'm sure," Harry says, tilting his head toward a seventy-something woman with darting green eyes wearing a bright white men's oxford shirt.

"We also have James Dietz. He is another docent. He and Ellis are best buds and have been here for years. I believe he's ex-military." A well-built, graying man with a crew cut and wearing the requisite red docent jacket sits quietly talking with Mr. Ellis. They are also speaking with a young, attractive woman wearing a docent jacket who looks to be the same age as Harry.

"That's Alyssa Hamm. She graduated last year and is another docent at the museum. I don't know much about her, but she was very good friends with Dr. Kim."

"Anyone with a grudge against Dr. Kim?" I ask, visually taking in our suspects.

"No! I mean—no, she was loved—by everyone."

"That's too bad," Hannah adds.

Just then a police officer calls out Harry's name, and he walks off to be questioned.

"Poor Harry," Ulysses says as he leaves. "His tour with his mentor from high school couldn't have gone worse."

"Mmm—mmm. I know. That kid always came into my physical education class with such a big smile, showing his dorky magic tricks to the upperclassmen. He loved being in my P.E. class," Bob says, assuming Ulysses is referring to him.

"Bob! I meant Dad is his mentor!"

Harry comes strolling back about ten minutes later looking even more disheveled.

"How did it go?" I ask.

"Well ..." Harry says, clearly unsure of whether he wants to share his thoughts with us.

"What is it?" I ask.

"Well, they asked if anyone was in a relationship with her, and I explained the museum gossip is that Dr. Kim was possibly romantically involved with Mr. Ellis."

"A lovers' quarrel, that is motive. I'm not willing to count out Mr. Ellis either," I say as I stare across the room at him. He is now wringing his hands together and sweating profusely, making his glossy dance-floor head look slippery.

"What? Dad, he was with us the whole time."

## SOMERSET SECRETS
### by T.W. Morse

"Yeah, but an insulin injection could take twenty to thirty minutes to cause someone's death, depending on her blood sugar levels at that time. Ellis had plenty of time to inject her and then get up to us in the lobby," I add, trying my best to whisper.

"How do you know that?" Harry asks.

"I just Googled it." I show everyone my phone that I'd been using to research. "Insulin wouldn't kill somebody who isn't a diabetic, but too much insulin can be very deadly for a diabetic like Dr. Kim."

While we huddled over my phone, the other three employees were asked to come out in ten-minute intervals too, just like Harry was. The last one pulled was Mr. Ellis.

"These other guys may have motive too; we just haven't found it yet. I say we investigate. Ask around about Ellis and Kim's relationship but also get the whereabouts of the others," Ulysses says.

"We'll ask Amber Meade. Old ladies love Ulysses," Hannah chimes in, rubbing Ulysses's hair.

"We should move quickly before Mr. Ellis gets back," Ulysses adds.

"Okay, we'll talk to the other two."

"Oh no! Mmm—mmm. Count me out. Whenever you guys ask questions," Bob squeals, making air quotes in the air, "I get in trouble or chased or shot at."

"Wait, you've been through something like this before?" Harry asks with raised eyebrows.

"Ah—once or twice," Ulysses chimes in.

"Bob, you sit back and watch over the students. We got this," I say, giving him a reassuring pat on the back.

"Mmm-mmm, sounds good for Bobby Nelson."

Hannah and Ulysses are already off to question the retired archaeologist Amber Meade. That leaves James

Dietz and Alyssa Hamm. I gesture for Harry to accompany me. I don't know them, and it would be good for him to do the introductions.

"Alyssa and James, this is my old school teacher from Somerset, Logan Adair. I was giving his school group a tour when we found Dr. Kim."

Alyssa is sobbing and can barely see me through her swollen eyes. She has a round face with lots of makeup, now being slowly washed away.

"I'm so sorry for your loss."

Alyssa sobs out a "Thank you."

"Do you think anyone wanted to hurt her?" I ask between sobs.

"Wait, she was murdered?" James gruffly asks as Alyssa's sobs now increase.

"I don't know, but the death looked suspicious," I respond, examining both of their faces for any signs of deceit.

"Nah, Kim was well liked. A bit of a flirt," James says while rubbing Alyssa's back in a very endearing way.

"Everybody loved her," Alyssa snorts out between sobs.

I frown with compassion but quickly turn back to James for more information. "A flirt, you say?"

"Yeah, I saw her leave from the parking lot a couple nights ago with a man. It was dark and I couldn't see for sure who it was, but they looked to be in a romantic embrace."

Alyssa looks stunned at James and then looks at me. "You don't think one of us killed her, do you?" she stumbles between sniffles and sobs.

"Oh, I don't know who killed her."

"Mr. Adair is only curious about the case; I'm sure the police will ask the same questions," Harry says just as Detective Walker comes into the break room, looking worn and sweaty even though the AC is blasting. Damn, it looks like my questioning is coming to an end.

He just points at me and curls his finger, beckoning me to come over to him. "You!" he yells across the room.

I point at myself and give my best confused face, similar to the expressions my students give me on most days.

I am led back into the lab. The crime scene guys are swarming through the place searching for evidence and clues while dusting for fingerprints. Maybe they've also realized that this was indeed murder.

"I heard of you," the detective notifies me while snickering over his pad of paper. At least I think it was a snicker. His straw hat reminds me of some '70s cop show that I just can't quite place.

"Ah—yeah? How's that?" I say, examining his features and folding my arms while standing up straight, trying to look confident.

"I read the papers. You are that teacher. The teacher who solves those crimes down in Somerset." Putting the Juul in his mouth and puffing a cloud of smoke in my direction tells me he isn't impressed. "I heard you were part of the group who found the body."

"I found some indications that Dr. Kim was murdered. Specifically, she had a needle mark on her hip," I blurt out, about to relay my findings.

"I know it was murder!" Walker says with an irritated inflection.

"You do?"

"I don't need no teacher coming in and messing with my scene. I saw the puncture wound. We also found a broken insulin bottle near the body. We got the ID tag log of everyone coming in and out of this lab. So, teacher, why don't you stick to the classroom because Detective Walker has got this wrapped up." With this, he points his straw hatted head toward the glass door where two officers are taking Mr. Ellis out in handcuffs.

"So, you do suspect Mr. Ellis?" Maybe Tampa cops know more than Somerset cops.

"I don't know how the cops do things down in Somerset, but up in Tampa, we follow the evidence. Mr. Oscar Ellis was the only ID tag logged into this lab other than Dr. Kim. We also found another bottle of insulin in his locker, and it was rumored they were having a love affair. Case closed—teacher. I guess you should leave it to the pros." He smiles and then gestures for an officer to escort me out. "You and your students are free to go."

## V.

"Ha! Ha! Oh my god! Logan, you got bested. I knew one of these days somebody was going to outsmart the great Logan Adair. See, the cops got the right dude without y'all's help—mmm—mmm," Bob says, laughing as we exit the museum for our waiting bus.

"Well, he did have his suspicions about Mr. Ellis and they were right, Bob," Ulysses says in my defense.

"It's also good for once that the police can take care of this instead of us," Hannah says, sighing.

I feel a little uneasy. It all just came together too easily. I wish I had a chance to speak with Mr. Ellis or—what did the detective call him?—Oscar. Why did he leave so much incriminating evidence? He must have known his ID badge logs him in and out of the museum lab. He must have known they'd search his locker. My thoughts are broken off by Harry clapping me on the back.

"It was nice seeing you and Mr. Nelson again. Sorry it couldn't be under better circumstances," Harry says as all of my students board the bus and we say our goodbyes.

Several of my students come up to Harry to take selfies, updating their social media accounts and calling it "the best field trip ever! It was raw!" Whatever that means.

After my students board, Hannah gives Harry a hug and Ulysses gives a fist bump, both wishing him good luck.

"Thanks again, Mr. Adair."

"No problemo—Ulysses and I would love to have you over for dinner sometime. How about next week?"

"Ah—I don't know. I've got finals coming up, and I'll probably be really busy here."

Bob slaps Harry on the back. "I insist, Harry. It was cool seeing you again. I'll be there too; you can have a brewski with your old teachers."

"Okay—I guess so. Yeah, that sounds good," Harry concedes as we finish boarding our yellow chariot and we take off back to Somerset.

Our ride home is—loud. Everyone is buzzing about seeing a dead body. Nothing fazes teenagers. I don't know how I'm going to explain this to all their parents and Principal O'Leary. Argh! He's going to find a way to blame me for all of this.

Bob is loudly snoring in the seat behind me, and Ulysses and Hannah are talking about what Amber Meade had said when they questioned her.

"For an old lady, she had a lot of spunk," Ulysses says to a nodding Hannah. "We asked her about Dr. Kim, if she had any suspicions, did she hold any grudges or have any enemies. The typical questions."

"She said possibly," Hannah adds, then proceeds to do an impression of the retired archaeologist. "'That doctor liked to, how do kids say it these days? Have friends with benefits?' I just about broke down laughing right then."

They both start to laugh at this before Hannah continues with her impression of Amber, "Margaret Kim was nice, but she definitely had the men eating out of the palm of her hand."

While they both continue to laugh at Hannah's impression, something hits me. Something Hannah just said struck a chord. What was it? Nothing comes to me. Something I heard earlier today, and it's important to the case. Why can't I remember? Damn! What was it?

## VI.

It's about a week after our field trip to the museum and the unfortunate death of Dr. Kim. Bob, Ulysses, and I are hosting Harry for dinner at our tiny condo in Somerset. Harry knocks at the door, and I invite him in.

Bob fist bumps him as he enters our living room while Ortiz, our hyperactive Boston terrier, howls and jumps at Harry's leg.

"Who's this?" Harry asks, looking past Ortiz's advancements at our other surprise dinner guest.

"Oh—this is an old friend of ours—Nathan. We've, ah, done some business in the past with him and invited him for my famous spaghetti and meatballs.

"Crazy weather, right?" I say as I take Harry's raincoat. "Any more news on Dr. Kim's murder?"

"No, it sounds like they got their man. It's all over the news up in Tampa. Oscar Ellis, museum docent, murdered beloved doctor," Harry adds as we all sit down for dinner at our cramped table.

"Mmm-mmm and what's Ellis saying?" Bob asks.

"He is still pleading his innocence. He claims he had a romantic relationship with Dr. Kim, but he says he didn't murder her," Harry explains, looking unfazed by our questioning.

"Salad?" Nathan asks.

"Ah yes, I will have some salad, thank you."

"He's right," I add as Harry piles his salad onto his plate.

"Say what?!" Bob blurts out.

"He's innocent. Isn't he?" I say, putting my fork down and giving Harry my full attention.

"I don't—I mean—what do you mean?" Harry stumbles out before putting his hands on his lap. He is sweating now and is overcome by a look of exhaustion.

"I mean Oscar Ellis didn't kill Dr. Kim. You did!" My disappointment in my former student exudes from my body, and I slam my fist on the table in rage. Both Ulysses and Bob back away from the table.

"Mr. Adair, I couldn't have killed her. You know me—you know me!"

"I thought I did." I shake my head in disgust but continue on.

"You were late to the lobby because you had just run from the lab. You were having a love affair with Margaret Kim. My suspicion started when I found out Dr. Kim's first name. Hannah had said it on the bus on the way home. It was Margaret. It struck me as odd. Only someone intimate would refer to Dr. Kim as Margie—like you slipped out that day when speaking about her.

"The other employees all call her by her title, doctor. You wouldn't call her anything but doctor too—unless, unless you were in an intimate relationship with her. I think Ellis was too. I saw how he waved to her and how she waved back. That was too much for you, wasn't it? You wanted her all to yourself. That is motive enough to kill.

"So, you planned it all out to murder her and frame Mr. Ellis. You exchanged key cards with Oscar Ellis using your sleight of hand magic tricks Bob and I fondly remember from high school. Swiped his card to get into the lab earlier that morning, so it looked like he had been there before meeting with us in the lobby. Meanwhile, he swiped yours elsewhere in the museum, giving you your alibi. You hid the extra insulin in his locker, and then snuck up behind Dr. Kim and injected her with a lethal dosage. Maybe you held her in her chair while she went into a diabetic seizure before she passed out. Then you wiped any fingerprints off the needle and then threw it across the lab before running up and joining us in the lobby. That's when you purposely bumped into Mr. Ellis, switching the key cards once again and continuing on with our tour like nothing had happened."

Harry smiles and starts to slowly clap his hands after I reveal my hypothesis. This is a smile unlike any I had ever seen before. It gives me a chill up my spine. Where was the student I once mentored?

"Ah, but Mr. Adair. How can you prove this? The evidence is significant against Oscar Ellis. You don't have me at the scene, and you can't prove Dr. Kim and I had a relationship either. These are just circumstantial accusations."

I shake my head and lean forward. "Well, first, you calling Dr. Kim by a pet nickname, Margie, made me suspicious of you. So, it won't be long before the police become suspicious too. See, I've already gone back to Tampa and convinced Detective Walker to check surveillance tape of the parking lot outside the museum. I remember James, your coworker, said he had seen Dr. Kim leave with a man from the museum parking lot. He claims they looked intimate.

Sure enough, we found the parking lot footage. You know what we found?"

"What?" Bob interrupts, grabbing a piece of bread from the table and tearing it in hunger before sinking back in his seat.

I frown at him before continuing on. "We found you and Dr. Kim in an embrace and then leaving together. Also, are you positive you wiped off your fingerprints from the insulin bottle you planted in Mr. Ellis's locker?

"Your fingerprints on the insulin bottle and the video were enough for the Tampa police to gain a search warrant to your place. I believe they are raiding it right now."

Harry slumps in his seat. "She was two-timing me!" Harry says, closing his eyes. "I had to do it!"

"You had to do what, Harry? Be a man!" I say goading him into his confession.

"I had to hurt her the way she hurt me; she had it coming. She embarrassed me. She started messing around with that oaf Ellis, and I knew—I knew I had to kill her!" As he finishes, he starts to sob. Ulysses and Bob both look at me puzzled.

"Nathan, I think he's all yours."

"Harry Tillerman, my—name is Nathan Brute; I—am a detective with the Somer—set sheriff's department—and I—am placing ya under a—rrest."

After Detective Brute leaves with Harry, Ulysses and Bob pounce on me with rapid questions.

"So that's why you suddenly wanted to be friendly with Detective Brute," Ulysses blurts out, half surprised and half out of breath. "I also didn't know you drove up to Tampa and checked the video with Detective Walker?"

"Yeah, I took a sick day from school. I didn't want to tell you guys. I had to make sure we got Harry to confess and make sure we didn't let it slip that we were onto him."

"So, they found fingerprints on the insulin bottle and issued a search warrant?" Ulysses says, smiling.

"Yes, after we found the incriminating tape confirming a motive, they checked the insulin bottle found in Mr. Ellis's locker for Harry's prints. Sure enough, they were a match. Detective Walker asked if we could keep him busy while they executed the search warrant. That's when I remembered the dinner invitation. Since it's in Brute's jurisdiction, we brought him into the action too."

Bob scrunches his face up and opens another beer. "This is too much. Mmm—mmm. Poor kid."

"So, when you said for both of us to call Detective Brute by his first name and to not mention he was a cop in front of Harry because he may feel—uncomfortable, that was also a lie?" Ulysses adds.

"Yup."

"When did you know it was Harry?" Ulysses adds, smiling.

"When I said I did, on the bus when Hannah mentioned Dr. Kim's first name being Margaret. Harry didn't mean for us to hear his pet name for her—Margie—it must have just slipped. I also thought Harry was not a mastermind criminal and the murder of his girlfriend was eating him up inside. He needed to confess his sins."

"We've got to tell Hannah; she will be so mad she wasn't here," Ulysses says, pulling out his phone and rapidly texting with his fingers.

Bob takes a long draw of beer before asking, "So, you didn't know for sure he'd confess?"

"Nope. Fingerprints can be planted, and we needed a confession because we couldn't completely disprove his alibi."

Bob whistles to himself. "Nice work, bro. Still I can't believe one of our ex-students committed murder."

"Me neither." On that, we both sit back in our seats and drink in a somber silence.

*SOMERSET SECRETS*
*by T.W. Morse*

# THE CASE OF BOB'S UFO SIGHTING

## ULYSSES
### I.

Hannah and I are helping Dad set up his classroom for Mangrove High's open house tomorrow morning. Dad thinks this is Mr. O'Leary's way of torturing the faculty by having open house for next year's freshmen on a Saturday morning. Dad's U.S. history classroom was next to the office and was one of Mangrove High's bigger classrooms. Because U.S. history is a requirement for all students to graduate, his classes are often full. This, in turn, means a lot of parents come through his classroom during open house. Dad wants his classroom to have a look of organization and feel welcoming to parents. This is taking a lot of work to achieve since his usual classroom style is closer to controlled chaos.

Hannah and I stop in our tracks and smirk to ourselves when we see Bob plow into the room wearing one of his signature black tracksuits. He starts to whisper in Dad's ear. Dad cringes and sighs with every word Bob says. Bob is definitely fired up about something. Dad whispers back with an irritated look. I can't hear what he is saying, but Dad's final response fills us in right away.

"Bob, you did not see aliens!" This is a sentence I never thought I would hear my dad utter.

"I sure as hell did!" Bob responds in a loud, angry whisper so that Hannah and I can hear while we reposition desks and chairs throughout the classroom.

**SOMERSET SECRETS**
*by T.W. Morse*

Just then Hope and Sarah walk in, which is a cue to us that we need to wrap things up and go to dinner. "Hey Hope, hey Sarah. Ah, Sarah, you know your boyfriend here thinks he saw aliens last night," Dad says after moving the last desk into position.

"We did," Sarah quickly affirms.

"No way, really?" Hannah asks with intrigue. Hope literally distances herself from Sarah by taking a step back, like her and Bob's crazy was contagious.

"Bobby, you didn't tell them what happened?" Sarah says, hugging Bob.

"I was just gett'n to it, girl, but my boy Logan started say'n it's malarkey, whatever that means. Let me tell you somethin', I always stick by you; you can't stick by a brother even when it concerns—aliens?" Bob says, whispering the word aliens. He probably thinks the aliens can actually hear him.

"Okay, okay. Tell us what happened," Dad concedes.

"Yeah, tell us about your alien visitation and your anal probe," I laugh, fist bumping Dad, but receiving death stares from all the women, especially Hannah.

"Bro! There were no anal probes," Bob says with a hint of uncertainty as he looks to Sarah for reassurance. "Mmm—mmm—Okay, let me tell you somethin'. Sarah and I were coming home from a little romantic jaunt," Bob says in his Barry White voice. And yes, he says jaunt.

"We'd be driving on Route 41 in south Somerset, taking Sarah home to her condo complex, Island View. As we park in her complex, we see this really big object floating above us with blinding red, green, and purple lights. The unidentified object just hovers above us."

Bob uses hand gestures to perform this, and I have to smirk to myself because with his black tracksuit he looks like he's doing an '80s break dance as a member of his favorite group, RUN-D.M.C. He always makes Dad and me watch old MTV videos of the famed hip hop group.

"Don't forget about the noise and the wind," Sarah interjects, her voice shaky as she buries her head into Bob's tracksuit jacket at the memory.

Bob continues his animated tale. "These cra-cra sounds and a heavy wind. Our car literally stops and loses power. Mmm—mmm—it loses—power," Bob says, contorting his face as he pleads his story to all of us in high, nervous squeaks. I actually get goosebumps and now wish I hadn't made fun of Bob because it's sounding—real. I take a deep gulp. Hannah crosses herself and grabs my hand to hold.

"So, these 'cra-cra' sounds?" Dad asks, making condescending air quotes when he says "cra-cra," not believing Bob for a minute.

"Yeah, it sounded like bagpipes in a car crash. Did I mention the wind too? The wind was like a hurricane," Bob says to a nodding Sarah.

"And your car went completely dead?" Hope now chimes in, looking a little white herself.

"Where was it exactly?" I ask, wondering whether it left marks somewhere. Dad and I make eye contact, confirming that he had the same thought.

"Right above a large park in Sarah's condo complex. They use it as a dog park, near the parking lot," Bob finishes.

"So, it just hovered? How long?"

"Jeez—mmm—mmm, about five minutes and then it sped away. As soon as it was gone, my car miraculously turns back on," Bob says with his eyes wide and scared.

"Oh-oh-oh, and that's not the weirdest part," Sarah adds. "When the car came back to life, Elton John's 'Rocket Man'

**SOMERSET SECRETS**
*by T.W. Morse*

came blaring on through Bobby's car radio." We all giggle at that. Wow, these two are perfect for each other.

"Okay, we'll check it out. We still have a little daylight left. We can go before dinner," Dad reassures them. I notice Hope's raised eyebrows. She must be wondering why Dad indulges Bob's whims.

## II.

The condo community of Island View is a lot like our home at River Creek: a tall Tucson-inspired two story building surrounded by a large parking lot. The only difference is their large fenced-in dog park in the middle of the parking lot.

When we arrive in Dad's Prius and Bob's Jeep Wrangler, the parking lot is practically empty. We are approached by an overweight, stout man with greasy, slicked back Jack Nicholson hair. "Sarah, did you see the UFO last night?" the man says, sounding like an out of breath, engorged bullfrog. He's wearing a bright orange golf tee and sneakers that are caked with dry mud.

"Hey Eric, these are my friends. I was actually going to show them around because Bobby and I did see the UFO last night. You know Bobby, but this is Ulysses, Hannah, Logan, and Hope. This is Eric Fuller; he owns Island View and lives here too," Sarah says.

"It doesn't appear that too many people live here," Hope says.

"Yeah, a lot of the condos are empty. They keep leaving; I've heard people complaining about the UFO sightings for a few weeks now. But I had never seen it until last night. Probably going to have to sell soon. Regents Bay is offering a nice, tidy sum. Sarah and a few residents are the only ones that still remain. Everyone is going off to live over at Regents Bay," Eric says.

"What's Regents Bay?" Dad quickly asks.

Eric lifts a thick, curled finger and points across the street to two high-rises being built. One is completely done; the other is surrounded by large red and blue cranes and only partially built.

"A lot of money over there," Eric grumbles with disdain before waddling away, looking back at us nervously as he retreats to the Island View clubhouse office.

"Regents Bay promises moving incentives and bonuses to people living in Island View, but I'm one of the few that keep rejecting their offers. I keep telling them I'm happy here. I look out for my elderly neighbor Ruth too, who doesn't want to move either. She was also approached by Regents Bay but refused like me. Her and I are two of the few residents that remain to stand up to those corporate bullies. I think they want to buy Island View to expand their high-rises to both sides of the street," Sarah informs us with a sickened look. "But I am less than a year into a three-year lease. So, I'm staying. Besides, if I left, who would look after Ruth?"

We can't blame her. Island View is just down the street from Hannah's and my favorite beach. It is probably prime real estate. "So where were you parked?" I ask Bob and Sarah, redirecting the conversation back to the case at hand.

"Right where Bobby's Jeep is parked now."

"And you saw the object there?" Dad says, pointing above the dog park.

"Object? Object? Logan, call it what it is, dude! It was an unidentified flying object, so it is a …" Bob says, wanting Dad to finish the sentence.

"Alright, is that where you saw the UFO?" Dad reluctantly responds in a sarcastic tone.

Bob smiles and nods.

Dad, Hannah, and I open the gate and enter the dog park while Hope waits with Sarah and Bob, who don't want to get too close.

"What are we looking for, Mr. Adair?" Hannah asks nervously. "Alien clues?"

"Ah—no, regular earthly style clues. But yet—but yet," Dad says with a puzzled face. He gets on all fours and examines the grass point blank and crawls around the park like a dog, examining different blades.

"You find something, Dad?"

"The blades of grass are bent here and here." He says this as he walks over from one side to another. "But not the grass near the corners. We need a higher view," he says with his determined, deep-thought expression.

"Sarah, does your condo face the dog park?" Dad asks.

"Um—yes. But I haven't been home. After what I saw last night, I couldn't stay the night here and instead stayed at Bobby's."

"That's fine. It's the second floor too—right?" Dad adds.

"Yes," Sarah says reluctantly.

I think I know where Dad is going with this. We all race up the stairs to Sarah's condo and burst in. It is very tastefully decorated with a hodgepodge of tan and white IKEA furniture.

Dad barges ahead of Sarah and rips open her beige curtains to gasps from everyone behind him as he reveals the view.

"Oh, what the hell is this?" Bob mutters. "I told you, Logan. You didn't believe me, but I was right," Bob chides.

Hannah crosses herself again and even says a prayer in Spanish under her breath. Hope takes Dad's hand and says, "Logan, what could do that?"

I myself am speechless and look up at Dad for answers, but for first time, I see my dad clueless about a case.

We all look down from the window onto the dog park and see a huge circular ring within the park, bending all the blades of grass down, undeniably leaving a huge crop circle from a UFO.

### III.

"What's next, Dad? A stakeout?" I eagerly ask as I finish my French fries at Penny University Cafe. I'm feeling a mix of nervousness and anxiety looking forward to a case involving aliens.

"Wait—wait, Ulysses—you want to go back—tonight?" Bob squeaks. "Mmm—mmm—you can count me out. Sarah can live with me and never go back to that place."

With this comment, Sarah holds Bob tighter and beams up at him. "You really mean it, Bobby?"

And with his Barry White voice, Bob says, "Mmm—mmm, for you, girl, you know that's right. Let me tell you somethin'—anything to keep my girl away from aliens." It is weird to see this relationship build so quickly. Bob and Sarah have only been dating since Christmas. I am not too sure whether Bob was genuine in his sudden offer of living together. But it is nice to see Bob happy, and they do appear perfect for each other.

"We're going back tonight," Dad adds confidently after periods of deep thought and periods of relentless typing on his phone. "We've got to solve this, don't we?" he finishes, winking at me and Hannah.

Hannah's parents, the owners of Penny U., walk over to our table. Sarah starts to update them on the details of the UFO sighting. Mrs. Reyes gasps and oohs and ahhs throughout the story while Mr. Reyes makes hissing and grunting sounds.

"No aliens—no such thing," Mr. Reyes insists in his Cuban-accented English. "Bob was just drunk. Yes. Drunk. Dumb American," Mr. Reyes concludes, with yes sounding more like jes.

"Papa!" Hannah pleads while Mrs. Reyes elbows Mr. Reyes in the ribs and aggressively pulls Mr. Reyes away into the kitchen.

"What else could it be?" Hope adds. "We have two witnesses and a crop circle."

"Don't forget Bob's Jeep going dead," I add.

"A variety of different things," Dad says before continuing. "I have two lines of investigation of what it could be, and we will follow those lines tonight. I'm confident the unidentified flying object will be identifiable soon enough," Dad adds.

"So, you're going to keep us in the dark?" I add.

"Well—as Sherlock Holmes says, 'Never trust to general impressions, my boy, but concentrate yourself upon details.'"

"Mmm—mmm, you can count Sarah and me out!" Bob squeaks.

"But Bobby, who's going to protect Logan and Ulysses from the big bad aliens?" Sarah pouts in her annoying baby voice while nudging her nose to Bob's. Hannah confidently raises her hand to this question.

"Mmm—mmm, okay, girl. I'll look out for my boys," Bob says now with a faux confidence that fools no one. Dad and I both just roll our eyes.

"I'll keep Sarah company in her condo and give you an aerial view," Hope adds.

"Good. Ulysses, Hannah, Bob, and I will stake out the dog park in your Jeep," Dad says.

"Why my Jeep?"

"I have my reasons. Let's go back now. It's about the same time as last night, right?" Dad inquires.

"Mmm—mmm—yeah—I think so. You think that matters?" Bob says.

"I think it does," Dad adds, looking like the confident Dad of old.

"Alien hunting! This definitely was on my bucket list," I shout excitedly.

"Ah, not mine. Ulysses, I'm not sure my karate will help us against aliens," Hannah says, smiling as we all laugh.

## IV.

We have been sitting in Bob's Jeep for more than an hour and nothing. Hannah and I are on our phones doing some silly snaps to our followers on Snapchat. Dad had told Bob to turn off the car. Bob is exuding nervous energy as his alien PTSD is in high gear. He's shaking his legs uncontrollably and munching obnoxiously on a wad of gum.

Hope and Sarah are our lookouts back in Sarah's condo. Bob frantically looks up and out of his Jeep. We have the top off and the windows rolled down, exposing us to Somerset's night sky. Not many stars are visible, and some ominous clouds are now rolling in.

"Dad, you are expecting something to happen tonight?"

"Yeah, Logan. Um, maybe we should pack it up for tonight. Go get a drink or somethin'—mmm—mmm," Bob says now, becoming more frantic by the minute.

"It's just a hunch, but I think …" Dad says, unable to finish his statement as a sudden blast of wind funnels through the Jeep and the sky above us fills with different colored lights, like the aurora borealis but brighter and closer. Dad's phone rings at the same time. It is Hope. Dad puts it on speaker phone and turns the volume all the way up to hear her over the wind. "Logan, they're here! GET OUT!!" Hope pleads before Dad's phone goes dead. Bob frantically tries to turn the engine over but shakes his head in frustration as beads of sweat trickle down.

"No-no-no-no. My Jeep won't turn on," Bob squeaks. As the bright lights creep closer and closer to our position, the wind continues to pick up around us like we are caught in the middle of a tornado.

Hannah shouts something to me, but I can't hear her even though she's sitting right next to me. The incredible amount of wind and whirring noises make it impossible to hear anything else.

I look to Dad, who shields his eyes and stares directly up at the lights. As the weird pulsating noise echoes over the park and vibrates the Jeep, it really does sound just like Bob's description of bagpipes in a car crash. A chill creeps up my spine and my hands become cold as ice as I look at Hannah, whose mouth is wide open, gaping with shock. Her mocha skin now looks chalky white. Fear of the unknown consumes us as we gaze up at the UFO.

"Screw this. Let me tell you somethin'—I ain't gett'n no anal probe!" Bob yells. At least I think that's what he says because his statement is followed by him jumping out of the Jeep, a little graceful considering the size of his large body.

He leaves us and runs toward Sarah's condo squealing, "ah—ah—ah!" the whole way while covering his head with his arms.

At this point, Dad also gets out of the car and waves for us to follow. Hannah and I look at each other, knowing we need to do what he says. It is hard to move since the wind is so fierce. Luckily, the bright greens and blues coming from the object above provide enough light to follow Dad. I am surprised to see Dad run around the park and away from Sarah's condo.

"Dad! Dad!"

"Mr. Adair!" We both yell and run after him. Dad is at a full sprint. Where is he running to? I look back and see the flying object still hovering above the park. It looks so weird. I am freaking out now as it is sinking in that we're watching this UFO hover about two stories up while wind and light come down all around us, filling the night sky with that eerie noise. Once we get several yards closer to the road with the new high-rise, Regents Bay, across the street, I can hear Hannah better.

"Where's your dad going?"

"I don't know, but I think he's onto something. Where's Bob?"

Hannah shrugs at this as we finally catch up to Dad.

We are now standing next to the construction zone of Regents Bay. We can see huge cement piping and construction material laying just beyond the orange construction fencing. Large scaffolding and the cranes sit in the distance like sleeping monsters to the left and right of us. The ground is partially paved, but we are standing in the part that is not. Instead, we've followed my dad into the mud and my new Sperrys now are caked in this crap. "Oh man!"

"What?" Hannah asks.

**SOMERSET SECRETS**
*by T.W. Morse*

"My Sperrys. Mud is all over them."

"Ulysses, we just got visited by extraterrestrials and all you can think about is your muddy shoes?"

I shrug at this comment. "Ah—yeah—they're Sperrys."

"Over there!" Dad yells as we follow him around the construction fencing just beyond the back side of the buildings to a large grassy field. Dad quickly ducks behind a taller section of temporary plywood fencing. We kneel behind him.

"I think this is where they will come," Dad whispers.

"Who? The aliens?" I ask, now gulping while Hannah grabs my hand tightly.

Dad smiles. "No, but they'll have that unidentified flying object."

"Ah, Dad, that's a UFO." Just then, we feel the wind again and look up to see the same UFO we had just left at the dog park now coming over the half-completed roof of Regents Bay. "We've got to get out of here!" I nervously yell over the noise.

"Wait for it!" Dad yells back as Hannah holds me tight.

The UFO is still hovering slowly with all its colors flashing, but this time it doesn't hover for long and instead lowers until it lands in front of our hiding position. To my shock, it isn't an unidentified flying object at all. It is a black helicopter with a silver dome on the bottom welded to its landing ruts.

"What the hell?!" Hannah gasps. "That's no UFO."

Just then an older man in a blue suit steps out of the pilot's seat and a stout man exits the passenger side. He's holding what looks like some kind of ray gun. "Eric!" I hiss.

"I know. I suspected him when I saw he had mud on his boots, mud that had to have been from this construction site. When I saw him, I wondered why he didn't want to sell. He had just seen a UFO. The reason is because he's in on it. I

142

also researched the owner of Regents Bay, and by coincidence, he has a helicopter and a pilot's license," Dad whispers to us now that the noises have stopped.

"Why are they doing this? Why UFOs?" Hannah asks with her fierceness replacing her earlier fear.

## V.

"Freeze!" Dad says with Hannah and me huddled behind him. I'm trying my best to hold Hannah back.

"Who's there?" An old weathered voice echoes through the night, now silent with the motor of the helicopter off. Our phones were active again, and we shined our flashlights on our culprits.

"It's that teacher and those kids I told you about," Eric says to the older man in his bullfrog voice.

"So, you sell out your neighbors for money?" I yell.

"Make innocent people think aliens are invading their condos!" Hannah adds.

"You used that EMP gun to shut off cars and any electronic devices in the area while you hovered over the dog park, which leaves the flattened grass crop circle. It was a nice trick, using the stereo system onboard the helicopter to make those weird alien-esque sounds too. And you mounted strobe lights with a silver, metal disk attached to the bottom of the helicopter, finishing off your UFO-inspired blackmail scheme. You both have a lot to answer for," Dad finishes in his stern teacher voice.

"Yeah," the older man in the suit says. "What are you going to do to stop us?" he finishes, snickering to Eric with a villainous laugh.

# SOMERSET SECRETS
## by T.W. Morse

"You're right; we won't be able to," Dad says defeated but with a sly grin. "But they will," he says, now confidently pointing to several police officers led by Detective Brute who quickly apprehend both men. Bob, Sarah and Hope are right behind the police.

"Where were you, good buddy?" Dad asks a still shaken Bob.

"Ah—I ran back to my girl," he says, squeezing Sarah to his chest. "I had to make sure she was—ah—alright."

"I was able to call the police just like you texted me before they arrived," Hope chimes in. "And Logan, you were right. The EMP pulse wasn't strong enough to reach my phone inside. I was able to speak with Detective Brute, and the rest is history," Hope finishes, giving Dad a big hug and kiss.

"Wait a minute. You knew Eric was in on it?" Ulysses says. "And you knew he used an EMP gun to shut off the electronic devices in the area?"

"Yes. I knew Bob didn't see a real UFO," Dad starts, rolling his eyes. "After speaking with Eric, I knew he had a hand in some sort of deception. The mud on his boots matches the mud at the construction site too. I also knew that the only thing that could prevent Bob's Jeep and our phones from working was an electromagnetic pulse, or EMP, gun," Dad says as he points at the ray gun that had been in Eric's hand and has now been confiscated by Detective Brute.

"These—are the rascals ma—king all that racket. We've had a—lot of com—plaints and UFO sightings around these—parts the last few weeks but ne—va took—it seriously. Residents claim—ing U—FO sightings, ma—larkey," Brute exclaims using one of Dad's euphemisms in his signature slow Southern drawl while distastefully spitting onto the muddy ground.

"Fortunately, the EMP wasn't strong enough to make our power loss permanent. These guys have been trying to scare out the last residents for a while so they can bulldoze Island View properties and put up a sky rise with views and access to the beach beyond. They would have made millions," Dad says, smiling in satisfaction to a nodding and frustrated Detective Brute. Brute has never been happy with us solving crimes on our own. He thinks we are getting into trouble on purpose. And he's half right, but what can you do?

"Who's the older guy in the suit?" Hannah asks with a puzzled look.

"Back at Penny U., I was researching on my phone and found out that the owner of Regents Bay is a guy named Cornelius Figgury. A Canadian developer who expanded his business to include Somerset, Florida. I also found registration information for his helicopter and pilot's license, so I put everything together, knowing they would try again to make Sarah and the others want to sell. She and a handful of residents were the only things in Figgury's way. If they could push Sarah out, the others would cave too," Dad adds as we all walk back to the parking lot.

Detective Brute and the other officers wave goodbye in appreciation as they haul Cornelius and Eric away in a couple of sheriff's cruisers.

"Mmm—mmm, I knew it wasn't aliens, babe," Bob says before kissing Sarah.

"Sure, Bob—sure," Dad injects, slapping Bob on the back.

We all laugh at this statement and pile into the cars for some coffee and pie back at Penny University.

*SOMERSET SECRETS*
*by T.W. Morse*

# BOB AND I ARE IN A TEACHER WORKSHOP FROM HELL

## LOGAN

### I.

"Hey Hope!" I say louder than I intend to over my FaceTime conversation with her.

Hope and I have only been dating for a few months now, but hearing her voice always soothes my tensions. While I talk, squirm in my seat next to Bob in the Somerset Inn's banquet room.

Bob and I are both waiting for a teacher workshop on school safety to begin. Our presenter is none other than Somerset's finest—Detective Brute.

Brute and I have had a few prior run ins, and we don't care too much for each other. He thinks that I put my nose into a few too many criminal investigations. And I'm certainly not the biggest fan of his either, given his overall attitude and inept ability to actually investigate those criminal investigations that Ulysses and I solved. You're welcome. Also his drawn-out Southern accent is wicked irritating.

"So, you guys having a good time?" Hope asks, breaking my train of thought.

"Not really. Detective Brute was supposed to come on about ten minutes ago. I don't know why this hasn't started yet," I say, regretting even coming in the first place. I always hate attending workshops. They always give us little to no useful information and deliver it in a condescending tone, treating us like we're inept. They should be modeling good teaching practices. I'd never treat my students like they treat us, at least I hope I don't.

"What's the topic?" Hope asks, smiling at my student-like impatience.

"The district is sending personnel from different area schools to hear the detective speak on proper school safety procedures. According to Bob, Principal O'Leary decided to send me and Bob instead of going himself. Then he wants us to come back to Mangrove High tomorrow and teach the other faculty members what we have learned," I explain, dreading the idea of me and Bob speaking in front of the rest of the faculty, especially on this topic.

O'Leary is probably back at Mangrove High, laughing like a tyrannical super villain at the thought of us sitting through this training, knowing full well how miserable we are. This was probably his master plan all along. Argh!

"I'm sure you'll do great," Hope reassures me, sensing my displeased demeanor.

"Yeah, and the food is terrible too. Let me tell ya somethin'. Don't invite teachers to a breakfast workshop and not serve breakfast. I mean come—on—son. Am I right? Cubes of cheese ain't good enough!" Bob chimes in, chuckling to himself as he practically shouts into the phone and grabs it from my hand.

"Hey Bob," Hope reluctantly greets him over my no-longer-private FaceTime conversation.

"Hey Hope! I—hope … you're doing well?" Bob says, giggling as I roll my eyes.

"Ha—ha, Bob, that never gets old," Hope says with subtle sarcasm. "Can you give the phone back to Logan now? Thanks."

"Okay—okay. Sorry—sorry—I hope to see you soon—girl," Bob finishes in his Barry White voice, usually reserved for his girlfriend, Sarah. I snag the phone back from him and smack him on his leg while giving him one of my stern frowns, reserved for my students and Ulysses. Bob only gives me a shrug like he did no wrong. I get that shrug a lot.

"Bye Logan," Hope says, smiling as I wink back at her. She drops the phone on the floor, and for a split second, I can only see a red and yellow flash before Hope quickly recovers the phone. "You still there?" Hope asks before blowing me a kiss and hanging up. I return my attention to a hyperactive Bob.

"Man oh man, what the hell is this?" Bob mutters to himself after downing another cup of bad coffee.

"What's the matter, buddy?" I say, now noticing the effects of the bad hotel coffee on Bob. His orange tracksuit leg is shaking uncontrollably. "Do you think you had one too many of those?"

Bob smirks as he raises an eyebrow. "C'mon, son, you know Bobby can handle his caffeine. I'm just want'n this damn workshop to get goin'."

Bob is right; Detective Brute was supposed to have gone on about twenty minutes ago. "Maybe something's wrong," I suggest.

"Oh no you don't," Bob says, straightening up. With his orange tracksuit on, he looks like a fat pencil. "I know that look, mmm—mmm."

"Ah, what do you mean? What look?"

"That look that you get when you want to investigate, which usually means putting me into harm's way."

"Bob—Bobby ..."

"Don't you Bobby me. I know from experience. Logan, let's just sit back. We get paid no matter if the detective shows or not. Let's relax and sip some more coffee."

I take what Bob says to heart but look at the stage and the anxious administrators all around us and know something is not quite right. I am also getting a bad feeling, which is never good, especially for Bob.

"Okay, Bob, you stay here. I'm going backstage to check out what's taking so long."

"Logan—you can't leave me here with all these administrators!" Bob announces, his voice becoming shrill. "All these white people are already look'n at Bobby like I'm guilty of something."

"Bob, the only thing you're guilty of is being extremely underdressed at an educational workshop. I'm going backstage. It should be fine," I say with a knowing grin.

"Alright—alright, I'm coming too. You always get into more trouble when I'm not with you. Mmm—mmm, dude, you're going to be the death of me."

## II.

Bob and I sneak around the stage. I look back at the audience. It is weird to see so many people in such nice suits. I guess they are paying administrators more these days. I notice a few of them pointing at Bob and me before we duck behind the stage. Backstage was just a corridor, lined with red and yellow faded hotel carpet. The smell of Bob's coffee wafts around us as we slink down the corridor. A maid is in the hallway maneuvering two large carts covered with white tablecloths. She keys into a first-floor room before I can speak with her. For a second, I thought she looked familiar, but my thoughts refocus when Bob pulls my arm and points at a door that is labeled Guest Speaker and has the usual electronic key card lock.

## SOMERSET SECRETS
### by T.W. Morse

"What should we do?" Bob whispers, looking more nervous than I had seen him in a while.

"Knock—I guess." I knock at the door with my fist, but as my hand touches the door, it swings open. So I proceed to knock on the doorframe. "Hello—Detective Brute! It's Logan Adair and Bob Nelson!"

"Logan, this don't feel right. Let's go back to our seats—please!" But with Bob's pleas the urge to go through and investigate increases. So I push open the door and slowly slink into the room. Bob tails behind me.

The room looks like a typical hotel room. The same red and yellow carpet flows throughout. The room is filled with a giant king bed and is flanked by two end tables. A wall-mounted TV is on but displays only a blue screen. A single black bag is on the bed and the only thing we can hear is a bathroom fan vibrating through the door on our right.

"Detective Brute!"

"Dude's probably in the bathroom. Gett'n pre-show jitters," Bob says while making the sign-language gesture for diarrhea.

"First, how the hell do you know sign language? Second, we should check on him then."

I took sign language back in college. I actually took it with my late wife, Jill. I am drawn away from this fond memory when Bob says, "I got a cousin who is deaf, and I know some basic signs." He shrugs.

"You call knowing the sign for diarrhea a basic sign?"

Bob smirks at this. "You should meet my cousin. He's a crude dude. I know some other good ones too."

"Shh!" I hiss. I take a step toward the bathroom door.

"Ah—Logan, maybe we should leave the guy in peace."

"Bob," I hiss again. "We have to check on him."

## SOMERSET SECRETS
### by T.W. Morse

Just then, the hotel room door slams shut. I can't see over Bob, but I quickly move around him, looking to see who just came in, but nobody is there. I pull the handle to open the door, but the door is locked. I wiggle the handle again—nothing. "Bob, someone just locked us into this room somehow."

"Logan!" I hear a screech from the bathroom. I see Bob through the bathroom door and he's leaning on the floor. A pit forms in my stomach as my legs start to wobble with the sight that is in front of us. Bob is feeling for a pulse on the bloodied body of Detective Brute. The detective is laying on his stomach in the middle of the bathroom floor with a huge knife sticking out of his back. Bob looks up at me with a contorted face of terror. As he gulps, he confirms my worst fear. "He—he—he—he's dead!

### III.

"Oh my god!" Bob screams, trying the handle and pounding on the door. "Help! We are trapped in here with a dead body!" Bob tries to ram the door but yells back at me, "Mmm—mmm, it's made of metal; we aren't moving this door."

As Bob screams, I look around the room for clues. The black bag on the bed only has a notepad, pen, and a folder labeled School Safety, which must include the detective's presentation material. Material he will never present. Damn! The detective could be annoying and often sarcastic with me, but nobody deserves to die.

"I'm going to call 911." I pick up the receiver to the hotel room, but I get no dial tone. I look down in shock as I see no telephone wire going from the wall into the phone. "Damn. The phone's dead."

"Say what!" Bob's voice cracks as his face contorts to look like a prune. "Logan, we are living in a horror movie. This is like some kind of escape room. Oh wait, I'll call on my phone." Bob says this while patting his tracksuit pockets. "Logan—Logan!" Bob says, spitting my name out of his mouth like the words are on fire. "My—my phone is back at the workshop table."

"It's okay, I got mine." I take my phone out but am puzzled beyond belief. I look up at Bob's prune face and my face starts to resemble his. "My phone's dead!"

"Oh—my god—oh—my god!" Bob runs to the hotel window and tries to open it, but it is sealed shut. The only view is of a red brick wall.

"I bet Detective Brute has his on him. We can call from his cell," I say as I rush past Bob and into the bathroom, quickly feeling around the dead detective's pockets. "Damn! The killer must have taken his phone."

With this information, Bob goes back to the door and starts pounding it again with manic persistence. "We are trapped with a dead body and can't call out!"

"Quiet, Bob. Did the body still feel warm?"

"Ah—yeah. Why?"

"Well, this couldn't have happened that long ago." I examine the body on the white tiled bathroom floor. A pool of blood is spread all over Detective Brute's back and onto the tiled floor. The detective's face is contorted; his gaunt features along with his gray skin make him look like a skeleton. I try my best not to step in the blood, but it's not easy. "I can see two sets of prints in the blood. Your Air Jordans that very distinctive and rare—"

"What?! My Air Jordans," Bob screams, looking down at his shoe and the prints of blood he is now leaving all around the room. "Oh—my gosh, my Jordans! This means the police will think I did it! Logan, they will shoot me on sight for this. It's one of their own!" Bob squeals, pulling me by the collar.

"Bob, calm down! I see another set of prints. They look like dress shoes with a pointed toe. Expensive." I follow the steps from the body. They go around the bed and I notice, for the first time, a door to an adjoining room. I see a bloody fingerprint on the door, which has a standard key lock. "Bob!" I hiss in a whisper. "The killer went out through this adjoining room. See, here is a fingerprint."

"That's good. I thought I would get framed for this."

"I got an idea," I grin. I run back to Detective Brute's body and fish around in his pockets. "Bingo!" I take out a set of rubber crime scene gloves and head back to the adjoining door. I take out two paper clips from my pocket and bend them to create the pick-locking tools that I need.

"Ah—Logan, what you doin'?"

"I'm picking the lock," I confess. "I think our killer was lying in wait in this adjoining room until the detective went to the bathroom. Then he snuck in and stabbed him in the back before retreating into this room."

"Do you think the killer locked us in this room?"

"It's a good bet that he or she did." Just then, the adjoining room's dead bolt clicks open. I gingerly open the door, being careful not to touch the fingerprint on the doorknob. The room is dark, giving off an ominous feeling with the fear of a murderer lurking around the corner.

"Ow! What are you doing?" Bob stomps on my ankle as he creeps too close behind me. I feel for the light switch on a nearby lamp. The room is identical to the detective's room with a king bed and the same drab red and yellow carpeting.

**SOMERSET SECRETS**
*by T.W. Morse*

Bob scrambles for the door to the corridor. "Logan!" Bob yells as he struggles with the knob. "It's locked too!"

I try the knob and realize: "We are truly trapped."

"Say what? Can't you just pick the lock again?"

"Bob, there is no lock to pick on the hallway doors. Someone has locked the key card locks. They must be using some sort of computer accessing the front desk in the lobby to keep these doors locked." I scan the room for any clues. Nothing. The bathroom and the bed all look clean, like nobody had stayed there at all. "This person is good."

Just then, the phone rings. Bob picks up the receiver. "Hey, we are trapped in a bedroom with a dead police detective—send help!" Bob exclaims over the phone in a voice trembling with fear. His face becomes a prune again, contorting in every direction. He holds the receiver out far from his body like it is a harmful virus of some sort. "It's him!" Bob hisses through grinding teeth.

"Who?" I say, taking a step forward.

Bob looks at me with his wide brown eyes, looking like they may pop out of his sockets. "It's the killer—and he's asking for you."

## IV.

I take a step toward Bob and take the receiver of the phone from his cold hands, putting it up to my ear. An electronic voice hisses in my ear like a reptile seeking its prey. "I see you have found the detective. You will never escape. Ha-ha-ha." The electronic laugh continues while I yell in the receiver, demanding answers.

"Who is this?! Show yourself—you coward! What kind of game are you playing?" Then the phone dies. I press and release the switch hook, hoping for a dial tone, but the line is now dead. How did the killer manage to make the line go dead?

"Who—who could this ki-kill-killer be?" Bob stutters in shocked disbelief.

I shake my head in confusion. "It sounds like this murderer is playing a game with us. It's like they know I would find the detective's body and investigate these rooms. The killer was waiting for us."

"Oh man. Logan, what did you get us into? Who is doing this to us?"

"The detective does have a long list of enemies. Convicted criminals that have been released, or maybe a hot case he's currently working on. I don't know—yet. I need time to process everything. Sit down and stay quiet, so I can take a minute to think." I sit on the bed in the adjoining room and look around, while Bob sits in a chair by the equally locked window.

As I sit on the edge of the bed, I pull the events together in my mind. We have one dead detective, two locked rooms, and no telephones. Both windows are locked and face a brick wall, limiting our escape. We pound on the door and get no response. Why? Why lock us into the rooms?

I guess it gives the murderer time to escape. He or she wouldn't get far, though. Ulysses, Hope, and even Sarah would report us missing in just a few hours. They would see Bob's Jeep is still in the parking lot. The killer wouldn't know he drove the jeep, and the police would search the hotel. Hell, the detective would also need to check out. When he doesn't, the police will swarm into this hotel. So why lock us in? Why? Also, why be smart enough to get an adjoining room but then step in the blood and leave a finger print on the doorknob? Some of this looks sloppy, while some of it appears methodical. It's so inconsistent.

**SOMERSET SECRETS**
*by T.W. Morse*

"Why lock us in? Why would the killer be ready to lock us in?" I ask out loud to a nervous looking Bob.

"I don't know, but can we work out how we get out of here first?"

"Yeah, you're right. I should be thinking about how to get out of this room, rather than why the murderer locked us in the room." I suddenly look up to see the adjoining room door swing shut and lock. I run to the door and try to open it—nothing.

"The murderer came back and locked us in here! Logan, where are your paperclips? Open this again."

"Bob, I don't have them! They were on the other side of the door, resting in the lock."

"No-no-no!" Bob starts to scream at the door, pounding it hard. I join him. "We've seen Hannah knock down doors and she's half our size. If both of us do it together, we can force down this door," I say, kicking at the door with my leg. "Damn, that hurts. How does Hannah do it?"

Bob kicks at it too, his bloody Air Jordans leaving red scuff marks on the door. I recover my drive and start kicking at the door again, with both Bob and I now taking turns. But we're having no luck; we are only successful at leaving scuff marks.

"Let's try our shoulders," Bob suggests. This is more productive, causing the door to splinter around the doorknob. But as we break through, I start pulling everything together in my mind. I blurt out, "Escape room—you said what this really is—it is an escape room." I realize this just as the adjoining door thunders to the ground and us with it. Bob and I now lie in pain side by side on the floor with the adjacent room door beneath our sore bodies. We hear a loud, "GOTCHA!"

## V.

My head is throbbing in pain as I look up, a little dazed, to see a large group of people huddled in front of Bob and me lying hurt on the ground. I do a double take and have to blink a couple of times to make sure that what I am looking at is real. There before me is a laughing Detective Brute—alive! The detective's scarecrow frame and pointed elbows jerk out as he lets out a deep Southern laugh. Ulysses and Hannah are bent over, laughing along with Sarah, Hope, and both Hector and Catherine Reyes. Even Deputy Diaz and some of the teachers from Mangrove High like Sam James, Helen Thatcher, and Edgar Cortez are standing in the room. Everyone then starts singing happy birthday—to me.

I am at a loss for words as I stand up with Bob, who is now singing next to me with a wide Cheshire grin. Once the singing stops, I am still at a loss for words as Ulysses continues to say, "We got you good! I knew this would work. Happy birthday, Dad."

"Oh, I don't know, U, I think your father figured it out right when the door burst open," Bob adds.

Ulysses's face goes stone cold. "No! Really?"

I approach Detective Brute; a very convincing dagger is still protruding from his seersucker suit. "You were a very convincing actor, Detective Brute," I say with my own wry grin.

"When your—boy came to me and told me—his idea—about prank'n you on ya' birth—day—I couldn't—re—sist," the detective doled out in his Southern accent, smiling for the first time since I've known him.

"Dad, you really did figure it out?"

"Yeah, Mr. Adair, what gave it away? Was it Bob?" Hannah asks, giving Bob a snide leer.

"Wasn't me," Bob says, holding up his arms defensively. "I deserve a damn Oscar."

"The clues were there all along," I say, dusting the remaining rubble from the door off my shirt sleeve.

"Oh yeah, what clues?" Hope asks, coming over and hugging me, planting a kiss on my cheek, and whispering, "Happy birthday."

"For starters, I remember Hope dropping her phone while we were on FaceTime together. I caught a glimpse of the same red and yellow carpeting that's throughout this horrid hotel. I should have realized that she must be nearby. But I didn't give it a second thought until the other clues started to pop into place. I also noticed the workshop attendees were dressed too nicely to be administrators."

"Yeah, you and Bob were just about to get a nice two-hour workshop on federal banking strategies," Ulysses chuckles, unable to hold in his laughter.

"I thought Bob and I were getting more stares than usual."

"We switched out the signs for the workshop once you walked into the hotel and then switched them back for everyone walking into the workshop," Ulysses confesses, unable to hold in his grin.

"Also, I noticed Catherine Reyes dressed as a maid. I just caught a glimpse of the back of her head before ducking into a room, but then Bob distracted me before I could make sense of it. I can see she was in charge of catering," I say as I gesture to two carts full of Penny University treats.

"Happy birthday, Logan," Catherine says with a beaming smile.

"You had me going for a while. But when Bob said we were in 'some kind of horror movie escape room,' I remembered that it was Bob who told me about the workshop today, and I knew my birthday was in two weeks and Ulysses's affinity for escape rooms. I put everything together along with the fact that the killer couldn't know that two amateurs would be checking out the whereabouts of Detective Brute, and if that was far-fetched, then maybe the whole murder was too," I say, almost out of breath as we started to eat the cake Hector and Catherine were both passing out.

"A friend from high school owns this hotel. He let us have a few of the rooms," says Deputy Diaz, Mangrove High School's resource officer, with a grin. "These two rooms are going to be renovated into one room starting tomorrow, so he was okay with the broken door."

I nod, relieved at the realization that Ulysses didn't just give us a huge birthday bill.

"Mr. James's theater department did Detective Brute's makeup—pretty convincing, wasn't it?" Hannah confesses. I smile and nod while giving her and Ulysses big hugs.

"I had you, Dad. I even unplugged your phone charger last night to make sure your battery was low today," Ulysses says, patting me on the back.

"Why do you think I kept you and Bob on FaceTime for so long?" Hope adds, smiling. "Had to help drain the rest of that battery."

"Yeah, we had him," Bob confirms.

"You were a pretty convincing actor, Bobby Nelson," I say, giving a friendly punch to Bob's shoulder.

"Ouch! You know that's right," Bob says, smirking and rubbing his arm.

**SOMERSET SECRETS**
*by T.W. Morse*

"Isn't your birthday in a few months?" I say to Bob while nudging him and giving a knowing smile to Ulysses.

Bob's mouth gapes open. "Ah—say what now?"

*SOMERSET SECRETS*
*by T.W. Morse*

# OUR CHEATING CLASS PRESIDENT?!

## ULYSSES
## I.

"Hannah—please! I'll do anything," I enthusiastically beg as Hannah and I hang out in the courtyard of Mangrove High School.

I know I shouldn't beg my girlfriend and best friend in the whole world to help me with my science fair project, but waiting for the last minute to complete it didn't help my situation. What can I say? I've been busy, and my freshman classes are hard. I'm also juggling playing guitar with Dad at Penny University Café between bussing tables there. All that is in addition to finding time to snap pictures for the school newspaper while getting wrapped up in a mystery or two. Busy doesn't cut it!

I reflect on this as I lay my head on Hannah's lap and gaze up at the sky. It is so clear, a nice relief from the rain we are always getting as we are now in the dreaded rainy season. I turn my attention to the busy breezeway as hundreds of students march like busy bees traversing through their hive to their next class. My freshman year is winding down, and I can finally take a breath from my own busy bee life, except for this damn science fair project for Biology.

"Please, Hannah," I add with a little toddler voice for an added pathetic touch.

"Ulysses Adair, I shouldn't have to do your science fair project because you waited until the last minute."

# SOMERSET SECRETS
## by T.W. Morse

"I know, but Ms. Thatcher will give me an F and my dad will be so pissed at me." I can tell she is wearing down. She hates disappointing my dad more than I do.

"Okay, but no more. I'm not doing this again. I'm really not." I give her my puppy dog face. The one that Ortiz gives when he wants a treat. "I'm really not." But a smile forms on her beautiful face and we kiss.

We were rudely interrupted by Amanda Cho, Hannah's so-called friend. I can't stand her; she's such a drama queen. Bob would call her a hoochie mamma.

"OMG, girl! Did you hear the tea on Robert Madison? Everybody is spilling it!" Amanda practically yells now as passersby look on in awe.

Everyone knows Robert Madison. He is the first black senior class president at Mangrove High. I ran with him on the cross-country team. He was the best on the team. With me being a freshman and Robert a senior, he embodied what I wanted to be in three more years. I practically worship him. You don't get more popular and successful than Robert Madison. He had just signed a full-ride academic scholarship.

Hannah clears her throat, changing her inflection to sound like Amanda, giving herself a mean girl/valley girl sound that was hard to listen to. "Oh my god, spill the tea, girl," she says. I gag and roll my eyes with this portrayal.

"Robert was caught cheating on his state exam in that silly government and economics class. He was told by Principal O'Leary that he could lose his academic scholarship and he won't be able to march at graduation."

"Wait, what!" I say in horror. "Why would Robert need to cheat? He's one of the smartest in the senior class." I ask a dumbfounded-looking Amanda.

## SOMERSET SECRETS
### by T.W. Morse

She throws up her shoulders. "I don't know." Just then the bell rings. "Girl—I gots to go or I'll be late for home econ—toodles." She gives Hannah a fake cheek to check air kiss before scurrying off, walking like a penguin in an overly tight mini skirt.

Hannah and I walk to *The Manatee Times* classroom. The room is right off of the courtyard, and she is walking with a bit of enthusiasm.

"Hannah—Hannah," I plead, trying to keep up with her pace. "I know that look."

"Ulysses!" she says, spinning on her heels. "This is a major story that we're going to take head on. We can clear his name."

"Who, Robert? I guess. But what if he actually did cheat?"

She ponders this by tilting her head. "We're reporters; we report the news. If the news shows guilt, then we report it; if it proves his innocence, then we report that. Come on—this will be fun."

"What about my science fair?" I plead, straggling behind her.

### II.

Hannah grabs her notebook and I get my camera, and we are off to investigate whether our beloved senior class president may, in fact, be a cheater. Mr. Scott, our newspaper editor and teacher, says we can investigate only if we don't get in the way. He promises us the front page if we uncover something good. Freshmen never get first page stories, so we are pretty stoked. I am still having trouble believing all of this, but I know Hannah is

***SOMERSET SECRETS***
*by T.W. Morse*

right, as usual, and we need to find out the truth behind Robert's alleged cheating.

"I say we start at the source. We find Robert. See what happened."

Hannah nods, "Good thinking; he may also have some insight in all of this."

Mr. Scott looks up Robert's schedule with a little nudging and convincing from Hannah.

"He's currently in weightlifting," Mr. Scott states.

Yeah, that's an actual class. I can't wait to take fun electives like that when I'm a senior. The weight room is off the gym. Did I mention who his supervising teacher is?

"Mmm—mmm—let me tell you somethin'. You two can't come in here waving that press badge around. The last story you guys published got me in trouble with O'Leary," Bob says in a high pitch squeal, blocking the weight room door. How he was the weight training teacher baffles the mind as his belly sticks out pretty far over his yellow tracksuit.

"Oh—Mr. Nelson," Hannah says, referring to him by his last name in an overly endearing voice. "That story about teachers taking double unpaid lunches from the cafeteria wasn't about you. It was just hard to run the story without including our dashing physical education teacher."

"Well—you know that's right!" Bob says, smiling to himself. "Alright, I'll let you kids in, but be quick about it. You know if O'Leary knew you guys were snooping around, he'd take you off the newspaper."

"Let us worry about Principal O'Leary," I reassure him, ducking under Bob's arm, which is blocking the door. Hannah follows. We are hit right away with a stink bomb of teenage sweat and grime coming off all the weight benches and machines. We scan the room and see a variety of male and female students in all shapes and sizes, all trying to get

## SOMERSET SECRETS
### by T.W. Morse

their P.E. electives completed. But there is a noticeable difference between those students just here for the credit and those taking this seriously. We spot Robert at the same time. He is punishing his body on the treadmill. His gym clothes are drenched in sweat, and he is running at a very high speed at a steep incline. I am envious. I run cross country, but I know I wouldn't last long on the treadmill going that fast.

"He must be running out his frustration," Hannah says, walking up parallel to the treadmill.

"Robert," Hannah says without startling him. That's all we need, Robert crashing off of the treadmill and getting a concussion from the school newspaper reporters. "Can we have a word?" she says, waving, with a raised voice over the thumping of the treadmill.

Robert pauses his treadmill as I give him a fist bump and hand him a towel. "Hey Rob, heard what happened. You got a raw deal, man."

"Thanks, Ulysses."

"Is there a place we can talk? We're here to help," I say with a sideways glance from Hannah. I know what she is thinking—he could be guilty—but I know this guy wouldn't cheat, especially when a scholarship is at stake.

"Yeah, we can go into the aerobics room," Robert says, slinging the towel over his shoulder, hiding his anger and leading us across the room to a heavy metal door.

Yup, Mangrove has an aerobics room too. Got to love the rich. We exit the smell and banging in the weight room and enter a soundproof room surrounded by body-length mirrors and highly glossed wooden floors.

"So, what do you want to know?"

Hannah quickly opens a pad of paper and uncaps a pen.

## SOMERSET SECRETS
### by T.W. Morse

"We want to help clear your name," she says, poised to write.

"Why don't you start from the beginning? Take us through the events leading up to the incident and everything during and after, if it's relevant." This works in detective stories—why not now? "Every little detail could help, so don't leave out anything."

Robert sits on the wood floor, lowering himself down by hanging onto a balance bar attached to the walls. We follow his lead, sitting on the floor in a tight circle as we listen to his retelling of the events.

"Mr. Reardon, my government and economics teacher, has always had it out for me. I don't know why, but he always gets this disgusted look on his face when he talks to me." I can relate, remembering similar looks that Principal O'Leary gives me.

"We were taking the big end of course exam."

"The EOC," Hannah says, writing in her pad rapidly.

"Ah—yeah. The EOC. I need to pass it to graduate."

"How well do you usually do in Mr. Reardon's class? A—B?" I ask.

"I do alright. Probably low A. I never usually get lower than an A, or at least I didn't used to. I worked really hard to qualify for my academic scholarship, and now I might lose it." With a dreadful expression, Robert looks down at his shoes. Right then, I know my instincts are right and he's innocent. Now it's just up to me and Hannah to prove it.

"Go on," Hannah politely nudges.

"Well, on the day of my EOC, I felt confident and good. I knew a lot of the answers and thought I had it. But, at the end of the test, Mr. Reardon accused me of using my phone and relayed this to Principal O'Leary. Since Mr. Reardon says he witnessed me looking up answers on my phone, my test became invalidated. Once O'Leary reports this to my school, I'll lose my scholarship and maybe even my admission all together. I am supposed to attend Southwest Florida University and run for their cross-country team. Now I don't know what I'll do. At least it'll be my teammate who gets the scholarship," he finishes, wiping away a tear.

"Oh yeah, who's that?" I ask.

"Jesse Keaton."

"Good guy. Isn't he dating Monique?" Hannah nudges me to get back on track.

"Were there any other witnesses or did Principal O'Leary go by Mr. Reardon's account?" Hannah asks as she furiously scribbles words into her notebook.

"Well, I was sick on the actual test day, so I was doing the EOC on a make-up day. There were three other students in the room, but we were all scattered in a big classroom. They may not have seen anything."

"Let us be the judge of that," I add.

"Well, let's see. There was Kylie Brown, Luke Chaffee, and also Jesse's girlfriend, Monique Chapman. There was only the four of us and Mr. Reardon. Luke and Kylie both finished before me and were excused, so they may not be the best witnesses. I was nearing the end of the test and was about to submit the exam when Mr. Reardon came up and started yelling at me. Monique can tell you that too.

"He said, 'How dare you use your phone while taking a state exam! Give it to me.' My phone wasn't even out. I swear I put it in my backpack on the floor before the exam, but suddenly Mr. Reardon had it in his hands and it was unlocked to the government practice questions I had reviewed before the test," Robert finishes his story while shaking his head in disgust.

"Where was Monique sitting?" I ask.

"Um—toward the front of the class."

"Could she see that your phone was not out?" Hannah says, while stopping to write for a moment.

"I don't think she could."

"Great! That means it's his word against yours," Hannah adds.

"I swear, guys, I didn't have my phone out. To make matters worse, Principal O'Leary claims my phone history has the questions I looked up in the search history. Why would I give up my academic scholarship?"

I share a look of despair with Hannah. "I don't know, man. Why would Mr. Reardon make this up? What motive would he have?"

"He hates me for starters."

Hannah closes her notepad and stands up like a rocket. "Robert, can you think of anything else?"

"Nah—I don't think so. If I do, I'll let you guys know. My parents died a few years back, and I've been with my foster family, the Coopers, for three years. They don't know what to believe. I can tell they are hesitant to fight this alongside me with all the evidence against me."

I nod, taken aback. I had a parent that died too. I never knew Robert lost both of his parents. I, at least, have Dad— he may have only us fighting for him. We have to solve this for him and restore his good name.

### III

We wait until school is over to continue our interviews. Luke Chaffee plays baseball, and Kylie Brown plays softball. I guess the reason they were taking Mr. Reardon's make-up EOC was because the baseball and softball teams were at a big tournament in

## SOMERSET SECRETS
### by T.W. Morse

Orlando during the original test. Our Mangrove High teams are really good. It's not unheard of for players to miss school for regional and state tournaments. We start with Luke Chaffee, a baseball player through and through. He is packing up his bat bag, slinging it over his muscular shoulder when we meet him at the fields. The red clay of the baseball fields covers his uniformed, stocky frame. Luke looks at us with vacant eyes, which glaze over as he checks out Hannah.

"Luke Chaffee?" I ask, forcing his vacant eyes off my girlfriend.

"Who's asking?" he replies, spitting brown gunk from a huge wad of bubble gum and tobacco lodged in his cheek. His stuffed cheek reminds me of the hamster I had when I was younger, storing food for the long haul, but this is super gross.

"Hannah Reyes and Ulysses Adair. We're with *The Manatee Times*, doing a story on Robert Madison, your senior class president accused of cheating."

"Oh, yeah." Another shot of brown gunk comes flying from his mouth. "Old-Bert. That's what the boys call him—he's always acting like an old—boomer. Telling us off for messing with little freshmen like you, Adair." I tighten my fist, but Hannah whips her hair back and steps between Luke and me.

"We are here to try and clear his name. It probably wouldn't be good news for Mangrove High to have this tarnish his reputation."

Luke shrugs and spits again, very close to my new Sperry shoes too. I clench the other fist.

"Did you see anything out of the ordinary?" Hannah now gives Luke a distracting smile while she opens her notebook. "Tell us what happened that day at the EOC."

"Well, Mr. Reardon had us log onto the test website. I remember Kylie was there too. We couldn't take it the day of the exam because of our big tourney up state, so we were taking our make-up. I hit for the cycle during our win," he now says, leering and winking at Hannah.

Hannah shrugs and looks confused. I see this and quickly explain through a whisper, "Hitting for the cycle is a baseball term. It's when a batter hits a single, double, triple, and a home run in one game." She nods, still looking a little confused.

"What else can you tell us—about the day of the EOC?" Hannah continues, reeling him back in.

"Some other girl was there besides us, but I don't remember her name."

"Monique Chapman?"

"Yeah, sure—I guess. I thought the test was a joke, so did Kylie, so we finished it fast and left together."

"Before you ditched it—did you see anything out of the ordinary?" Hannah asks, looking perturbed at the admission that he didn't take the test seriously.

"Nope."

We were just about to head over to the softball field when Luke thought for a moment. "Wait!"

His vacant eyes strain to focus—I think it's hard for him. The wad in his cheek grows after he takes a sneaky look over his shoulder and quickly grabs more chew from his back pocket.

"Reardon."

"What about him?" Hannah asks, poised to write on her pad.

"Before the test, he had us log onto the website we used to study for the EOC on our phones. He wanted us to practice on them before the exam."

Hannah abruptly stops writing. Looking frustrated with Luke, she cries, "That's it!?"

Luke shrugs and heads away.

"So gross!" Hannah says, stomping off as I trail behind. "That lug didn't give us anything new."

"Well, we have a reason government-related information was on Robert's phone," I say, now out of breath, trying to keep up on our way to the softball field.

Kylie Brown has just gotten in her little blue Porsche. Somerset and their rich cars.

Hannah says she knows her from karate. Hannah, being a second degree black belt, helps instruct the younger kids. Kylie's little brother belongs to her dojo and he's trying to earn his yellow belt. Kylie often comes to the dojo, giving her brother rides to and from, Hannah informs me as we jog toward the Porsche. Hannah and I wave Kylie down just as she starts to back out of the softball stadium parking lot.

"Hey Hannah. What's up?" A bubbly blonde with a tight ponytail and flushed red cheeks sits sweaty and dirty in the tiny front seat of a car worth twice my dad's salary.

"We were hoping you could tell us about Robert Madison's accusation of cheating."

"Why is that your business?"

"We are investigating for *The Manatee—Times*," I say, catching my breath.

"What, so you can write about poor Old Bert?" Boy, I didn't know the seniors called Robert Old Bert—worst nickname ever.

"We heard from Luke that you and he finished early; do you remember anything that could exonerate Robert?" Hannah asks, putting a hand on Kylie's door. Kylie, knowing how dangerous Hannah is, is taken aback. My girlfriend may look sweet and innocent, but she has taken down people twice her size. If Kylie attends the dojo practices, she will definitely know this.

"Nothing—I mean, I saw nothing," Kylie says with a nervous tinge in her throat.

"So Mr. Reardon said that you guys could look up test questions prior to the EOC on your phones?" I ask, taking advantage of this fear.

"Yes. Yes, he did. He said we could all take our phones out and review for a few minutes."

"What else?" Hannah says with a leer.

"Nothing—ah, I mean, he said we could review, and while we did this, he was circling behind us, observing us. He stood behind each of us for a few minutes. I was sitting in the aisle next to Old Bert and Luke was behind me. Monique was in the front near Mr. Reardon's desk."

"That's it?" Hannah says, taking her arm off the car.

"Yes, I swear. Look, I didn't see Old Bert cheat. I left early though. Monique may have some more answers for you. Can I go?"

Permission is granted through a sly nod from Hannah, and Kylie seizes the moment as we watch the Porsche speed away.

"I don't think we're any closer to solving this," I say, feeling the dread of failing Robert.

"We need to get to Monique. She may have heard or seen something. She was the only other one present when Mr. Reardon accused Robert. Where do you think we can find her?"

"I'm friends with her on Snapchat and will send her a snap," I say, grabbing for my phone in my pocket.

"How are you friends with her?"

"She's on the cross-country team too, with Robert and me. Are you jealous?"

"Ah—no," Hannah says as we make our way back to her dad's blue truck parked in student parking.

"Good idea. I'm sure she'll want to help out since Robert is a cross-country teammate."

## IV.

We made our way over to the other side of Somerset. It was a run-down area—well, for Somerset. Probably it would be prime real estate in another city. Monique Chapman's condo reminded me of the place Dad and I live, Florida Tuscan, surrounded by warehouses and strip malls.

"I know Monique pretty well; she's a sweetheart. She and I did some fundraising for the Mangrove cross-country team at the beginning of the year."

"Which number is her place?" Hannah says, readying her notebook for the interview.

"Her snap said number 33, ground floor corner unit. Yup, this is the right place." I knock on the hard metal screen door that time forgot. A tall, pretty black girl with long dreads comes to the door.

"Monique, how's it going?"

With an overly suspicious glare, she hangs onto the front door and doesn't invite us in. "Hey Ulysses, whatcha want?"

Hannah starts off like always by rapidly rattling off our purpose and asking what Monique may know. "Monique, my name is Hannah Reyes. Ulysses and I are with *The Manatee Times* at Mangrove High. We're investigating the cheating scandal of your class president, Robert Madison. We understand you were present at the EOC, and we're wondering if you could shed some light on what happened between Robert and Mr. Reardon."

Crash! The door that Monique had been hanging onto slams in both of our faces.

We both stare at each other. "Sweetheart, huh? I would love to know how you describe me," Hannah says.

"This isn't like her. Maybe she knows something," I confess. We continue to knock, louder and louder. Nothing.

"Monique!" I yell through the window of what looks like a living room. I think I see some movement inside. "Monique! We are here to prove Robert was innocent! Help us! I'm sure you don't want your senior year tarnished by having your class president's reputation smeared and his scholarship taken away!"

I shrug at Hannah as I can tell her patience is running thin. Her karate focus is starting to take over, and if Monique doesn't let us in soon, Hannah will probably burst down that door with a roundhouse kick or something.

We wait in silence for a while. "I know you, Monique! The Monique I know would help us find the truth!" Still nothing.

"Come on, Ulysses, let's go. She's not going to help us," Hannah says, releasing her anger by kicking the side of the house. Just then, the door that had just been slammed in our faces opens a crack.

"Please, Monique, just a few minutes of your time," I plead one last time. She slowly nods, looking scared.

"Okay. Come in." She directs us to come into the condo, rapidly looking to the right and left for anyone watching the place. She points to a comfortable couch in a living room full of pictures and pillows. Monique must have seen me looking around at all the pictures. "I live with my aunt. She loves taking pictures," she speaks out of the side of her mouth while wrapping her arms around her body. Her eyes won't meet ours, like she is ashamed of something.

"Can you tell us what happened on the day of the EOC?"

She continues to look at her shoes before starting to speak. "Maybe you should record me."

Hannah catches my eye as we both are taken aback with this request, wondering now what we have stumbled upon. Hannah takes out her iPhone and presses record.

"This is Hannah Reyes and Ulysses Adair with Monique Chapman, at her house on May 1st. Okay, your turn, Monique. What can you tell us about the government EOC make-up exam in Mr. Reardon's classroom?"

Monique starts to rub her fingers and rock back and forth. "It was me, Robert, Luke, and Kylie. We all had missed the exam for one reason or another. I was sitting up front with my back to Robert, Luke, and Kylie. Luke and Kylie sat behind Robert. Mr. Reardon asked if we wanted to practice before we started. He directed us to the app where you can take practice questions and then circled behind us, watching us over our shoulders. I presumed at the time it was to make sure we were all on the site and on task."

"That is what Luke and Kylie both said too," Hannah adds.

"When the test started, Mr. Reardon made the announcement to put all phones away and asked me to hand out paper directions for completing the exam. I saw Robert put his phone in his backpack. I'm sure of it."

"Is that what you said to O'Leary when he questioned you?"

Monique looks at us, scared and afraid to answer.

"Then how did it get out of his bag?" I continue. "And why did Mr. Reardon say he saw him searching on it? Did you see anything like that? Luke and Kylie left early; what happened after they left?"

Monique's face takes on a distressed expression and she's about to speak when we hear a CRASH! as a rock breaks through the window directly behind the couch where we were sitting. We all quickly dive to the floor.

The rock misses Hannah's head by a matter of inches. Monique starts to scream. We hear a car squeal away outside. Hannah gets to her feet faster than me, but we both race out of the condo in pursuit. It is now twilight and the sun had faded quickly. We can't quite make out the license plate or even the make of the car.

"I think it was an older car," Hannah says.

"That's not much to go on," I add.

We both head back to the corner condo. Monique was shaking in the doorway, crying. "I can't help you. I'll get hurt. Enough people have gotten hurt."

"Wait, Monique, what do you know? Who threatened to hurt you?" I say as the door once again slams in our face.

"Do you think Mr. Reardon framed Robert?" Hannah asks.

"I don't know." I think on this on our way back to the truck. "It is his word against Robert's, unless Robert did in fact cheat." I shake my head at this. "No, I think Reardon has a hand in this. But what's his motive? Why would he say Robert was cheating if he has no motive to do so? What would he gain?"

Hannah shakes her head in disgust. "Well, we have no evidence. It's his word against Robert's if Monique doesn't step up."

"We'll figure this out; we've got to—for Robert's sake."

"What now? Our only good witness is scared off," Hannah says.

"The other two didn't see anything, and as my grandma says, they're numah than a pound of thumbs," I add, with frustration filling my face, as we hop back into the old truck.

"Let's bring it to Dad; he may be able to help us." We drive back to my place to see Dad, who can hopefully help us piece this all together.

## V.

Dad and Hope both listen intently as Hannah and I take turns walking them through our interviews with Robert, Luke, and Kylie, and then we retell our incident with Monique and the rock through her window. At this part in the story, Dad cringes and stirs in his seat and Hope cries out, "You could have been killed!"

"So what do you think?" I say to Dad as he strokes his newly grown beard. Hope puts her head on my dad's shoulder, flattening her Afro.

"Poor kid. Why would he throw everything away?" she says.

"That is, if he's guilty," Dad says. "I know Neil Reardon pretty well. I can't think of anything that would motivate him to lie. It sounds like Robert did cheat."

"What! Nah. I know Robert. How can you say that when we have presented all of this evidence?"

"Yeah, Mr. Adair, what about the rock through Monique's window?"

"Coincidence."

"Really, a coincidence?!" What is Dad thinking? He's usually all over a case like this and he always tells me to never believe in coincidences. "Is it because the person we think orchestrated this is a fellow teacher?"

"Ulysses!" Hope says with disappointment in her voice.

Dad frowns and shakes his head. "Maybe Ulysses is right."

## SOMERSET SECRETS
### by T.W. Morse

"What? You think so?" Hope says with a stir.

"Run over the case again. I don't like coincidences," Dad says, now getting out his whiteboard and drawing all the desks and their whereabouts along with the locations of Robert, Luke, Kylie and Monique.

"That's what I'm talkin' about!"

Just then, Bob bursts through the door, without knocking.

"What's happenin' my peeps? Bobby Nelson is in the house! Whatcha all doin'?" Bob says, plopping down on the couch between Hannah and me, pushing us to the ends like a whale parting the sea.

We fill Bob in on all the goings on as he nods his lack of a neck, looking like a black pumpkin going back and forth. He looks like he is intently listening, only adding his usual grunts of "Mmm—mmm" or saying, "Let me tell ya somethin'," or "that ain't right," when he was upset at hearing of the rock going through Monique's window.

Dad continues to look at the whiteboard, shaking his head. "What's the motive?"

"So he loses his academic scholarship? Just like that?" Hope says, curling up on a chair, looking sad.

Bob sits back and closes his eyes. "Yeah—poor kid. Let me tell ya somethin', Jesse Keaton is a good kid and deserves it too."

"Wait, what did you say?" Dad says, turning on his heels.

"Jesse Keaton gets the academic scholarship now. Since Robert was caught cheating, it goes to the next best cross-country senior at Mangrove High with equally good grades. Some rich Somerset dude with millions to spare ran cross country at Mangrove High years ago and left a substantial academic scholarship to cross country runners that show high marks."

"I thought I mentioned that Jesse Keaton gets the scholarship?" Seeing my dad's expression and his blank look, I know he is in deep thought. "But he wasn't in the room during the EOC, so how does that matter?"

Dad spurs to life and writes on the whiteboard, circling the name Jesse Keaton. "Because I know how and why it happened."

## VI.

The next day, Dad, Hannah, and I take a page from an Agatha Christie novel and assemble all the people relevant to the case in Dad's classroom near the front office.

Luke and Kylie are present, speaking with each other and looking a little confused and impatient, as always. Monique sits near Dad with her arms crossed, once again looking scared. Hannah and I both sit in front of her on top of a few desks with Robert by our side. Dad waves at the open door to Bob, who was showing Mr. Reardon and Principal O'Leary into the classroom.

"Should I go and get the others?" Bob says in a half whisper. Dad gestures in the affirmative.

Mr. Reardon is looking a little cocky. He's wearing a golfer's outfit, and he has a golfer's swagger about him that exudes cockiness. He has slicked back hair and overly orange tanned skin, probably from playing too much golf, which gives him a slimy appearance. Monique jumps a little and hides behind Dad, while Robert clenches his fist. Hannah puts a hand on his shoulder to calm him down.

"Why are we here, A—dair?" Principal O'Leary screeches in his unusually high-pitched voice.

**SOMERSET SECRETS**
*by T.W. Morse*

"We will get to that soon enough—sir," Dad says with a slight irritation he always displays for Principal O'Leary. "Ulysses—Hannah, you guys want to take it? It's your case."

I look at Hannah, and she nods for me to begin. She looks a little nervous, especially around O'Leary, who always has it out for Hannah—and me too.

"We started this investigation for *The Manatee Times* in hopes of clearing Robert from the accusations of cheating."

Mr. Reardon, who had just sat down, shot up. "He did cheat; I saw it. This is ridiculous. I'm leaving."

"Principal O'Leary, we have evidence that proves Robert is innocent," Dad says. "Please allow us to present the evidence and you can decide Robert's guilt after we're done."

Principal O'Leary looks back and forth from me to Dad and back to me. "Sit down, Reardon. The A—dairs are annoying and stick their noses into other people's business, but they have had—some success in the past. We're going to hear them out."

"But sir!" Mr. Reardon protests.

"Sit down!" Principal O'Leary screeches.

O'Leary looks at me with his tunneling eyes. "Ulysses A—dair, this better be good."

I brought out the whiteboard Dad had started the night before, showing the diagram of Mr. Reardon's classroom. "During the makeup EOC, we saw four people complete the exam. Luke and Kylie saw nothing suspicious and finished early. They did both say Mr. Reardon directed the four students to take out their cell phones to review the information on the government EOC app before the test. Correct?"

"Ah—yeah—so?" Luke says with sarcasm.

"I don't see how that can mean anything," Kylie says, glancing at Hannah with fear.

"Oh, we'll get to that," Hannah says, taking over. "We then interview Monique. She was the only person, other than Robert and Mr. Reardon, present at the time that Mr. Reardon accused Robert of cheating. We went to her house. She was visibly shaken and was about to share some information important to the case when a rock was thrown through her window, causing her to be so frightened that she kicked us out of her house." Everyone looks at Monique as she looks away fearfully. "What made Monique so afraid? Who sent the rock into her window?"

"All good questions," I say, tagging in. "First, let's review what Monique said."

I played the recording of our interview with Monique from the day before. "It was me, Robert, Luke, and Kylie. We all had missed the exam for one reason or another. I was sitting up front with my back to Robert, Luke, and Kylie. Luke and Kylie sat behind Robert. Mr. Reardon asked if we wanted to practice before we started. He directed us to the app where you can take practice questions and then circled behind us, watching us over our shoulders. I presumed at the time that it was to make sure we were all on the site and on task."

"So? That's what happened," Kylie says with a stern glance from Hannah.

"Yes, but she added something you and Luke didn't. Monique said Mr. Reardon watched you by pacing the room and standing behind you while you all reviewed the questions." I walk over to Robert, who handed me his phone. "Robert has an old phone. It only requires a four-digit password. I presume Mr. Reardon saw Robert enter his four-digit password when practicing before the test. Then, after Luke and Kylie left, he circled the classroom again, lifting

## SOMERSET SECRETS
### by T.W. Morse

Robert's phone from his bag without him noticing and punching in his four-digit code. Then he circled back around the classroom to place the phone on Robert's desk before accusing Robert of having his phone out all along."

"That's a bald-faced lie! I don't have to listen to this!" Mr. Reardon yells.

"Yes, you do. Sit down, Neil," Dad says with quick authority. Mr. Reardon sits with frustration.

"What proof do you have? This doesn't sound very definitive," Principal O'Leary sneers.

"We'll get to that," Dad says before waving for me to continue.

"I think it went down like that. I think, after Mr. Reardon took Robert down to the office, he came back for Monique. See, Monique is dating Jesse Keaton."

"Why does that matter?" Principal O'Leary sneers again.

"Jesse Keaton receives the academic cross-country scholarship now, by default. Mr. Reardon knew this and knew Monique well. Reardon threatened her. He tells her to back up his story or else. He probably said it's a win-win for everyone. Her boyfriend, Jesse, can now go to college for free and—" I am about to finish when O'Leary cuts me off.

"That's a great story, but what is Mr. Reardon's motive for this? Why would he risk his job and reputation to frame a kid for cheating so another kid can get the scholarship?" O'Leary says, shaking his head with confusion.

Bob appears at the door. Behind him is Jesse Keaton and a stout little woman. Mr. Reardon starts to squirm in his seat.

"Because, Principal O'Leary, Mr. Reardon is engaged to Jesse Keaton's mother, Lori Keaton." Gasps pop off around the room. I nod to Dad to bring it home.

"I remember that about a year ago Neil mentioned how his fiancée, a waitress, was struggling to work two jobs. He said they couldn't afford a wedding or even a new house because his fiancée's son was going to run at an expensive university. She had already taken out a second mortgage on her own run-down home because she had another daughter who was also in college. I only found out at the Christmas party several months ago that his fiancée was, in fact, the mother of one of my former students, Jesse Keaton. When Bob mentioned to me that the next in line for the scholarship was Jesse Keaton, well, I put two and two together. Low paying teacher, desperate mother of two, paying for expensive college bills. Life would be so much easier if she could have her youngest get that scholarship."

Principal O'Leary stands up and separates himself from sitting next to Mr. Reardon.

"Neil, tell me it's not true," Lori Keaton pleads.

"I—I didn't plan this. I was in the back of the classroom observing everyone, and it just popped in my head as I saw Robert punch in his four-digit code."

"You also staked out Monique's condo, just in case she talked," Hannah accuses him, pointing her finger in disgust.

"Yeah! That rock almost hit Hannah's head!" I say as I hold onto Hannah's arm to prevent her from doing anything too drastic.

Principal O'Leary escorts Reardon and the others involved back to his office. Soon after, everyone else leaves Dad's classroom. Hannah starts to busily type up the article for *The Manatee Times*. Dad places an arm around my shoulder. "I'm proud of you guys, finding the truth and helping out Robert like that."

I fist bump Dad. "Let's go and celebrate at Penny University. I told Robert we'd be by. He wanted to buy a round of coffee smoothies as a thank you for proving his innocence."

Hannah lifts her head up after completing her article. "What will happen to Mr. Reardon?"

"Well, he probably will never teach again," Dad says somberly.

"I feel bad for the Keatons too. Jesse never asked for this. Now he lost a scholarship and is graduating with his name attached to this scandal," Hannah adds.

"College is expensive. The drive to get a higher education without breaking the bank can often drive people to do bad things," Dad adds.

*SOMERSET SECRETS*
*by T.W. Morse*

# HORRIFIC ADVENTURES IN BABYSITTING

## ULYSSES
### I.

My neighbors, Mr. and Mrs. Hernandez, asked Hannah and me to babysit their baby, Sabrina, today.

As I wait for Hannah to meet me outside my condo, I feel the pit in my stomach growing. I have hardly any experience with babies, but Hannah can't get enough of them. The pit in my stomach is making me breathe a little faster, and I feel a little faintish because when I think of babies, I think of crying, slobbering pooping machines. They are a ton of responsibility that I don't want. The Hernandez baby is no exception.

Our condo at River Creek has poor insulation with thin walls and floors. The Hernandez family lives right below us and baby Sabrina is known to begin wailing way too early on most mornings. I've been asking myself why I said yes, but I quickly remember the answer when I see Hannah at my front door with a flirtatious smile that makes my heart flutter. Hannah and I have been best friends for several years, but we've only been dating about a year. But in that year, it has seemed like we've always been together.

"Are you ready for this, U? I can't wait. I'll change her, of course—you know, diapers and everything. I'll even feed her. You just help out where you can. I got this," Hannah rattles off without taking a breath. She often talks until breathless, which leaves her mocha skin a little pink. I just smile and nod. I gave up trying to protest a while ago.

"Where's your dad?"

## SOMERSET SECRETS
### by T.W. Morse

"He's at a Miami basketball tournament with Bob. He'll be back in a couple of hours. You want to head down to the Hernandezes'? They were expecting us around 3:00 and it's almost that time now."

"Do I!" Hannah replies with a little too much energy. I think she's been drinking a few too many café con leches at Penny U.

We traverse the seventeen steps from our second-floor condo to the first floor Hernandez unit. Each building has four units, two on the first floor and two more on the second. Ours and an empty condo are on the second floor and the Hernandez family is below that with another empty condo next to them on the first floor.

I was glad to leave my condo behind, mainly because I am never allowed to be alone with Hannah at my condo without my dad or Bob present at all times. Those were Hannah's father's strict instructions. Mr. Reyes is not a guy you mess with either. His Cuban accent makes him sound like a Hollywood movie hitman, so when he says, "Ulysses, you are never allowed to be alone in your house with my daughter—do you understand?"—you nod, gulp, and be thankful he doesn't extinguish your life, right then and there. The thought of this is washed away when Hannah grabs my hand and beams up at me as she firmly knocks on the door.

A weary eyed Mr. Hernandez answers the door. He is about my height but much heavier, and the bags under his eyes make him squint hard to see us with the intense Florida sun shining in behind us.

"Oh, Ulysses and Hannah. I am so glad you are here. Gloria—Mrs. Hernandez—is meeting me at the restaurant in a couple of hours. But I have to go into work before I meet her. Come in—come in," he says in a thick Puerto Rican accent, gesturing us rapidly to come in out of the heat.

"Sabrina is sleeping. Thank god." He says this with a sigh of relief.

He starts to show Hannah and me around the condo. It looks almost identical to ours, but a bit newer and less lived in than ours. Hannah is nodding at Mr. Hernandez's directions and swinging my arm as he speaks.

"Sabrina can eat when she wakes. Her food is here." He opens the fridge, but Hannah starts to list her resume—rapidly.

"Mr. Hernandez. I am so happy you are letting us babysit. I want to let you know that I am first aid and CPR certified. I have a second degree black belt in karate, and I took a babysitting course online. Ulysses and I have also babysat for a couple up in Maine last Christmas." Her face is turning pink as she runs out of breath.

"Um—okay?" Mr. Hernandez replies with a touch of confusion.

I smile at this, but it quickly evaporates because Hannah notices and elbows me in the ribs.

"Well, I'm glad Sabrina will be in such good hands," Mr. Hernandez says before Hannah gives me a disapproving look. "But I better be going. You sure you're all set?" he says before dashing for the door.

"Oh, we are good!" Hannah says ecstatically as I give a slow nod and a thumbs up.

"Alright, then. We should be home by 9:00. You kids have fun." And just like that, a facial transformation comes over Mr. Hernandez. He now looks so relieved and relaxed as he leaves us for his date with his wife.

## SOMERSET SECRETS
### by T.W. Morse

## II.

After Mr. Hernandez exits, Hannah and I are just about to sit down and watch some TV when we hear a wail. Hannah rushes to Sabrina's room with me trailing behind her. We come into a very—very pink nursery with a chubby ten-month-old propping herself up to look through her crib bars. Her face is drenched in tears and her hair is matted from sleeping. She sees us and knows right away that her dad is not here, and she starts to wail even more.

"Hey there, Sabrina. My name is Hannah, and this is Ulysses. We are here to babysit you," Hannah reassures her in a soft voice as we surround the crib and look down as Sabrina looks up. Her cheeks are now even redder from her latest cry, but at Hannah's soft tone, Sabrina quiets and cocks her head, sizing up her new sitters before starting to wail again. "Ah!!—Ah!!" This goes on intermittently for about twenty minutes as she is being changed by Hannah and then as we try to feed her.

"Here comes the airplane," Hannah says, making motor noises with her lips, trying her best to feed her spoonfuls of green peas.

"Ah!!" is Sabrina's only reply.

"What should we do?" I ask.

"Um—how about we sing her a song?" Hannah says, trying to not sound desperate.

"I'm not sure if I know any baby songs," I say, putting my hands on my head as the sound of Sabrina's cry rings through the tiny condo.

Hannah starts to sing "The Wheels on the Bus," which I have to say Hannah nails—but Sabrina is not having it.

**SOMERSET SECRETS**
**by T.W. Morse**

"Ah!!—Ah!!" continues to be her answer.

Then a light bulb goes off in my head. "How about I go and get my guitar?"

"Yeah, good idea," Hannah mumbles out the side of her mouth between verses of "Twinkle, Twinkle Little Star." As I turn to leave, I notice Sabrina now splattering peas in Hannah's direction.

I sprint out of the Hernandez condo and up the flight of stairs to my home. Just as I reach for my front door, the door to the condo next to ours slams shut. That's weird! That condo has been vacant since we moved in. I hadn't heard about anyone new renting it. I brush this thought aside because I hear a more intense wail coming from Sabrina. I key into my place and grab my old acoustic guitar before quickly backtracking to find Hannah picking out little pieces of peas from her hair and Sabrina still crying. But now her lips are quivering in disgust. I sit down at the kitchen table next to her high chair.

"Play something," Hannah pleads.

"What should I play? I've never played for a baby before."

"Ulysses Robert Adair! Anything!" Hannah says in a low voice; her frustration is clearly building.

"Okay—okay." Then it comes to me. The song my mom, who passed away a few years ago, would always sing to me as I went to bed: the Beatles' "Ob-La-Di, Ob-La-Da."

As I begin to play, the screaming instantly slows, and by the time I sing the first ob-la-di, Sabrina stops crying and starts to smile, flinging her hands with the beat. Hannah smiles and joins in with the chorus. We have found something that soothes this cranky baby.

After the song, Sabrina is in a far better mood. She finishes her peas and allows Hannah to change her again while she smiles and mumbles to herself in a rhythm that almost sounds like the beat to the song.

"This isn't so bad," I say to Hannah.

Her eyebrows raise at my comment. "This is why people wait to have kids, Ulysses," she says with a smile.

We settle on the couch as I start to play "Twinkle, Twinkle Little Star" when we hear a thud from above us.

I abruptly stop. "What was that?" Hannah asks. Even Sabrina cocks her head upright and looks at the ceiling.

"I don't know," I say.

"Is your dad back from his game?"

"Ah—no. I don't think that was from our place. I think it was from the other unit across from us, the condo directly above this place," I say. I then relay the story of the front door slamming to Hannah. I also mention how that condo has been vacant since we moved in.

"Should we check it out?" Hannah wonders, a look of curiosity coming over her face.

"Well, what do we do with Sabrina?" I ask, which puzzles both of us for a moment. "I guess we could bring her," I add.

"Yeah, they have one of those baby carriers. You could put her into it," Hannah says, holding up a large backpack-looking thing with a bunch of straps.

"Me!?"

"Yeah, that way if we run into trouble, I can defend us," Hannah says, smiling.

"You know, I'm not completely defenseless." With that comment, Sabrina lets out a giggle while Hannah stares at me in disbelief.

Just as I am about to protest further, we hear another thump from above. "Okay—okay, I'll wear the baby carrier, but don't mention this to my dad or Bob. They would never stop making fun of me."

"Alright. Let's go!" Hannah says over-excitedly. It takes us about twenty more minutes to figure out how to put on the baby carrier. First, we can't figure out how to adjust the straps, then we put it on upside down. It is a long, hot mess. But we finally figure it out. Sabrina actually loves being in the carrier, and since I played the guitar, she will not stop smiling up at me. Sabrina is facing out in the baby carrier, kicking her feet with joy. Hannah and I take a moment to giggle at the sight of the two of us looking so parental.

Before long, we are once again out the door of the condo, in search of the mysterious thump coming from the empty condo above.

### III.

We ascend the seventeen steps back up to the second floor. The extra weight from carrying Sabrina in the baby carrier is more noticeable than I expected. I am huffing for air by the time we reach the top step. "You are one heavy baby," I say. Our condo is on the right of the stairwell and the empty condo is to our left, number 208.

I give Hannah a raised eyebrow and nod toward the door for her to knock. She gives a hard knock while Sabrina continues to smile at her while waving her free arms in the baby carrier like she's trying to do the knocking. Nobody answers. Hannah knocks again.

"Maybe we were just hearing things," Hannah offers. "I'll try again." This time her knock is louder and longer. We hear several steps inside, and I think I hear a whisper before steps are heard coming toward the door.

"Someone is in there." And just as I say this, the door creaks open. A sweaty man with a bent nose and a sandpaper beard pokes his head through a crack.

"What do you want?" he sneers through the crack.

"Hey neighbor!" I say a little cheerier than I intend. "My name is Ulysses, and this is my girlfriend, Hannah. I live next door to you in 206." I say this pointing to our door and sticking out my hand for a shake. The man doesn't take my hand. He just stares at us with some beady cat-like green eyes. "And this is baby Sabrina. We were just babysitting. I didn't know that someone had moved into this unit," I add to break the icy tension.

"Yeah, just started today," he finally grunts out.

"Welcome to River Creek," I say while Sabrina makes motorboat sounds. Hannah tries her best to peek around him. But he comes out of the condo completely, shutting the door behind him.

"Sorry, kids, but I got a lot of unpacking to do. Why don't you get back to babysitting and leave."

Hannah's eyebrows begin to wrinkle, and she is just about to give a tongue lashing to this new neighbor when he opens the door and slams it in retreat.

## IV.

"That was weird," I comment to Hannah as we walk the few steps next door to my condo.

"Why are we going to your place?"

Sabrina and I both smile at Hannah. "A little eavesdropping never hurt anyone."

"Eavesdropping?" Hannah asks in a horrified voice, like we were going to commit murder.

# SOMERSET SECRETS
## by T.W. Morse

"What? I'm just going to put a glass to the wall and see if I can hear anything," I reply.

"I don't know. Maybe we should just babysit. The guy probably just dropped a couple of boxes." But just as Hannah says this, we hear a muffled scream. "What was that?" she says.

"I think that was a woman." The scream was so brief it actually could've been a man dropping a box on his toe. "I think this calls for more than a glass to the wall."

"What did you have in mind?" Hannah asks as I unstrap Sabrina and re-strap her onto Hannah, adjusting the straps to fit her better.

"The River Creek property manager was too cheap to put a screen on all of the communities. Next door's lanai has no screen. Dad and I put a screen on ours ourselves last year," I finish saying with a sly grin.

"So? Oh, wait a minute. Ulysses Robert Adair! You aren't going to do what I think you're going to do."

I nod with a very conniving grin. "Our outdoor lanais are only about three to five feet apart. I will carefully remove our screen and then leap next door to this guy's lanai. Peek in through the sliding doors and see where the thump and scream are coming from, easy peasy."

"What the hell," Hannah says, covering Sabrina's ears and crossing herself in a Catholic prayer. "This sounds a little half-baked."

"Oh no—we are fully baked."

"Why don't we just call the police for once?"

"Oh yeah, what if it's nothing? We could get in trouble for filing a false police report. You know how Detective Brute feels about us."

"And you think swinging like Tarzan from lanai to lanai is better?"

# SOMERSET SECRETS
## by T.W. Morse

"Me Tarzan—you Jane," I tease, while receiving Hannah's stern look and Sabrina's laughter in reply. "At least Sabrina thinks I'm funny."

With this last comment, Hannah puts her hands on her hips. "It definitely sounded like a woman's scream. And you are usually right about this stuff."

I nod and start to walk toward the lanai door after grabbing a butter knife from the kitchen. "If something happens, call the cops and maybe come over and do some karate on this guy."

Hannah kisses me. "Good luck."

I start to open the lanai screen with the butter knife, being careful not to rip any of it and to preserve the hard work Dad and I had done. I slowly and quietly take out the rubber string that binds it to the thin metal.

"I'm through," I whisper. Hannah nods while bouncing Sabrina, who is loving every minute. I slowly climb onto the ledge of my lanai. I momentarily look down. Boy, two floors are high! Probably not high enough to kill me, but I'd probably end up with a broken arm. My thoughts immediately drift to playing the guitar and how a broken arm could be a problem. My grip on my lanai grows stronger at this train of thought.

The distance to the empty condo next door is closer to three feet. I can almost reach it with my fingers. I take a moment for a deep breath before flinging my body from my lanai to my new neighbor's. Eat your heart out Spider-Man. I now cling to the neighboring lanai, gasping for air and rethinking the logic of my actions. Maybe this wasn't the brightest move. I take a glance back at Hannah and Sabrina. Sabrina is squirming with excitement, but Hannah looks very wide eyed with concern. I hold my thumb up in reassurance. She just shakes her head in disgust.

"Be careful," Hannah silently mouths from my lanai.

Getting back may be troublesome. Especially since my luck just ran out: the clouds above start to open up to a hard-stinging Florida rain.

The rain pummels me, instantly soaking my clothes and making it hard for me to see. Getting back will now be extremely dangerous. The railings and the lanai will surely be too slippery. I put that thought aside and readjust my footing to pull myself up onto my new neighbor's lanai. That wasn't too bad. I look over to Hannah and shrug as she covers her face and looks more frustrated.

There is just enough stucco siding to hide my legs and body as I climb over the railing, which is not so easy with soaked clothes clinging to my body.

I continue to use the siding to hide behind. I ever-so-slowly peek around the corner, trying my best to not give my position away. The glass sliding door is now the only thing between me and my new neighbor. The glass is little dingy since the condo had been empty for so long, and it was hard to focus my vision while being stung by rainwater. I quickly look in. No lights are on. I try my best to scan the area, looking out for the sweaty, grumpy guy who is supposedly my new neighbor. Trying to find where the scream and thud came from too.

"What the hell!" I quickly look back at Hannah in panic. She is now standing in the doorway of my lanai to keep her and Sabrina out of the rain. She looks at me confused, as she's unable to hear the horror in my voice.

"What?" she mouths.

What do I say back? I'm too shaken to say anything. I rub my eyes and take another covert glance inside the condo just to make sure my eyes aren't playing tricks on me. Sure enough, the scene is the same. Laid out on the vinyl floor directly in front of the sliding doors is a body, bound and gagged.

## V.

The body appears to be of a petite woman. She's wearing jeans and a bloody white t-shirt. Her face is swollen and smeared with blood too. Strands of her long blonde hair are matted to her bloody face. What looks like a red bandana is stuffed into her mouth while zip ties bind her hands and feet. She appears to be unconscious. Just then, I see the guy Hannah and I ran into come in the living room where the women lays. I quickly hide behind the safety of the stucco wall, praying this guy doesn't see me.

What was this? Some home invasion or kidnapping? I can't yell, but I try to make hand gestures across the way to Hannah. She and Sabrina only look at me confused. Then it hits me, my phone! I take it out. I'll try to call Hannah, or better yet the police, but my fingers are too wet! The fingerprint recognition doesn't work. Dammit! I can still punch in the code, but it's difficult to type with the pounding rain. Again, I am frustrated when I see that I only have two percent battery left. Ulysses, why don't you ever charge your phone?! Argh!

Too wet to text. Who should I call then? If I call the police, I won't be able to explain myself fast enough before my phone dies. So I decide to call Hannah.

She answers with a worried cry, "Ulysses! What did you see?"

"That guy has got a woman tied up in here. You got to call the police," I ever-so-quietly whisper.

"What!—I can't hear you. The rain on the lanai is too loud." With this, Hannah and Sabrina duck inside my condo. "That's better. What did you say?"

"I said the guy has a woman tied up. Call the police," I say in a slightly raised voice. With the rain, I'm not sure Hannah can hear me, and my whispers are no longer considered quiet. The sound of the rain may have made me raise my voice a little too loud. My phone is now dead. Great! Before I know what is happening, the sliding door bursts open next to me. The sweaty neighbor charges out onto the lanai after me.

"What are you doing here?" he growls with scary, pulsating eyes. He grabs me and pushes me hard against the lanai wall. My head flings back hard against it. My head, now throbbing, is causing me to see little white dots. The guy becomes a little blurry to me as I slink to my knees, trying to recover from the pain in my head.

I rapidly think back to a move Hannah had taught me from karate and do a desperate quick punch square into this guy's crotch. He wails in pain, kneeling down to one knee too, cursing me under his breath.

I quickly regain my balance and stand up, but he just as quickly recovers and comes after me again. He reaches for my neck as I fling my arms helplessly at him, trying to punch and slap him away. Some of punches land on his face and chest, but his strong, wet hands tightly ring around my neck as we both jockey for position on the small landing of the lanai. I try to gasp for air as he increases his grip tighter and tighter around my neck. I try my best to punch him so he will let me go, landing some strong blows and making him loosen a little. Suddenly, we both hear a crash through the condo behind us.

**SOMERSET SECRETS**
*by T.W. Morse*

My assailant looks over my shoulder with concern, but it is too late for him. The next thing I see is a blur of Hannah running, with Sabrina still strapped to her chest in the baby carrier, jumping in the air and doing some kind of side karate kick to this guy's face. This makes him back off of me in pain, stumbling backward and then flipping end over end off of the lanai. "Ah!!" is the only sound we hear as he falls down to the wet grass below.

Hannah and I both rush to the lanai ledge and look over to see this guy's condition. My attacker lays unconscious on the soaking, wet ground below with his right leg and left arm contorted in grotesque, unnatural positions.

"You rescued me again!" I croak out from my sore throat, touching my neck as I still feel the remnants of his hot hands.

"I called the police too," Hannah says proudly, smiling with a twinkle in her eye and kissing me. Sabrina looks up at me from her baby carrier with a huge grin, making her own karate chops into the air as she imitates our hero—Hannah.

## VI.

Meghan sits upright across the kitchen table, chewing on some of Dad's wicked good meatloaf. Her bruises are fading and her spunky blonde hair is no longer matted with blood. She seems pretty cool, talking to us about her history. Oh yeah, Meghan is our new neighbor, you know, the tied-up woman. Her name is Meghan Pearson and she seems pretty lit. She's a veterinarian and new to Somerset. Meghan was trying to escape her abusive boyfriend.

Meghan moved into River Creek, next door to us, the day Hannah and I babysat for the Hernandez family. That was three days ago now.

The thud Hannah and I heard was her abusive boyfriend. He found out that she moved into River Creek and broke into her condo, gagging her and binding her up with the intent to murder her. Luckily, Hannah and I were downstairs at the time, babysitting. If we were next door, we would never have known, except for the scream. Meghan had moved her gag from her mouth and tried to call for help before her ex-boyfriend, Vincent Crowley, knocked her out cold and replaced the gag again.

Vincent was arrested shortly after the police came and got a statement from us and Meghan. They booked him for attempted murder and kidnapping. The sleaze bag is now handcuffed to a hospital bed, laid up with a broken arm and leg and two cracked ribs thanks to my very fierce girlfriend.

Hannah and I got a stern talking to from Detective Brute for taking matters into our own hands. Even Dad was peeved at my lanai jumping antics in the rain. But all in all, Hannah and I did good, and that's all that matters. We were able to save a woman from an abusive relationship and certain death, and we ended up with a new friend and neighbor who is also a new vet for Ortiz, who now is warming up to Meghan. Ortiz has currently taken up a begging position under the table on the floor near Meghan, licking his lips at the smell of the meatloaf above.

Hannah and I did not mention baby Sabrina's role to anyone, especially Mr. and Mrs. Hernandez. In particular, we did not mention the part where Sabrina was strapped to Hannah while Hannah drop kicked Meghan's abuser off of a second-floor lanai. We didn't want child endangerment charges filed against us, so we kept that one to ourselves.

After all, Hannah and I have become pretty attached to our new biggest fan.

*SOMERSET SECRETS*
*by T.W. Morse*

# THE CASE OF THE EMPTY CHURCH

## ULYSSES
### I.

Somerset, Florida, in the summer time is described as—what is the right word?—freaking hot! No, that doesn't do our summer justice. Other places are hot, but Florida is different. The humid air is thick, reminding me of a homemade quilt wrapped around you in front of a blazing wood stove up in my home state of Maine. Minus the cold air, comfortable, humane temperatures, and oh yeah, add sticky, oppressive humidity!

I had just taken a shower on my third day of summer vacation, and I already need another because my humidity quilt is now wrapping its thick, sticky blanket around me, making me sweat out of every pore. Why bother with any deodorant? Got to love Florida.

I am biking to Hannah's place, trying to bike fast so the wind will cool down my sweating face. Luckily, our summers always have pounding rain in the late afternoon; you can set your watch to it. Every day, sometime between four and six, we get about an inch of rain, often accompanied by powerful thunderstorms. Cool, wet relief! Got to love Florida.

I finally see the ginormous old fish factory, smeared with royal blue paint, covered in a rusty tin roof, and with powerful neon Edison light bulbs brightly spelling out Penny University Café. I drop my bike, stashing it in my usual spot in the back of the warehouse near the Penny U. dumpster.

A wrought-iron staircase leads to the Reyes family's apartment above the business. Their ancient blue truck parked haphazardly in the alley lets me know everyone is home. The truck is plastered with a magnetic version of the café marquee, providing them their free advertising.

It is Sunday and the café closed at five. It is now six and I hadn't called ahead. I thought I would hang with Hannah before the Florida sky opens up, which is happening a little late today. I smell rain coming in the air as I bounce up the stairs feeling the humidity quilt wrap around my neck, making it difficult to breathe. I knock rapidly because, like clockwork, I feel the first drops splatter me.

Mr. Reyes answers. His demeanor and voice exude that of a Cuban hitman, but he is a softy at heart—sometimes.

"Yes?"

His yes always sounds like a "Jes" in his thickly accented hitman growl.

"Oh, it's only you" is all I get as he leaves the doorframe. The door remains ajar, and I'm unsure whether to come in or not. Meanwhile, I'm beginning to get wet, so I decide to come in quickly just before the sky opens up above me, leveling everything with sheets of blinding rain.

"That was close," I say under my breath, as I'm spared from being a soaking victim. As I enter the apartment, air conditioning hits me like a gulf wave. The air nips at my wet skin, giving me goose pimples and finally relinquishing my humid blanket.

The apartment, like Mr. Reyes, welcomes me with cold open arms. I reflect on how we transition from oppressive heat to oppressive A/C throughout most of the year. I smile at the thought of this before making my way to Hannah's room. "Got to love Florida," I mutter under my breath.

Hannah sits with an opened laptop at her desk, which sits under a board of karate ribbons and trophies. Above that are bookshelves with her textbooks and novels lining the wall. Her abundance of books weighs down the cheap shelves, the boards bowing in the middle, looking like they could collapse at any moment.

    I walk over, give her a quick kiss, and then sit on her bed, which is covered in cobalt sheets. The sheets, combined with her cobalt painted room, make it dark like a cave, only a lamp on a bedside table providing light. The Reyes family lives in the second story of Penny U.'s massive converted warehouse, and windows are a rare commodity. I always feel Hannah's room is so dark and appears more boyish than my own. The only traditionally girly stuff is an army of stuffed animals that line the head of her bed.

    "What ya reading?" I ask, throwing one of her stuffed animals up in the air over and over again, a faded green turtle that spins nicely in the air. My makeshift fun provides a welcome escape from the boredom that only a rainy summer day can bring as Hannah's Einstein poster, tacked above her bed, sticks his tongue out at me.

    "I'm reading a fascinating article about the history of the old Somerset Baptist Church down on Sutherland street," Hannah rattles out as the laptop screen illuminates her large reading glasses. Her hair is pulled back in a tight ponytail, distracting me from my new game of stuffed animal toss as the turtle drops on my face.

    "Why are you reading a lame article? We're on summer break! Let's watch some Netflix together."

    She ignores what I say and continues on, "Papa is thinking about buying this church. Sutherland is over on the Bonita Springs line. He and Mama are thinking about expanding Penny University Café, maybe even making it a bar and grill."

    "That would be cool."

    "Yeah, they chose this old Baptist church because it's been vacant for years and we'd get a pretty good deal."

# SOMERSET SECRETS
## by T.W. Morse

"Why has it been vacant?" I ask, thinking properties in Somerset rarely stay vacant because of the high prices they fetch. Some rich one-percenter could scoop it up, demolish it, and build a brand-new condo complex or strip mall in its place. Out with the old, in with the new. Got to love Florida.

Reading my thoughts, Hannah whispers, "They say it's haunted." Just then—CRACK!!—thunder finds us in the small apartment.

I sit up in a flash and am at Hannah's side in one move with a newfound anticipation, the hair on my arms now erect.

"Papa believes this stuff and wants me to research the history of the old church. He's deathly afraid of ghosts."

I couldn't picture the gruff hitman-sounding Mr. Reyes scared of ghosts. I smile to myself. "Your dad thinks it's haunted?"

"His Realtor claims that's why it's so cheap. I guess some developer purchased it two years ago, but when he tried to have it bulldozed, all of his trucks and wrecking ball became mysteriously inoperative. His workers claimed they saw strange things too, and one security guard even said he heard a little girl crying at night. I'm trying to find some *Somerset Daily News* articles to back up the claims," she says, sighing and blowing a stray wisp of her hair from her mocha cheek.

I put my hands on her shoulder and start to kiss her neck just as Mr. Reyes opens her bedroom door. I quickly remove myself from Hannah's neck and take a large step back as my heart falls to my toes in instant fear.

## II.

"Always!" Mr. Reyes growls and then pauses for effect, adding a sinister glare and squinting his eyes almost shut. The wrinkles in his nose give him a menacing appearance that give me a chill to my very core. Even though I tower over the man, he can still put the fear of God in me that no one else can match. "Keep this door open!" he finishes with a hiss.

"Papa, Ulysses and I are just researching the Baptist church. I don't think you have anything to worry about," Hannah reassures him in a sweet, calming voice.

At this news, Mr. Reyes steps into the room and closes the door behind him. For the first time, he looks a little pale and unsure of himself. "You told—the boy?"

"Papa! It's Ulysses! If Mama heard you refer to Ulysses as the boy—well, I don't know what she would do, but you know you would be in mucho trouble." They both continue on in very low hushed Spanish that I don't recognize. My eyes widen with admiration at the courageous way Hannah stands up to her father. Clearly, she has courage I immensely lack in this area.

"Are you sure?" he hisses in a low whisper. Either he is whispering because I knew he was afraid of ghosts at this empty church or he didn't want Mrs. Reyes, who I had just heard come home and is now in the next room, to know his fears.

"How about we all go over there and check it out tonight? The rain should be letting up soon, and we can see everything for ourselves," Hannah suggests.

"Ah—tonight?" Mr. Reyes replies in a heightened, raspy voice.

"Yes, Papa, if you want to buy the church and expand Penny U., we should check it out for ourselves and not buy it sight unseen. The Realtor gave us the combo to the lock. We can check it out tonight and call the Realtor in the morning with our answer."

"Reals?" I quip.

"Yeah, who's up for some ghost hunting?" Hannah asks, smiling as she leads us from her bedroom.

Mrs. Reyes, the baker/cook/everything else at Penny University Café, lies on the couch in the living room, looking exhausted and vegging out on some PBS period drama on TV.

"Hey Mama—Papa, Ulysses, and I are going to check out the new property together."

"Your father is going?" Mrs. Reyes teases, with a sly grin.

"Yes?! I'm going!" he growls. "I better check it out if I'm going to buy it—no?" Mr. Reyes says, puffing out his chest and marching from the small apartment. I catch grins between mother and daughter before Hannah and I follow Mr. Reyes to the truck downstairs.

"I'm driving," Hannah yells to her dad. She hasn't had her license too long, and let's just say her driving is an acquired taste.

Mr. Reyes looks both fearful and dejected, but he still hands over the keys to her. We all sit in the front cabin of the truck, like an overstuffed burrito with me in the middle. Mr. Reyes's boney elbows soon find an armrest on my rib cage. I try to move closer to Hannah to his disapproving grunts.

The beat-up truck drives along Edison Boulevard, which runs parallel with Somerset beach. The rain has stopped and the inch of water is now rapidly receding. It is amazing how fast the rainwater is absorbed into the sandy soil of Florida. In Maine, where I was born, rain hangs around for days, creating temporary rivers and lakes. In Florida, it's gone in a matter of minutes, and within an hour, it looks like it never rained. Got to love Florida.

We drive fast. Both Mr. Reyes and I hang on to the dash with white knuckles and mouths agape as Hannah swerves, speeds, and slams on the brakes, sometimes all at once.

The summer sun is just setting, and traffic is becoming heavier, giving our stomachs temporary relief from all the swerving of Hannah's driving. Hundreds of the elderly and European tourists that invade our city in the summer each year are now driving home from the beach. I've been hearing more German on our beaches lately than English. I call them sunset peepers. They are all heading back to their hotels and home rentals, causing some minor traffic. Got to love Florida.

"Whatcha doing?" Hannah asks.

"I'm just giving my dad a quick text," I say.

> **Me:** *"Going with Hannah and Mr. Reyes to look at a haunted Baptist church over on Sutherland Street. B home soon."*
> **Dad:** *"Did you say haunted?"*
> **Me:** *"Yeah, probably nothing. Love ya."*
> **Dad:** *"love you too. B safe."*
> **Me:** *"No worries."*

"I bet Bob and your dad are glad they don't have to go. Could you imagine Bob at this place?" Hannah says smiling, having looked at my texts over my shoulder while we idled in traffic.

"Yeah, he wouldn't last two minutes. And he'd complain the whole time," I add as we both laugh.

**SOMERSET SECRETS**
*by T.W. Morse*

"There are no ghosts," Mr. Reyes barks, almost to reassure himself rather than us.

"I couldn't find any news reports of anyone dying or any other suspicious behaviors, Papa. I think we'll be fine," Hannah says, revving the engine before sending us hurtling forward and back and forward again as she commences with her erratic driving.

"That doesn't mean it's not haunted," I add, raising my eyebrows at an ill-amused, grumpy Mr. Reyes.

### III.

We roll onto Sutherland Street, and Hannah finally puts the car in park. My heart can rest; I can tell Mr. Reyes is now breathing easier too.

"Oh my," I exclaim, sounding like Dad as I take in the scene before us. The old run-down church stands tall and imposing. Mr. Reyes gulps while Hannah smiles broadly.

"Bet! This place is lit! Look at all the parking and the location. It's right off Route 41 and close to the beach; we are sure to get steady traffic," Hannah rambles off in an ecstatic rant.

Mr. Reyes and I look at each other, wondering if we're looking at the same building as Hannah. The church does have a large parking lot, but the pavement is crumbling and would be hard to traverse in this condition. It does have a tall, narrow steeple, providing a picturesque place of worship at one time, but now it's covered in graffiti and long sheets of peeling paint, like a skinned, sunburned tourist. Large plywood covers the windows and front door, which are also covered in spray paint. Just then, we see a streak of lightning illuminate the sky, backlighting the church in the darkening sky.

Mr. Reyes turns to Hannah as we cautiously leave the truck. "Maybe we should g—" He doesn't finish his thought before we hear a follow up to the lightning,

BAM!!

Mr. Reyes grabs my arm, and we turn back toward the truck with fear running down our spines. Mr. Reyes mutters Spanish swears under his breath as he drags me along.

Hannah, now brandishing a large flashlight, switches it on and holds it under her chin while yelling to us, "You two aren't afraid of a little—thunder? Are you?" She continues to giggle and make ghoulish sounds. "Wha—ah—ah!"

Mr. Reyes yanks the flashlight from Hannah and mumbles in disgust under his breath. "Let's go. ¡Vamos!"

Just then, we are all blinded by headlights rolling up to the truck, and I immediately recognize Dad's silver Prius. Out come Dad, Hope, and a hesitant Bob dressed in a bright green tracksuit, making him look like an engorged watermelon. Hannah and I give Hope and Dad hugs, while Bob reaches for a hard fist bump.

"We wanted to help out, see if you guys and Hector need a hand checking this place out," Dad explains, smiling at our surprised faces.

Mr. Reyes enthusiastically shakes Dad's hand, "Si, very happy, very happy to have you." He smiles broadly at Hannah, who now looks crestfallen at the diminished prospects of scaring her father as much as she would've liked. "They say it's haunted, no?" Mr. Reyes adds.

"Haunted? Nobody said anything about being haunted! Mmm-mmm," Bob squeals.

"You wouldn't have come if Logan said it was," Hope pipes in.

"It's not haunted, Hector. You and Bob shouldn't believe in that stuff. It's probably a squatter or something," Dad says with a confidence that I admire.

I examine the church. "I know of a lot of kids from Mangrove High go to old, abandoned buildings like this to buy drugs. Got to love Florida," I say, adding my two cents.

"Are we done talking? Let's go in!" an impatient Hannah encourages.

Dad, Bob, and I all turn on our phone flashlights, and with Hannah's large flashlight, we make our way over the torn-up parking lot, avoiding the huge blocks of pavement like they're land mines.

"I've got the combo to the front door lock," Hannah says in a hushed tone as Dad and Mr. Reyes pull off a plywood board.

"I don't think we need it," I add as we all look at the door. On the ground in front of it is a broken lock.

"Do you think squatters did that?" Hope asks.

"Yeah, it certainly wasn't ghosts," Dad adds.

"Hello!—Hello!—Is anyone here?!" Dad yells into the empty church. We hear a flutter of wings as we are startled by birds that fly out, scaring Bob and Mr. Reyes.

"Oh, what the hell!" Bob squirms as they hold each other in fright.

"Bob, it's just birds!" I reassure him while everyone shakes their heads and snickers at their reaction.

"I knew that, all is good," Mr. Reyes says, puffing out his chest and distancing himself from Bob.

I look at Dad and Hannah. "Are we going in?" I ask with a gulp, feeling my own trepidation.

## IV.

The church was musty and damp from the lack of air conditioning. The smell of sweat fills the air.

"Maybe we should split up," I suggest in a hushed voice. The church makes even my whisper echo around us. The place is pitch dark but for our flashlight and phone lights sending beams in every direction. More birds flutter, causing another jump from Bob. The pews are scattered around the nave and some are even tipped over. Cobwebs connect every surface and sometimes find our hair.

"Ah! Logan, it's in my hair! Get it out!" Hope screams as she walks into a cobweb. Dad quickly pulls them out, reassuring Hope that nothing remains of the webs or spider who made them.

"I do not like this. I do not need to buy," Mr. Reyes says nervously.

"Papa, you've got to have imagination. Remember what the warehouse looked like before you and Mama transformed it into Penny University?"

"She's got a point, Hector. I see a lot of potential here," Dad adds. Mr. Reyes nods in appreciation. He admires both Hannah's and Dad's opinions almost as much as Mrs. Reyes's.

"This place is massive. Maybe we should split up," I suggest again, tripping over Bob, who in turn bumps into a pew.

"Yeah, Hannah, Hope, and I will go and check out the back rooms near the altar. You three check out the side rooms," Dad says.

Already regretting my comment about splitting up, I say, "You want Mr. Reyes and Bob with me?" I am ready to protest, but a deep painful gulp prevents me, and they are off before I can get the words out. I guess I am left with the two scaredy-cats. Yay me.

This is like an episode of *Scooby-Doo,* but instead I'm stuck with two guys that both act like Shaggy. Wait, does that make me Scooby? I don't want to be Scooby. I want to be Fred, hunting for ghosts with my Daphne.

"I guess we should go this way," I suggest hesitantly, leading Bob and Mr. Reyes with my phone light around the pews to a side doorway.

The door swings precariously on its hinges, broken and already ajar. It was, of course, dark and ominous like the rest of the church. Bob and Mr. Reyes cautiously follow, pushing me to lead the way. "Okay—okay, you don't have to push," I say with a growing frustration at these two grown, frightened men. Dealing with a scared Mr. Reyes was one thing, dealing with him and a petrified Bob is a whole different story. Their fears feed off each other.

Both guys slowly follow me as we progress through the opening. The floorboards creak beneath our feet as we traverse the side rooms in almost pitch dark.

"What was that?" Bob yelps.

At first, I don't hear anything; then I make out a faint moaning coming from the end of the corridor.

Mr. Reyes crosses himself. "We should turn back, yes?"

"Mmm—mmm, I agree. Let me tell you somethin'— Ulysses, we should find your dad," Bob whines. I am just about to agree when I see a glimpse of something down the dark corridor. I quickly flash my phone light, and we all gasp at once. We see what appears to be a small figure, dressed in a white, tattered sundress, dash into a room at the end of the corridor. Both Mr. Reyes and Bob grab my arm, twisting it as they squirm.

## SOMERSET SECRETS
### by T.W. Morse

"Oh—what the hell is this?" Bob squawks in my ear. And in the same ear, he yells, "Logan! Help!"

"Bob, quiet," Mr. Reyes says, now recovered. I think he is holding a finger to his bearded face, but because of the lack of light, I can't quite tell. I hear his raspy whisper, "Quiet. It may come back for us."

"What?—What was that. Ulysses?" says Bob, now quivering as he continues his death grip on my arm.

"I don't know, but I think we need to check it out." Not sure what makes me say this, but my curiosity feeds a confidence I'm not sure I really like. I wiggle my arm away from Bob's grip. "Come on," I command, feeling both Mr. Reyes and Bob exchange glances at each other.

The corridor seems to go the length of the church and eventually leads to a door. I flash my phone ahead to uncover a closed, highly glossed red door. I reach for the handle, but Bob takes my wrist. "Should you open that?"

I wriggle away again. I look over to Mr. Reyes; he nods yes. Or I think he does; it is very dark down here.

I am just about to turn the handle when I hear Bob mutter, "Ulysses, I don't know—I don't know. Don't do it—please."

I open the door ever so slowly. It, of course, loudly creaks with every movement, like a loud scratching of a chalkboard that penetrates the emptiness of the church. We all huddle in the doorframe, wide eyed like deer in headlights.

Inside the room is completely dark but for the stream of light from my phone, which allows us to catch a glimpse of something sitting in a metal chair. I can barely make out what looks like a life-size doll sitting bolt upright with her head looking down at her dangling bare feet. She is wearing the same worn white dress we saw earlier. My phone flashes onto the doll when we hear it. Giggling! It's coming from the room. The giggling sounds like that of a little girl as it echoes

**SOMERSET SECRETS**
*by T.W. Morse*

around the empty room, creating a menacing, maniacal atmosphere.

All of a sudden, the life-size doll shoots its head up like it has just woken up. Simultaneously, the giggling stops and the same menacing little girl's voice asks, "Why are you here?" A cold chill spikes through my spine, and my body temperature freezes in the humid, hot summer air. Then the little doll voice yells, "GET OUT! GET OUT! GET OUT!"

Before I know it, both Mr. Reyes and Bob do a 180 and start to run back the way we came, bumping over each other in the process and leaving me behind, unable to move. I can hear Bob yelling down the corridor, "I don't do ghosts! I don't do ghosts!"

"LEAVE! LEAVE NOW!" the ghost doll chants.

I don't think twice as I turn and exit right on their heels, running for my life.

## V.

It seems like we've been running for awhile, but it was only a few feet back to the pews and the larger sanctuary.

I need to find Dad, Hannah, and Hope and get the hell out of here. My mind is racing. Did we just encounter a ghost? I shudder just thinking about it.

When I get back to the nave, I find it lit. I don't know how it is lit, but it is. It no longer has a menacing look either; it actually feels welcoming, other than a few cobwebs here and there. I stop to catch my breath and am quickly startled to find Hannah introducing her father to an older Latino man and woman. Both had seen better days and are wearing dingy, old clothes that hang from their emaciated bodies. They look fearful and tired.

I watch Hannah rattle off Spanish to the couple, only catching Bob's and my names. I recognize a few more words but am still shaking from the episode with the girl, so I'm unable to process much.

Hannah notices our confusion and translates for us. "I was just explaining that the puzzled looking black man in the bright tracksuit is Bob Nelson, a friend of the family, and the tall handsome one is my boyfriend, Ulysses Adair."

"Say what?" Bob utters, while holding a stitch in his side. I also discover the source of lights, a bunch of campfire lanterns hung all around the nave. A couple of them are illuminating the boarded up stained glass, showing the beauty of the craftsmanship that remains in this old, empty church.

"Bob and Ulysses, this is Luis and Alina Bello. You just met their little girl, Christina," Hannah explains.

"We—how do you say—sorry," Alina explains as they both hold out hands to me and Bob to shake. Bob first looks hesitant, but he eventually accepts.

"The whole family has been living and hiding out in the church. They were first hidden away by the preacher, but he died a few years ago of a heart attack. The church was then abandoned by the parishioners, who had moved on to the other Baptist church in Somerset, leaving the Bellos hidden away. Your father found their secret room behind the altar. The Bellos have been scaring and sabotaging any new developers and Realtors trying to access the property," Hannah explains.

Both of the Bellos are now speaking in rapid Spanish to Mr. Reyes and Hannah.

"Ulysses, they don't speak much English. They go to soup kitchens on most days, but they are in constant fear of immigration enforcement catching them," Dad explains.

"Got to love Florida," I grumble under my breath.

"They have a large garden in the back too, where they grow most of their own food. They even have a chicken that lays eggs," Hannah translates for Alina, who speaks rapidly, making my two years of Spanish classes completely useless.

"That poor family," Hope adds.

Just then, Christina comes up to her parents, hugging her father's leg. "Sorry—I scare you," she offers in apology with a devilish grin.

"Girl, nobody scares Bobby Nelson, it all good."

I shake my head in disbelief. "Her English sounded a lot better a few minutes ago when she was trying to scare us to death," I say to a giggle from Christina. This girl is really good at making trouble.

"This may work out well for all of us," Mr. Reyes confesses, turning back to us.

"How Hector?" Dad asks.

"Luis says he was a chef back in Mexico. I explained to him that we will help him get an immigration attorney, so he can stay here legally. The only thing I ask for in return is he and his family work and live at the church—after our renovations, of course. But until then, everyone can stay at Penny University. We have the space in the lower levels. Your mama and I can fix it up nicely," Mr. Reyes says and then translates his comment into Spanish.

"Oh Papa! Mama will be so proud of you," Hannah adds, giving her father a long hug.

"What is Pe—penny U-no—virsty?" Luis asks, looking puzzled.

*SOMERSET SECRETS*
*by T.W. Morse*

# WAKE UP! IT'S MURDER!

## LOGAN
### I.

I hate getting phone calls in the middle of the night. My mind always races to the worst possible scenario. Did Ulysses sneak out of the house and meet up with Hannah? Maybe he got in a car wreck! My thoughts play out to this scenario as my phone wakes me from a deep REM sleep at 2 a.m. My mouth goes dry. My retro ringtone makes a sound like an old rotary phone blaring in my ear.

"Logan—get it. I have patients early tomorrow morning," Hope, half awake, grunts in my ear as she pulls the blankets over her head.

I feel around on my bedside table, knocking over the TV remote, a picture frame, and my wallet before finally grabbing the obnoxious vibrating phone. I squint at the caller ID. It reads "Best Friend In the Whole World—Bobby Nelson," with a picture of him in a black tracksuit with his arms folded and wearing a black fedora, trying to look like the fourth member of RUN-D.M.C. Bob hijacked my phone a few months ago and changed his name and picture to something more to his liking.

"What the hell?!"

"What? Who is it?" Hope grunts.

"It's Bob."

"Oh! For the love of god! Don't answer it! Decline it! Nothing good will come from answering that call," Hope pleads.

## SOMERSET SECRETS
### by T.W. Morse

    I am about to hit decline, but then I think on it for second. Why would Bob be calling me at 2 a.m.? "I'm sure he has a good reason," I say as Hope covers her ears with a pillow and I click the answer button on my phone, already regretting my choice.
    "Bob, this better be good."
    Heavy breathing turns to gasps over the line, "Logan—Logan, I need you man. I—I don't know what happened. First, I was winning at roulette and enjoying myself, and now…" He pauses and adds long, whimpering sounds to his deep breaths, crying out his words.
    "What, Bob? What happened?"
    "She's dead!" Bob hisses in my ear.
    "Who's dead?" I sit bolt upright, now fully awake.
    "What?" Hope does the same, and I switch to speaker phone.
    "Logan—Logan, you gots to come down and help a brother out. I didn't kill her, but—she's been murdered!"
    "Who's been murdered?"
    "Layla. Layla's dead. Oh my gosh, I—!" We hear a loud bang at the door, cutting out Bob's plea.
    "Police! Open up!"
    "Logan—Logan, the police are here! THEY'RE GONNA THINK I DID IT!!" Bob lets out the highest squeal yet, releasing the remainder of his emotions. "Let me tell ya somethin'—I didn't do it, or I don't think I did it!"
    "Bob, calm down! I will not let anything happen to you. Do you hear me? I will make this right. Where are you?" I have never heard panic like this in Bob's voice, and he's an overly panicked guy.
    "Logan—Logan, I knew you got my back, bro. I'm at the casino. You know the one, Seminole Suns. I don't remember

even getting back to my room last night. Wait, this isn't even my room! Logan, help me!"

We hear the door burst open and a voice over the speaker phone say in a very authoritative voice, "Sir, hang up that phone—you're under arrest!"

Bob whispers a hissing last cry for help, "Mmm—mmm—Help me, Logan!" Then the line goes dead.

## II.

Ulysses and Hope are trying to keep up with me as we practically jog through the Seminole Suns Casino parking lot. The exterior of the place is straight out of the seventies, in a hasn't-been-remodeled-since way, not in a cool-retro way. Everything inside looks drab and beige, with a little burnt orange mixed in. We quickly traverse the swinging lobby door. Slots and loud cheering provide the typical constant background noise of the casino, still going strong at nearly 2:30 a.m. I had made good time in my Prius, and Ulysses and Hope were more than glad to help.

"Where should we go first, Dad?"

"Bob said he was not in his room, and he was in fact in the dead girl's room. He said her name was Layla, probably an alias."

"Should we ask the concierge?" Hope asks, pointing to the nearby front desk.

"No," I say as I nod my head toward three sheriff deputies lingering off to the side and an ambulance pulls in behind us. The crime scene guys are probably already up there. "Let's wait and hang back a bit."

## SOMERSET SECRETS
### by T.W. Morse

I find a large potted plant, more of a tree than a plant, and probably left over from the seventies too. We wait for the EMTs to make their way into the lobby. A young Hispanic sheriff's deputy motions for them to follow him and they head toward a bank of glass elevators. Between the elevators is a wall mural. In keeping with the décor, it is beige with brown accents. It looks like it might be of a Native American, but who can tell with all that beige?

"We'll see what floor they get off on and take the stairs. See, there they go." The elevator stops at the fourth floor. "Fourth floor—let's go." We dash for the stairway and all climb the stairs two at a time. Hope and Ulysses are well ahead of me; I guess my age is catching up to me.

"You good, Dad?"

I give a thumbs up because I think I might need to sit down if I speak.

We finally arrive at the fourth floor. "Before we go through, keep an eye out for anything out of the ordinary. Take a mental note of things you see." We observe deputies along with men and women in CSI gear going in and out of room 412.

We walk casually, or we try to walk as casually as you can at nearly three in the morning outside a murder scene in a casino. The deputy at the door goes inside the room for a moment, giving us a chance to speed walk up to the doorway. We look inside and see the dead woman laying on her back with her arms spread out, lifeless. She is wearing a gold glittery skirt. She has long blonde hair, blown back like an overused Barbie doll. She is wearing clunky jewelry that doesn't coordinate well with her skirt. The room looks clean, other than the murder.

A CSI photographer is snapping pictures as two deputies stand guard in front of Bob, who is handcuffed to a chair. He is wearing black slacks and a ribbed white tank top. His head is hung low and he looks half dead himself. In the bathroom door stands a tall scarecrow of a man. The scarecrow slowly looks up from his notepad to see Ulysses, Hope, and I gawking in at his crime scene. Detective Nathan Brute then says in his overly slow, deep, Southern drawl, "Mr. A—dair—I knew—when I saw—your friend—Bob. I knew—you—wouldn't—be—far behind."

"Logan! Help me," Bob squeals before Brute gestures the deputies to take him away. "I don't remember anything from last night! I don't even know how I got here!" Bob pleads with the officers while being handcuffed. That's the second time Bob mentioned he didn't remember anything. He must have been drugged.

"Don't say anything, Bob; I'll make this right," I yell to Bob as the deputies Mirandize him and take him away. Bob enthusiastically nods in agreement, but I know he'll be singing like a canary if Brute pushes him the slightest bit.

"Detective, Bob doesn't remember going back to this room. He can't remember last night at all. You know that means he was probably drugged. "

"That's—quite an—assumption, Mr. A—dair. I —know that Bob—woke in the—same bed—as a dead woman. And—I know you all—don't belong in a crime—scene." Brute points to another deputy with his long, emaciated arm and he escorts us out of the room.

"Who called this in?" I yell back. "You know this stinks! You know Bob didn't do this! Keep an open mind!"

The deputy luckily only walks with us as far as the elevator. Once in, I turn to Ulysses. "What did you see?" I know my resourceful son had been snapping pictures covertly with his phone, bobbing behind me as Brute and I spoke.

## SOMERSET SECRETS
### by T.W. Morse

"Got some real clear ones of the body. It looks like she was strangled. There's bruising around the neck."

"What's that mark?" I zoom in with my fingers. "I can't see. It's too blurry."

"This is horrible," Hope says. "We shouldn't be getting involved. Taking pictures of a dead body?"

"Hope—it's Bob. We need to clear his name. We need to find the real killer. Especially before the press gets wind of this," I say as the elevator doors burst open.

"It's what we do," Ulysses adds with a wink. "Are we sure he didn't do it, though?" Ulysses asks with a Cheshire grin.

"U!?" I say, giving him my sternest frown.

"Even I know Bob couldn't kill anyone," Hope says, elbowing Ulysses.

"Agreed."

"Dad, did you notice anything in the room?"

"They both were dressed. I think it was a staged scene. Bob must have been drugged and then put there. But why?"

"Where do we go next?" Hope says now, warming up to our escapades.

"Now we go to the concierge desk and check out some security footage. But we'll need you to do some acting," I say to Hope, taking her by the hand.

### III.

"Oh I don't know, Logan," Hope protests as she comes out from the bathroom after changing out of her old clothes and into a large straw hat, dress, and heels, which we just bought in the lobby boutique. Hope now looks Southern sophisticated, or at least that is the role I want her to play. She struggles to straighten her hair and adds some makeup for added effect.

"Hope, you'll be great. You got this," Ulysses says, offering further reassurance.

"So let's go over it again. We don't have much time before Brute gets down here."

"Okay, so I go up to the concierge and claim some big goofy black guy stole my purse."

"Yes, and give a proper description of Bob." I think I saw a lavender shirt crumpled on the hotel room floor. "Say he was about five foot ten, African American, about forty, short beard, wearing black slacks and a lavender shirt. Say you think he stole it around eleven last night, near the roulette tables. Bob loves roulette. He's always quoting Wesley Snipes, 'Always bet on black,' from that dumb '90s airplane hijack movie."

"I'm good," Hope says, but I notice she's shaking either from nerves or exhaustion. "I just have to lie to a casino concierge, face possible obstruction of justice charges, and meddle in a police investigation. I could lose my license to practice medicine if I'm caught, but no biggie." She says this with pure venom in her eyes as she slinks away from us and over to the concierge desk while Ulysses and I once again sneak behind the tree in the lobby.

"Good, she's made contact," Ulysses says, joining me in peeking between branches. We're trying to not look out place but more than likely we stick out like a sore thumb. We both unstick our heads from the tree and find a couch in a far corner of the lobby, out of sight from any onlookers. Hope dialed my number before speaking with the concierge, so Ulysses and I put the phone up to our ears after I mute our end. I told her to describe everything she observes.

"Oh-my-gosh."

"Yes, ma'am, how can I help you?"

"How can you help me? Wow, for starters, you can help me get my purse back!"

"Your purse, ma'am?"

"Yes, there was this oaf of a man at the roulette tables last night. I'm sure he stole it."

"This might be a matter for the police ma'am."

"No!" Hope insists before adding some tears for effect. "My group is going back to New York tonight, and I don't have my ID. If I can at least know what room number this oaf is staying in—you must have a gazillion cameras?"

"We do have a fair share, ma'am."

"Then I demand to look at them. Do you know who I am?! Haven't you heard of my services?"

"Your services—ma'am?"

"Yes, damn—it! I am Dr. Adair, known as the scalpel to the stars. I've done plastic surgeries on half of Somerset. I have just expanded my practice to New York and am back in town with some of my clients, only to have this happen."

"Oh, she's good," Ulysses quips. "I bet you like her using your name?"

"It's better than her own, if she's caught," I say before we continue our eavesdropping over the phone.

The concierge clears his throat, now sounding a little impressed. "I will have someone escort you to our security room. But you must hurry because we've had another incident in the hotel. A matter for the police. This is Mr. Taylor. He is a security officer, and he can take you to our back room to view our security feeds."

"Thank you." We hear nothing but footsteps until they reach the security office.

"What time do you need to view?" a stern sounding security officer asks.

"About 11:00 p.m. Look for a big, black, overweight oaf wearing a lavender shirt." I guess that description works too. Ulysses is snickering beside me as Hope's now getting more comfortable.

"Yes. Him!" We both hear over the phone. "He's the one I think stole my purse. Can you follow him with the cameras throughout the night?"

"Yes, we can even speed it up for you," the security officer offers, just as Ulysses taps me on the shoulder and a spike of fear shoots up my spine because Detective Brute and a deputy are riding the glass elevator down to the lobby. They're most likely headed to interview the concierge and look at those security feeds.

I hit end on my phone and send Hope a text, "GET OUT! BRUTE IS COMING!" I wait to see if she has read it. It seems like a long moment before my screen notifies me that the text is read.

But my relief doesn't last long because she quickly replies, "STALL!"

I show Ulysses the text message, and we run to the glass elevators to intercept Brute as he exits.

"Detective—Detective! You know Bob; you know he's not a killer!" I say, half out of breath.

"Mr. A—dair. I know—this case is a little weird, but—I got to look—at the facts. And I'm as busy—as a one-legged cat in a sandbox." One-legged what? I briefly give Ulysses a dumbfounded look. His expression shows that he's just as mystified by Brute's unusual turn of phrase.

"Point one, who called it in? Point two, give Bob a blood test. He's got some kind of drug in his system, maybe some kind of roofies. And—" But the detective interrupts my lecture as he motions for the deputy to remove both of us from the hotel before I can finish.

"And don't—get mess—in'— in my investi—gation, or I'm—gonna tan your hide!"

After the deputy escorts us from the casino into the dawn of the outdoors, Ulysses turns to me with a confused look. "Tan your hide?" I only shrug and scan my phone frantically for a message from Hope. Sure enough, there is a message waiting for me. I am dreading what it might say. Was she caught? Or did she get out?

## IV.

"I'm at the car." Ulysses and I both jog over to my little silver Prius to find Hope hiding in the back seat. She remains crouched below the window until we leave the parking lot.

"How did you get out of there?"

"When I got your text, I pretended to get nauseous."

"But you're okay, right?" I ask, concerned.

"Yes, Logan! Oh my god, let me finish! I said I needed to go to the lady's room because I was feeling sick from all the stress. The security guard quickly showed me to a bathroom. I was betting on him wanting to get far away from any illness, which he did. When he left me, I saw a maintenance door in the back of the hallway to the bathrooms and dashed out. I was practically at the car by then. I knew they have parking lot cameras, so I ducked behind a big truck and crawled into the back seat of the Prius without prying eyes seeing which car I fled in, just in case they suspect my involvement with the case."

"A girl after my own heart," I say before winking at her in my rearview mirror.

"So, what did you see in the video feed?" Ulysses asks, getting us back on track.

"I first saw Bob at the bar near the casino floor. He was throwing back a few drinks and speaking with the bartender. That's when he met Layla. They spoke for a while and then they both made their way over to the roulette table, like you said."

"Did you see anyone suspicious? Maybe slipping something in his drink?"

"It was weird. Layla was hanging on Bob for a long time, I mean, really hanging on him."

"The bartender could've given him something. Maybe—we can try and interview him later," I say before nodding in the rearview mirror for her to continue.

"There was this large man in a fancy white suit, bigger than Bob. He exchanged some words with Layla while Bob was at the roulette table."

"An argument?" Ulysses adds.

"Um—yes, it looked that way. He even took her forcefully by the arm. Bob stepped in and said something to the guy and he backed off."

"Way to go, Bob! That could be enough for Brute to let Bob go," Ulysses says.

"I don't know. We need to find that guy and see how he knew Layla. Anything more?"

"Well, the security guy sped up the recording at that point to follow Bob throughout the night. It looked like he and Layla were locked in each other's arms, laughing and having a wonderful time, all the way to the elevator. He better have been drugged, Logan, with the way he and that woman were hanging all over each other. Poor Sarah! Anyway, I didn't see any footage after that. The security guard said the cameras on the fourth floor are broken somehow. That's also when you had texted me, and my story with the security guard was starting to run thin because I think he was starting to notice I was not in any of the footage."

"The cameras don't work on the fourth floor! That will piss off Brute and make it worse for Bob. Wait! Maybe the murderer knew the cameras didn't work. Maybe that was part of his plan the whole time," Ulysses says.

"I don't know; it's possible."

"What's the plan now?" Hope enthusiastically asks, having caught the investigative bug.

"Can you contact Sarah? Being Bob's girlfriend, she might be able to speak with him easier than I could. And she should be made aware of what happened. Can you then go with her to the station to try to see if he remembers anything more? Ask about this big guy in the suit and the bartender. I will try to come down later today and speak to Brute after Ulysses and I do a little follow-up work.

"Okay, but what are you guys going to do?" Hope says, confused.

"You may not want to know—actually, the less you know the better," I say, giving a worried glance over to Ulysses. After we drop Hope off at her house to freshen up and call Sarah, we make our way over to Penny University Café.

"Hannah's up, right?" I ask.

"Oh—yeah. Mrs. Reyes has been waking up Hannah every morning this summer to help with the baking at Penny U."

"I'm sure Catherine won't mind us taking Hannah for a quick mission."

After we pick up Hannah from Penny University, once again I feel the guilt sweep through my body as I hear Ulysses make a lie up to convince Catherine Reyes to let her daughter assist us in another investigation and take her away from her baking duties.

Ulysses fills Hannah in on our previous night/morning escapade while she shakes her head and lets out the occasional, "Poor Mr. Nelson" or even a "Hope did what?" Ulysses tries to not over-embellish, but you know how teenagers can be. "So he cheated on Sarah?"

"I don't think so," I reassure her. "We think Bob was slipped something like a roofie, debilitating him. He probably didn't know what he was doing."

"What's our next move, Mr. Adair?" Hannah asks with an enthusiasm only she can bring.

"I want to start with that bartender. He may be our guy or at least may have some insights to the identity of the large man in the white suit who had an argument with Layla."

We arrive back at Seminole Suns and backtrack through the lobby. The lobby is quieter now at 7 a.m. than it was at nearly 3.

I have Hannah and Ulysses wait in the lobby, near the tree that continues to define our day. "You guys wait here. I'm sure teenagers aren't allowed in the bar."

"We'll ask around about the big guy in the white suit," Ulysses offers with a quick approving nod from Hannah.

The bar is near the casino floor. The incessant background noises get louder as I approach, with the clinking of chips, ringing of bells, and people cheering filling the air. I remember Hope said Bob first went to the bar. I enter the bar, which is set up more like a 1920s speakeasy.

The high gloss wooden bar is manned by a little man with slicked back, greasy hair, wearing suspenders topped by a bright green bow tie. His crooked name tag reads Chase. He looks like he is closing up and coming off his shift as he wipes an already clean bartop with a white rag. Chase looks exhausted, which means easy pickings.

"Chase?"

"Yeah, who's asking?"

"Logan Adair. I'm investigating the incident from last night."

"Another cop?"

So he thinks I'm a cop. Well, if I don't say I'm not, then I can't be accused of impersonating one.

"Do you remember this man last night?" I flash a picture of Bob on my phone.

"Oh—yeah, who could forget Bobby Nelson? He had a few drinks. I told the other cops that too."

"How many drinks?"

"A couple."

"So about two drinks?" Chase nods. Knowing the amount that Bob drinks on a daily basis leads me to think Bob wouldn't have blacked out on two drinks alone. This confirms my suspicion of him being drugged.

"He spoke with the victim too, didn't he?"

"Yeah—I already said that to the other officer, the tall skinny one. Why you asking too?"

"Oh, Brute. Well, he asks and then I come around and confirm the stories." Chase nods, believing my half lie, as I stretch myself further into trouble.

"Yeah, Layla."

"Oh, you know her?"

"Yeah, I knew of her."

"What can you tell me?"

"I hear things," Chase cryptically replies with a hushed tone over the glossy bar. "She's got a reputation for seducing and stealing, if you know what I mean."

"A grifter?" Chase nods. "How do you know this?"

"A friend of mine, Benny, told me."

I nod in understanding. "Benny—ha. This Benny got a last name?"

Chase leans back. "The copper wasn't interested in Layla and Benny."

"No?"

"Yeah, he was only interested in the black guy, Bobby Nelson."

"Yeah, well, I'm interested in a lot things. What's Benny's last name?"

Chase looks at me with a growing suspicion. "Booth. He has nothing to do with this. He only knows Layla and what kind of girl she is. Benny's a friend of mine."

"Benny, he's a big guy, right? Wore a white suit last night?"

I see the anger build over Chase's face and know his silence is all the confirmation I need. This Benny Booth was the large man in the white suit that Hope saw on the security cameras who got into an altercation with Layla last night.

"What's your name? Ah, Logan Adair. I'm calling the police to see if you're a cop."

"I actually never said I was a cop—you did," I say as I make a quick retreat from the bar. I see Hannah and Ulysses in the lobby and wave for them to join me so we can get the hell out of this casino.

## V.

We all walk into the police station to check on Hope and Sarah and to see if they were able to speak with Bob. Maybe some of his memories have been jogged. The station is bustling, and we find Hope with her arm around Sarah as they sit on a bench near Detective Brute's desk.

"Any news?"

Hope somberly shakes her head. "You?"

**SOMERSET SECRETS**
*by T.W. Morse*

I raise my eyebrows to indicate I have something, but then I nod to Brute's desk to let her know it's not safe to talk here. I see him reviewing the pictures taken of the crime scene and don't want him to know we've been meddling. I need a closer look at the mark on Layla's neck. The photo Ulysses took was too blurry. I need to see what Brute sees.

"Ulysses and Hannah, I need you to distract the detective. Can you do that? It needs to be big," I whisper in both their ears. They look at each other and then whisper something to each other out of my earshot. A couple minutes later, Ulysses gives me a wink and then nods at Hannah.

Hannah and Ulysses make their way over to a water cooler far away from Brute's desk. "Bastardo infiel!" Hannah exclaims with forceful anger out of nowhere. She starts to cry and turn red. Spitting her words, she continues, "How dare you, Ulysses!"

"Babe, it will be alright, calm down."

"Calm down! I will show you calm down!"

With this, Detective Brute jumps from his seat, "Well—butter my butt—and call me a—biscuit! You kiddos—betta calm down."

As soon as the commotion starts, Hope gets up from the bench, sensing my need to look at the file. She immediately takes on the position of lookout. My heart starts to beat rapidly as I dash to Brute's desk and open the file. A close-up picture of a rap sheet with Layla's mugshot is staring right up at me. Her full name is written at the bottom: Angela Wells a.k.a. Layla Snow. It lists some interesting accomplices and their addresses too. I read that she was arrested a year ago for petty theft and larceny and three years ago in Orlando with similar charges. Typical charges for a grifter; that's interesting.

I flip through the file and find the picture of her dead body on the hotel bed. A much better quality than Ulysses's cell phone. The bruises on her neck are different shades of purples and yellow. The size of the bruises indicate that the hands used to strangle her were massive. Then I see it: the imprint of a rectangle on what looks like the ring finger on the right hand. I look up to make sure I still have time. I cringe at the scene in front of me. Detective Brute and several other police officers are trying their best to hold back a sobbing, screaming, and cheated Hannah as she tries to tear apart my cowering son. Oh Ulysses, don't ever cross that girl.

I quickly look down and use an empty water glass as a magnifier for a quick moment before Hope hisses, "Logan!"

I dart around Brute's desk, running over to Ulysses as Hope and Sarah assist with Hannah. Hannah quickly sees that her need for acting has come to an end and shrugs off the officers as they escort her, Hope, and Sarah out of the station.

"Little A—dair—you, your daddy—and your girl—are not welcome here—no more," Detective Brute says, pointing a bony finger at the door as Ulysses and I also vacate.

We all meet back at Penny University.

"You were great!" I say to Hannah, who looks a little worn out.

"I'm so sorry, Ulysses; I know you would never," Hannah says to Ulysses as she cups his face with her hands and kisses him. All I can think is: Boy, you better never. That's one murder I don't want to investigate.

"So what do you guys have?" Hope asks as she takes a long sip from her hot latte.

"Well, I know for sure it wasn't Bob. I think I know why and who, but I can't prove it yet."

**SOMERSET SECRETS**
*by T.W. Morse*

"We've got to question this Benny Booth," Ulysses says, breaking away from an overly apologetic Hannah, who is now resting her head on his shoulder.

"I got his address," I say with a wry grin.

"How'd you manage that?" Ulysses asks. I ignore the question to avoid bringing them further into my law-bending activities.

I instead change the subject and turn to Hope and Sarah.

"Hope and Sarah, I need you to go back to the police station and wait for my text. When I send it, bring the detective and a few large officers." Hope looks at me sideways as I kiss her and then dash with Ulysses and Hannah out the door.

"Where are you guys going?" she yells after us.

"No time! Look for my text!"

## VI.

"Ouch!! This bush has thorns," Ulysses says as I bring my finger to my mouth to tell him to stay quiet. We are sitting in wait outside a beautifully landscaped house. We hear a waterfall off in the distance; there must be a pool in the back.

"Dad, where did you get this address?"

"I'll share that with you later—duck!" Our luck finally pays off as a blue BMW convertible zooms in the driveway. A massive man exits the car. He's so large I can't imagine that he comfortably fit in the vehicle.

"Benny Booth?" Ulysses whispers.

I nod in silent response.

"Should we go and speak with him?" Hannah adds, still in hushed tones as we watch from a safe distance.

## SOMERSET SECRETS
### by T.W. Morse

"Yeah, let's go—I got an idea." The idea I have is dumb, reckless, and very unsafe but necessary to quickly prove Bob's innocence. We need to clear his name before his arrest is processed. Even a whiff of a scandal could cost him his job if Principal O'Leary ever found out. Before we approach Benny's house, I send Hope a quick text. She responds immediately with simply, "OK." That is the signal to proceed. We walk up to the gravel driveway, and I whisper to Hannah, "Whatever you do, don't interfere until I give you a thumbs up."

"Yeah, sure, Mr. Adair."

I say it again with more urgency. "No matter what you see, no matter what happens to me, don't interfere until I give the thumbs up."

"I got it."

"Wait, Dad, what do you mean?" Ulysses adds, but I continue to ignore him as I pound on the door. The door is thick and heavy, a lot like its owner. The door swings open to reveal Benny filling the doorframe.

"What," he grunts, looking at us and sniffing to himself.

"Benny Booth?"

"Yeah—what of it?"

"Benny Booth who was at the Seminole Suns Casino last night?"

"Maybe—you a cop? Are ya?" I can't cross that line of impersonating an officer, especially with Ulysses and Hannah looking on.

"Ah—no. We are friends of Bob Nelson."

"Who the hell is Bob Nelson?"

Ulysses takes a step back while Hannah doesn't care how big this guy is and moves into her ready stance, prepared for anything.

"Bob Nelson was your patsy."

# SOMERSET SECRETS
## by T.W. Morse

"My what?" Benny asks, looking confused.

"I'm going to take you through last night's events, Benny." Now he is turning a little red, making his massive head look like a tomato.

"What do you and these kids know?"

He is about to slam the door when I say confidently, "Everything." Ulysses gulps as he looks at me and then back at Benny. "I know you and Angela Wells go way back."

Benny snorts and releases a deep laugh that only a large man like him could make. The laughter sounds like a sinister, crazy Santa.

"Well, you know her by her alias, Layla Snow."

"Layla! What do you know?" he asks, his forehead furrowing to create a menacing glare as he leans down to my level. He brings his right hand up and cracks his knuckles directly in front of my face. I stare at his massive hands and relay everything I know to Benny Booth.

"Layla and you were partners, grifters, setting up marks, and stealing what possessions they have on them, probably with the help of that bartender, Chase. You would drug them at the bar, and she would take them back to her room where she would steal their wallets. That was until last night. What changed last night? Layla get greedy? She keep more of the money from previous cons? That's when you saw your chance. You drugged Bob at the bar before confronting Layla at the roulette table. How am I doing, Benny?" He doesn't speak; he just looks like a bull about to charge.

"That's when you followed Bob and her back to the room. The room you two always use for your jobs. You knew the fourth-floor cameras didn't work—you probably sabotaged the cameras weeks ago yourself, so you knew you wouldn't be seen. You probably had a key too. You snuck in there right as Bob passed out. You took your chance at payback. If

Layla wouldn't give you your due, you would take it! And you took it alright, by strangling her." But I can't finish as two massive paws grip tightly around my neck.

My throat is tightening as I am lifted off the ground. My eyes are starting to bulge out. I can see Ulysses jump on Benny, but Benny takes one of his paws and flings Ulysses away like a bug, only to return full pressure to my throat. I feel myself slowly lose consciousness, but I muster enough energy to stick up my right thumb.

Like a tiger, Hannah kicks Benny hard in his knee, causing a SNAP! And then Benny grabs his knee and cries in pain, taking both mitts off of my sore, bruised neck as I drop like a rag doll to the ground. From my vantage point on the ground, I see Hannah kneel down on one knee and punch Benny in the crotch. "Hi-Yah!"

"AHH!!" he screams, almost as loud as the many police sirens screeching into Benny's driveway. For good measure, Hannah does a roundhouse kick across Benny's face, breaking his massive nose, while Hannah says, "That's for Mr. Nelson!"

Hope comes running from the police cars and into my arms. "Good job!" I say with my scratchy sore throat.

"Are you okay?" Hope asks with concern as she examines my neck.

Two sheriff's deputies handcuff Benny Booth to an ambulance gurney, while Detective Brute stands like a scarecrow, staring at us like we're some meddling crows getting into his corn field.

Hannah is jogging in place now; the adrenaline of being able to use her skills is coursing through her tiny body. "Mr. Adair, why did you make me wait?"

"Yeah, Dad, you got a death wish?" Ulysses wonders, rubbing his bruised arm.

"No, but I do have the same marks on my neck that Layla Snow had. I'm now the evidence we need to prove Bob didn't commit the murder," I say, pointing to the massive hand marks imprinted in purple and yellow on my sore neck. "I noticed Benny was wearing a large ring with a square-cut ruby on his right hand. It was the same size and shape as the mark I saw in the police photo. I knew Benny was involved in the crime, but I wasn't 100 percent sure until I saw the ring on his hand. I wanted to bait Benny into leaving marks on me. I'm always glad that Hannah has my back," I explain in a hoarse whisper as I put a hand on my guardian angel.

"That's why you didn't want me to get involved until you gave me the thumbs up," she says, shaking her head.

"He could've killed you," Hope pleads.

Detective Brute looks closer at my neck as officers take photos of the marks. I tell him everything I told Benny.

"I guess—it looks—like I owe ya—an apolo—gy. I—will re—lease Mr. Nel—son when I get back to the sta—tion."

## VII.

Later that night at Penny University, we all wait for Bob to be released. We sit on the outdoor deck that overlooks Somerset Marina. The sailboats sway in the distance as the clink of dishes and seagulls fill the air. Edison bulbs are strung all around, making the café sparkle. Hannah and Ulysses sit with Catherine and Hector Reyes, sipping café con leche and embellishing the day's journey.

I rub my throat, sipping some tomato juice. Catherine swears it will help my throat. I stare out to the Somerset docks just as the sun is setting. Bob comes around the corner, holding hands with Sarah and wearing a huge smile.

We all run over to him and hug him even though he stinks of casino and prison.

"Mmm—mmm, I owe you guys—Logan, Ulysses, Hannah, even Hope—I heard you put your neck out for me. Come on—son," he says bashfully.

"Yeah—we love our big oaf," Hope says, smiling up at me.

"Let me tell ya somethin', y'all are family and I am so happy you guys came to bat for me," Bob admits, wiping away a tear. We all hug and rejoice again before Ulysses and I take the Penny University outdoor stage with our acoustic guitars and start a little impromptu concert.

"I guess I'm the one singing tonight, since Dad likes to get strangled by murdering criminals," Ulysses announces through the mic. Everyone laughs while I cough with a still very sore throat.

I see Catherine and Bob talking privately, and she hands something small to him. But my attention quickly fades back to Ulysses as he begins to count us into "Better Together" by Jack Johnson.

Catherine and Hector slow dance with Sarah and Bob as Hope and Hannah sway with the rhythm of the music. We are about to kick it up by singing "Sweet Caroline" when Bob yells, "I have ah—an announcement! Mmm—mmm, last night and today got Bobby Nelson think'n, mmm—mmm. Let me tell ya somthin'. I nev—a want to be alone again like that. I've got the best girl in the whole world and she's need'n to know that every day of her life, so Bobby Nelson's try'n or I'm gett'n to sayin'—" Bob kneels down in front of Sarah and slips a ring onto her finger. "Sarah Evans, will you marry this big, tracksuit-wearing oaf?"

My mouth drops as I look over to Ulysses, who is smiling from ear to ear, and even Hannah is beaming. My knees start to buckle when I see Hope wink up at me.

SOMERSET SECRETS
by T.W. Morse

"YES! You big lug, YES!" Sarah says as all of us cheer, sharing in their joy.

Bob scoops Sarah up into the air as Ulysses and I start to play Bruno Mars's "Marry You." I guess we have a wedding to look forward to during our next school year.

---

*If you enjoyed this mystery, please remember to leave a review.*
*Also look for my next adventures with Logan and Ulysses in*
**Wedded to Murder:**
**The Adair Classroom Mysteries**
**Vol. IV.**
*by T.W. Morse*

*Follow on Twitter @twmorse2*
***Website:*** https://adairclassroommysteries.sitey.me/
***Facebook:***
https://www.facebook.com/Adairclassroommysteries/

SOMERSET SECRETS
by T.W. Morse

# WEDDED TO MURDER:

# THE ADAIR CLASSROOM MYSTERIES VOL. IV

## -SNEAK PEAK-

# PROLOGUE

# ABBEY AND THE WASP

The room is humid and damp, enclosed by poorly laid cinderblock walls, making it smaller than it appears from the exterior. The pungent smell of old sweat wafts through the air. It's the kind of smell that lurks in sad, lonely places.

On one side of the dank room is an old, splintered door, while on the immediate opposite side stands an imposing metallic door that looks like it belongs in a bank, not in a basement.

Years of dust and debris can be easily seen from the bright hanging fluorescent light. A cold, metal table sits in a corner. A blue backpack with the name Abbey stitched on the top lays next to a perfectly folded pair of jeans and pink tank top.

In the center of the room is a larger table and a single cold metal chair; in it sits a quiet, thin, odious-looking man surrounded by the complete silence of the room but for a wasp stuck in the fluorescent light zipping above his head. "How did you get there?" he whispers as he tilts his head up to see the wasp rattling for freedom above him, while he continues to sweat in the basement heat.

## SOMERSET SECRETS
### by T.W. Morse

    The man had just put on his old, faded tuxedo upstairs and now sits with growing interest directed at this desperate wasp. His body is sweating as he intently watches the wasp buzzing around the plastic light casing, unsuccessfully and desperately searching for freedom. He admires the wasp's tenacity. The wasp never gives up, but he knows his end will come soon, either a result of exhaustion or the light burning it alive. The wasp flies relentlessly, building into a flurry of wings and sound in a multitude of directions. The man snickers to himself as he licks his dry lips and repositions his glasses while rubbing his sore eyes, now strained with the constant glare of watching the light above and the slow death of this wasp.

    How ironic, he thinks as he continues to smile while the wasp struggles for freedom. How long before it gives up? Or will it burn to death? He turns his attention away from the buzzing light to adjust his strained eyes on the monitor displaying the black and white picture in front of him at his work desk. The large desk is covered in countless wallet-sized pictures of young women. He loves to be surrounded by his girls. They give him … purpose, as he softly touches them.

    The man's eyes rest on the old monitor. On the screen, a young woman with wet jet-black hair and a dirty face, wearing nothing but a torn wedding dress, frantically and desperately searches for an escape from the man's make-shift prison cell. The woman had been relentlessly scratching at the walls, screaming, pleading for her freedom. "Hello, Abbey," he whispers.

    The dark cell is only lit by a single dull lightbulb dangling above the girl's head. She can't believe her situation. Her hands won't stop trembling with fear as her lips quiver. She scrambles around the cell, again desperately searching for an opening. "HELP! HELP ME! PLEASE!" her voice trembles out in a desperate plea. Her throat is sore and burns with every shout, making it impossible for her to scream loudly.

The walls appear to be made from rough padded cloth. She stares at her shredded fingers, dripping with blood as a result of her attempt to break free.

Abbey then turns to the metal door and begins to pound on it. The beat of the door seems to echo through the cell. Her tears are now stinging her eyes as she begs for help. All Abbey can say is "Help—help me—please," but it comes out as a desperate, low whisper.

Abbey begins to feel lightheaded from the heat and humidity of the cell, which have increased immensely in her attempt to escape. The lack of oxygen in the sealed space finally catches up to her, and Abbey slowly slumps to the floor in defeat.

The floor offers a cool reprieve as she finally gives in to the exhaustion that now consumes her entire body. Abbey lays on the floor lifeless and trapped; she finally closes her eyes and surrenders.

The man watches the young woman as beads of sweat drip off his brow and slowly fall onto his wire-framed glasses, causing them to slip. He repositions them further up onto the bridge of his hooked nose. His glasses became luminous with the glow of the video screen. He licks his lips in satisfaction.

This woman would not be his last, he thinks. Oh—no, he chuckles to himself. This would be his first of many—oh, yes—many—many more. She would be his first—present to himself. "Buzz—buzz my little wasp," he says out loud to himself and the dying wasp above. A sinister smirk covers the man's face as he licks his lips again before opening the metal door to enter the cell.

**SOMERSET SECRETS**
by T.W. Morse

Made in the USA
Middletown, DE
09 September 2025